D1013182

C

WITHDRAWN

CHARITY, COLORADO

AN EVANS NOVEL OF THE WEST

CHARITY, COLORADO

CHELSEA QUINN YARBRO

M. EVANS AND COMPANY, INC.
NEW YORK

For **Sandy** and **Sauncie** and **Roxann**
and all the other good people
working to save the Contra Costa County
equestrian trails

Copyright © 1993 by Chelsea Quinn Yarbro

All rights reserved. No part of this book may be reproduced or
transmitted in any form or by any means without the written
permission of the publisher.

M. Evans and Company, Inc.
216 East 49th Street
New York, New York 10017

Library of Congress Cataloging-in-Publication Data

Yarbro, Chelsea Quinn, 1942—
    Charity, Colorado : a western novel / by Chelsea Quinn Yarbro
      p.   cm. — (An Evans novel of the West)
    "Sequel to The law in charity."
    ISBN 0-87131-746-X : $18.95
    1. Sheriffs—Colorado—Fiction.   2. British—Colorado—Fiction.
    I. Title.   II. Series.
  PS3575.A7C48   1993
  813'.54—dc20   93-30622
                                                                CIP

Typeset by Classic Type, Inc.

Manufactured in the United States of America

First Edition

9 8 7 6 5 4 3 2 1

Chapter One

As he swung the last barred door closed, Jason Russell smiled at
Daniel Calvin. "Excellent. Very well done." He slipped the heavy
padlock into the hasp. "All of them barred and lockable. At last."

"Better nor them old doors," said Calvin, indicating the plank
doors that lay in the small front office of the Charity jail. He
scratched at his sinewy arm and regarded Russell with wry
amusement. "You fixing to fill it up, Sheriff?"

"Not if I don't have to," said Russell. He tossed the ring of
large new keys onto his desk.

"Spring's here, and that means more people coming," said
Calvin, dropping his mallet back into the deep pocket for it in his
leather apron. "Last spring we got over sixty new people in town.
This year'll be the same or worse."

"Worse?" asked Russell, opening the bottom drawer of his
desk and pulling out a cashbox. "I was one of the newcomers."

"It used to be a nice little place, away from things. Now it's
turning into a town," Calvin muttered.

"Four-hundred thirty-nine people are hardly a mob, Mister
Calvin," said Russell as he counted out the twenty-eight dollars
the smith was due. "Here. And another dollar for a job well
done."

Daniel Calvin waved the extra money away. "Oh, no; thank
you anyway, Sheriff, but I don't hold with getting paid more'n I
ask for. It's not fitting; makes me beholdin', which I don't want
to be. No offense intended." He added the last quickly and deliberately.

"None taken," Russell assured him. He put the dollar in his pocket. "Then perhaps you'll let me stand you a drink one evening."

"I don't hold with drink, neither," said Calvin, raising his chin. "But I would take kindly to a glass of cider." He backed toward the door. "No rush on it, though, Sheriff."

"Later in the week, then," said Russell, putting his cashbox away again.

Calvin nodded emphatically, then opened the door wide, letting in the smell of wet streets and spring. "God keep you," he said in parting, stepping gingerly into the mud.

Russell lifted his hand as he went to close the door, pausing to look at the squat church of Sagrada Caridad across the road. He noticed one of the nuns scraping her shoes on the walkway bricks, and he smiled to himself. As he stepped back into his office, he looked once more at the bars Daniel Calvin had installed, feeling relief. He went to the pot-bellied stove and added a small log to the embers, watching it start to flame. As the first warmth began to spread, Russell went back to his desk and sat down. He took out his writing paper and began to compose a letter to his nephew. He pared a quill and put it into the holder, but then sat, his face blank, as he tried to think of something to tell the inquisitive boy. Finally, with a sigh, he began.

My Dear Nephew Reginald,

It is—he almost wrote "relieving," but at the last instant substituted—*gratifying to know that your father is willing for us to continue our correspondence. It would be unacceptable to me to exchange letters with you if he did not approve, as you, I am certain, would not wish to displease him in this regard.*

Your last letter, which arrived here a week ago, fully five months after you posted it, contained many thoughtful questions and I will do my best to answer them. Your curiosity is certainly welcome and you have no need to apologize for your various inquiries; I am most happy to provide you with whatever information I possess that may be of use to you. In your letter you ask about the Spaniards here, and yes, this town sits on land that is technically part of the land grant given to the ancestor of Don Maximillian, who died a few months since in the winter. There and Congress has yet to rule on them as the land becomes part of the United States. Don Maximillian has a daughter who has inherited his land and his fortune. She is married to the youngest son of the mayor, an arrangement that the family does not wholly like.

There are few Red Indians here, so I cannot advise you in that regard, although I have come to believe that many reports of the savagery of these people is grossly exaggerated. But as I have never seen Red Indian warriors in battle I am not to be considered informed in that regard. I do have the good fortune to know one Red Indian, a William Red Pony who has been—

A sharp knock on the door caused him almost to drop his pen. He called out sharply, "Who's there?"

"Lorinda Dooley," came the answer accompanied by a cough. "I've got to speak to you, Sheriff."

Russell set his pen aside, frowning as he did. "What is it? Come in, come in." He rose and was halfway to the door when Lorinda came into the room, her face averted, her long flowered shawl pulled tightly around her thin shoulders. "Well?" he asked. "What is the matter, Lorinda?"

She still would not look directly at him. "I have had a man at my house. He insisted that he spend the night with me. You said I should report any bad behavior." As she turned toward him defiantly, Russell saw that there was a large bruise on her face.

"He did that to you?" Russell demanded, moving more quickly to help her to the single visitor's chair. "Are you going to charge him? Do you wish to make a complaint?"

"Yes," she said, coughing again. "But not for this, for stealing from me." She slumped as she sat. "You know what it is like in this world, Sheriff. Every man in town thinks I deserve what I get because I'm a whore, but they'll draw the line at stealing." She pulled a large lace-edged handkerchief from her old-fashioned reticule and blew her nose.

Russell did not attempt to argue with her. "How badly are you hurt?"

"A few bruises. One blow struck me low in the back, and it hurts more than the others. I had Henry Clayton look at them, just in case. There's also one on my ribs that hurts but the rest..." She ended her explanation with a shrug.

"What man did that to you?" Russell asked insistently.

"He had to," she said after a brief and thoughtful hesitation. "He was like a man ordered to act. That was how it was with him, as if demons were inside him, forcing him to strike and curse. He was pitiful, in a way." Her voice was weary and her eyes shone more with contempt than tears. "He was a foreigner. He spoke badly, with an accent. I'd never seen him before. But I know that kind of man, who quotes Scripture while he does his business, as if that makes it less a sin." She started to laugh, though the sound was more like a sob.

"And he robbed you?" Russell asked, going to the stove where the kettle sat, growing warmer. "I can make you some tea, if you'd like it."

"I'd like it, but not yet," said Lorinda, bringing herself back under control. "I want the man caught for the thief that he is. I may be the town whore, but I earn my money, the same as others. They might not like what I do, the good people of Charity, but they don't like thieves any better. He took money from me, after he was sure I was dazed. Which I was," she added sullenly, "but I saw what he did. I couldn't stop him, but I saw him."

"What does this cove look like?" asked Russell, slipping back into the slang of the London of his youth. "Describe him to me. Everything you can remember."

Lorinda gave a defiant chuckle. "Everything?" Then she shrugged again, covering a cough with her hand. "He's a big man, maybe a head taller than you are. He's big everywhere—big hands, big arms, big body, big legs. He talks something like the Widow Schmidt, that kind of accent, so he's probably some sort of German. Stinks, too. Old sweat and grime all over him." She made a face. "And he called me filth."

"How long was he in your house?" Russell inquired as he sat down once more and took out his notepad, scribbling as he listened. "When did he arrive?"

"He came a little before sunset, on a big red horse that looked more like it pulls plows than gets ridden. He had three glasses of whiskey, very quick, talking to no one. His face got red as a plum, and he kept rubbing at his nose. When I went up to him, to know which of the girls he fancied, he was surly, but he said only the owner of the house would do. Well, I don't like to take newcomers. It always bodes ill when a newcomer wants me instead of the other girls. They're all younger than I am, and prettier, too." She shook her head morosely. "And I was right, wasn't I, Sheriff?"

"If he stole from you, yes." Russell studied his notes. "So, then, he asked for you and you accepted."

"And you're curious why I did that, aren't you?" she asked with defiance. "You want to know why I agreed if I thought it boded ill, don't you?"

"I am a bit puzzled," Russell admitted.

"We had two months where we made little money, and I have to pay the good Sisters to care for Rosemary." She gave him a hard stare.

"I see," said Russell, making no other comment. "Did you take him to your room?"

"I had to," said Lorinda. "It was a good night, too, the first in a long time. We had a number of customers and none of the girls wanted to spare their rooms, and I won't have them using mine. It was a bad idea." She touched her hand to the bruise on her face. "He locked the door and told me to undress. That's usual enough. He didn't want me to touch him, or take his clothes off, which was as well with me."

"His clothes were dirty," said Russell as he wrote.

"Yes. There were bits of food in his beard." She made a face. "It didn't look like he ever combed it."

"Bearded," said Russell. "Full beard? Spade beard? Long? Short? What?"

"A beard that hasn't seen scissors in a year, I'd reckon," said Lorinda, wrinkling her nose in distaste.

"Unkempt?" suggested Russell.

"Like a bird's nest," said Lorinda. "I haven't seen one like that since...since before I came here," she finished lamely. "He's a hairy man, the hair a brown going grey, all over him, like a roan horse."

"About how old, would you say?" Russell held his pencil to write, hoping to get enough from Lorinda to identify the man.

"Hard to tell with someone like that, but thirty-five, forty. He looks older at first, but his body isn't that old, if you understand me. No sagging, no wrinkles where you see them when men get on in years."

Russell thought of his own body, nearer fifty than forty, and nodded in agreement. "All right, late thirties. What about his eyes?"

"Blue. Light blue, almost like water. Very strange eyes, Sheriff, eyes you remember. They're burning cold, like ice." She pulled her shawl more closely around her shoulders.

"Like ice," Russell repeated, his face suddenly smooth and distant. "I have seen such eyes, a long time ago."

"Then you know what I mean," said Lorinda, and fell silent for a minute or two.

Russell shook off the memory. "So, we have a man with an accent, probably German, late thirties, a bit over six feet, big build, brown hair going grey, a wild beard—what more?" He consulted his notes. "Did he quote Scripture while he was drinking or only when he was alone with you?"

"He quoted Scripture all the time." She absently gnawed the nail of her little finger, tearing with her teeth. "He has a bad tooth," she added.

"Protestant Scripture?" asked Russell, hoping that Lorinda was aware of the difference in texts.

"Scripture Scripture," she answered bluntly, breaking off to cough again. There were bright spots in her cheeks, as if she had been slapped moments before. "About women being silent and submissive and men being tools of their own lust. I didn't listen to most of it."

Russell frowned as he looked at her. "Have you been taking the medicines Doctor Clayton has given you?" he asked as gently as he could.

"When I remember," Lorinda answered. "There's nothing he can do if it is consumption, anyway." She folded her arms. "I have them boil all the glasses and plates in the house when they're used, and I make sure the bed-linen's boiled proper. But I do that anyway." Her green eyes were defensive now, and she sat straight in the chair, her arms folded. "I don't need Henry Clayton telling me what to do."

"Of course," said Russell, not wanting to distress her. "About this man? who quoted Scripture and robbed you?"

"He's nothing," she said contemptuously. "But I want my money back. He got what he paid for, and he can't take my earnings, not if I can stop him." This time her silence was hostile. "Will they let me get my money back, Fletcher and his cronies? Or will they find an excuse to forget—"

"They do not take complaints; I do," Russell reminded her. "I don't care what the mayor may think, I am obliged to apprehend the thief because that is the law, and I have taken an oath to uphold the law. Not the whim of the council or the mayor." He looked over his notes again, and this time he added what she had said about the tooth. "Which one, again?"

"This one," she said, pointing to her own mouth. "The dog tooth."

"Left side?" Russell asked.

"I think so." She relaxed a little. "If you catch him, I want to spit in his face. You bring him to me before you lock him up, sheriff."

"I have to catch him first," Russell said, deliberately avoiding giving her a direct answer. "Do you think any of your girls would be able to tell me more about this man if I asked them?" He held his pencil poised.

"Maybe, maybe not," she said, sighing a little. She lifted her hand to the splendid chaos of her red hair. "I'm losing my looks," she observed in a tone that required no response from him. "My bosom's dropping, and I'm too pale. My hair's still good and my ankle has a nice turn. I got two, at best three years, and then I will have to let my girls take over. I don't have time enough to earn that money back, and I don't bring in the men the way I did a couple years ago." She fiddled with the knotted fringe on her shawl. "It worries me, why that bastard wanted me. I got prettier girls working for me, and ones that know more tricks than I like to use. Maybe he was going to rob me from the first."

Russell hesitated. "You said the man had never been there before."

"Yes," she admitted.

"Then how could he know he would have the chance to rob you? He had no reason to think that you would take him to your own room, or that you kept your money there." He watched her as she considered his question.

She got out of the chair and walked down the little office. "Blamed luck?" Her laughter was desolate. "They'd say I deserved it, most of them in this town. I'm afraid to hear what Padre Antonio will tell me when I go to Confession. And I know that once it's learned that I've been robbed, there's others that'll try it."

Privately Russell agreed with her, but he shook his head. "You aren't so helpless as all that, Lorinda. You can deal with anyone who tries to take advantage of you."

"Now it's happened, you mean?" she asked, her face showing two bright fever spots in her pale cheeks. "Certainly. I have a pistol and I have a knife. But if I used either of them, the town would see me swinging for it." She glared in the direction of Sheriff Russell. "And you'd have to let them, wouldn't you?"

"Not if you were not found guilty," said Russell as reasonably as he could. "If you were found guilty, I would still not be willing to see you hanged."

Lorinda would have spoken but she coughed instead. She put her back to the wall for support. Finally she made herself stop. "If that man comes back again, I want him arrested."

"Of course," said Russell, watching her more closely. "Has Henry Clayton given you anything for the cough?"

"Nothing new. There's nothing he can give me." She jerked her shoulder in an attempt at a shrug. "You have to catch that thief, so that I can make the right arrangements for Rosemary. Sister Mercedes is a good woman, but she can't conjure money out of the air."

"No, and you cannot drive yourself to an early grave for your daughter, either," said Russell. "I will do everything I can to get your money back, and I give you my wo.. that I will arrest this man if he returns to your house."

"Scripture and all?" Lorinda suggested darkly. "There are those here would forgive him the theft if he quotes enough Scripture for it."

"They won't feel that way if I remind them that God does not love a hypocrite." He indicated the stove. "Come nearer, if you like."

"I'd better not. I'll just cough more when I step outside if I do." She favored the sheriff with a quick, shy smile. "I didn't think you'd listen to me."

"But I've told you I would," said Russell at his most reasonable. "Why would I lie to you?"

"Men say all manner of things to whores. You get used to it." She shoved herself away from the wall and looked at his notebook with curiosity. "Did you really write it all down?"

"Yes," he assured her. "Everything you described. And I will use it. I will s:e that Luis has the description as well, and Smilin' Jack. Between the two of them, that should cover all the towns from here to Denver."

"Smilin' Jack Johnson never did a whore a favor in his life," said Lorinda with bitter certainty.

"But he abides by the law. He will not be doing this for you, Lorinda, but for me, and for the law."

She looked at him steadily for several seconds, then said, "You are serious, aren't you? You expect Smilin' Jack to look for this fellow." Her laughter bit. "All right. And I will tell my girls to keep watch for the man again."

"Good," said Russell, getting another cup from the wall and filling it with boiled tea. "I'm sorry it isn't coffee. I've been told that some is being brought to me, genuine," he told her. "No chicory." He held it out to her.

"Boil the cup before you use it again," said Lorinda as he fingers closed around the white porcelain. "What kind of tea is this?"

"It's the only kind I have left, that black India tea. Not much flavor to it, really, but it's hot."

"That it is." She went back to the hard chair and sat down, her attention on the mug she held. "I wish I had some spices. I was planning to get some, but now...." Whatever else she might have said was lost as she drank.

"Perhaps something can be arranged with Sun Fan-Li at the hotel. He'll be ordering spices." He cocked his head toward the window. "It's only April. You could have spices by the middle of May."

"Do you think the Widow Schmidt would let her cook deal with me?" demanded Lorinda. "She runs a respectable house, and I do not."

Russell poured himself a second cup of tea, not so much because he wanted it, but to make it apparent to Lorinda that she could have more if she wanted it. "Respectable house or not, you both want spices and the spices are cheaper if bought in larger quantities," said Russell. "I'll speak with Missus Schmidt, if you like."

"She'll have that clerk of hers throw you out on your ear," warned Lorinda, shaking her head. "Don't be foolish, Sheriff. You done more than ever I expected when you said you'd try to find the thief." She finished her tea and set the mug down on the top of the small book case between the stove and the door. "Mind you boil that, now."

Russell went to the door, holding it for her. "I wish you had rather more faith in me, Lorinda Dooley."

The look she gave him might have been flirtatious if she had looked less exhausted and ill. "I have great faith in men, Sheriff. It just isn't your faith, that's all." She gave a toss to her lovely mess of red hair, then went out into the chilly sunlight.

Chapter Two

Henry Clayton brushed the last bits of food from his mustache before drinking the little, precious glass of port that Dorabelle Schmidt had offered him at the end of his meal. He touched the rim of his glass to Jason Russell's and smiled as he had his first sip. "I've been told that Don Maximillian left an enormous cellar of wines, with ports and sherries," he said.

"I wouldn't know," said Russell, letting the port ease down his throat.

"What does Dona Elvira say?" asked Clayton.

"Missus Frederick Fletcher has said nothing on the matter," Russell said, a bit more sharply.

Clayton chuckled. "She may have married that young idiot, but she's never going to be Missus Frederick Fletcher, not here in Charity. She'll be Dona Inez, Don Maximillian's daughter, until she's a wizened old granny." There was only enough port in his glass now for one last sip. "What if Congress honors the Spanish land grants? Have you thought what that could mean to George Fletcher?"

"Do you think Congress will?" Russell inquired. "No one expects it."

"Who knows?" Clayton regretfully drank the last of his port. "Who knows?" he repeated.

Russell took his last sip, too, and changed the subject. "Lorinda Dooley was in my office two days ago."

"Um-hum." Clayton set down his glass. "The fellow gave her quite a beating. He must have known what he was doing; the worst damage was where you couldn't see it." He hesitated, once again wiping his mustache. "She's a sick woman. She's in no condition for such treatment."

"Who is?" Russell challenged. "Or have you forgot all the times you've read me lectures for getting scrapes and bruises."

"You're over forty," Clayton said. "A man of your age has to be careful—"

"No one wants to get bruises and broken bones, not at any age," Russell said flatly.

"The young make a quicker recovery," said Clayton. "They heal better and faster than aging men do."

"Lorinda Dooley is thirty and consumptive, and life has not used her kindly."

Clayton shook his head. "What is it about men in the law, that they either despise whores or defend them?" His question was asked of the poorly stuffed stag's head by the door, as if this way he could not give offense to his friend.

Russell set his little port glass aside. "In Australia, I saw many women who had been whores, as I had seen them in London when I was a Runner, and in India after that. They were all poor women, though some of them did well for themselves, after a fashion. They were ignorant women, almost all of them, who had traded on the one thing they could call their own—their bodies. I cannot look on them with contempt anymore. If I were legitimate, perhaps I would still; I don't know."

"I didn't mean—" Clayton began, then looked squarely at Russell. "Yes, I did, Jason, and I ask your pardon for it."

"No reason for pardon," said Russell. "If you should ask anyone's pardon, it's Lorinda Dooley's."

"But surely they know the risks of whoring," said Clayton, sitting a little straighter. "They accept those risks when they take their first coin."

"They know the certainty of starving, of seeing their families starve with them. What is shame to that? You've been over the world. You know what the world is." He leaned back in his sturdy wooden chair. "Henry, think a little."

"You're a radical fellow, Jason, under that quiet demeanor." He signaled to the bartender. "Bring us each a whiskey, Kinsman."

The young man nodded and set about his task so grimly that he seemed to be readying poison rather than drink.

"A shame about his wife," said Clayton softly. "But there was nothing I could do. The fever was too far advanced, and she was too weak to fight more. No one could have saved her." This last was said defensively.

Russell nodded as if he had not noticed the change in his friend. "True enough." He pulled out a coin for the bartender as he brought their drinks. "Thanks."

The young man accepted the coin with a single nod then went back to the bar.

Whatever Henry Clayton was about to say was interrupted as the door to the bar swung open, then was shoved closed by Charity's single dandy, Frederick Fletcher. This evening he was sporting a fine new waistcoat of brocade, and his coat had been sent all the way from Boston. He accepted the sudden silence as his due as he strode to the bar. "I want a bottle of Widow Schmidt's German Schnapps," he announced, looking around to see who had heard this.

"Oh, dear me," murmured Russell. "Not again."

"That boy's going to rot his liver before he's thirty if he keeps this up," whispered Clayton. "He hasn't the constitution for hard drinking. The slender ones never do."

"What does his wife think, I wonder?" said Russell in the same under voice, not expecting an answer.

Linus Cooke, who had come to Charity three years ago to set up his own saddlery, gave Frederick Fletcher a single, scornful glance, then gave his attention once again to Jock Bruder, the shoe- and boot-maker.

"Well," said Frederick as he rounded on the men at the tables, his elbows resting on the bar behind him. "How many of Charity's good citizens come here."

"Here's your Schnapps," said Kinsman, shoving the bottle and a glass toward him so that one of his elbows was dislodged.

Frederick swung around to face the bar and reached out, grabbing Kinsman by the front of his shirt. "Louis, I am waiting for apology for that."

"For what?" asked Kinsman, looking anywhere but at Frederick. "You ordered your drink and I've served you."

"You did that deliberately," said Frederick softly, in what he thought was a menacing tone.

Russell was already on his feet and pulling his baton from its holster as Kinsman answered, "You do this every time, Mister Fletcher. Can't you just let it alone."

"Everyone in this town tries to insult me," said Frederick, delivering a condemnation to all the men in the bar. "I won't have it."

Russell put his hand on Frederick's shoulder. "Let go of Mister Kinsman, Mister Fletcher, do." His tone was light and persuasive. "Right now."

Frederick did not release Kinsman, but he directed his wrath at Russell. "This has nothing to do with you, Sheriff. Leave us alone." He tried to turn back to Kinsman; his leg buckled under him as Russell smacked the back of his knee with his baton. Frederick cursed fulsomely.

"If you are willing to stand up and be civil, this need not go any farther," said Russell pleasantly. "I'll make a place for you with Doctor Clayton and me at our table."

By now Frederick was back on his feet, straightening his clothes. "Get away from me."

"It's nothing, Sheriff," said Kinsman. "Maybe I did jolt him. I don't know." He looked embarrassed and angry.

Russell hesitated. "If you wish, Mister Kinsman?" He nodded, then pointed out a table in the corner near the entrance to the hotel lobby. "You will be more private there, Mister Frederick."

"I want to stay—" Frederick began mulishly.

But Russell had already picked up his bottle of Schnapps and his glass and was carrying them toward the table; his baton was back in its holster and he had taken Frederick by the sleeve. "You will be more comfortable here."

Frederick was still blustering. "You have no right—"

"Who better?" asked Russell cordially as he pulled out a chair for Frederick. "Enjoy your evening, Mister Frederick, and be good enough to permit the rest of us to enjoy ours."

"Fine state of affairs," grumbled Frederick, his handsome features sullen.

"Yes indeed," said Russell with undiminished affability, "shocking. A sheriff keeping the peace." He put his hand on

Frederick's shoulder, not quite forcing him into the chair. As he stepped back, he added with a smile, "I hope you will not decide to be awkward."

Frederick stared at his bottle of Schnapps as if trying to ignite it with the fury in his eyes. He said something under his breath, but had sense enough not to be heard.

"I have heard that his oldest brother is coming back to Charity this summer," said Clayton as Russell once again took the chair across the table from him. "Missus Fletcher—his mother, not his wife—has been overjoyed since his letter came."

"That would be Newton or Horatio?" said Russell.

"Horatio," said Clayton. "I met him briefly. He's very like his father in appearance. I have no impression of his temperament." He tasted the whiskey. "I'll be glad when new supplies arrive: this is the worst she has served us yet."

"It was that snowfall last week," said Russell with a gesture of acceptance. "There are probably supplies stranded below the passes. In Australia, it was often worse. Most of our supplies came in by boat, and—"

Clayton interrupted. "What about your horses? The rest of them should be along any day."

"Once the passes are open enough, yes, I suppose that's so." Russell smiled in spite of himself. "I'm glad we've got the barn up. I can keep the horses there until we're finished with the stable." He touched his tongue to the whiskey, making a face at the harsh, medicinal taste. "This is worse than some of your damned potions."

"It is," agreed Clayton. He started to speak and then once again fell silent.

"What is it, Henry?" Russell asked as the physician's hesitation continued.

"I went to the Howes' dairy today." He admitted it in the same guilty rush that he would admit to having procured more opium.

"Cora Vreeland?" Russell guessed.

"I should not approach her," said Clayton, becoming quite nervous. "I know that there is nothing I can offer her." He silenced Russell with two raised fingers. "A widow, and so young...and I am...well, nothing she would be wise to—"

"Have you said anything to her?" Russell asked, his tone quiet.

"No," said Clayton. "It isn't right."

"You've told me so before," said Russell, his voice even more neutral. He drank the last of his whiskey and moved the glass away.

"What I've said before is still true," Clayton insisted. "I have only my skills to offer, and under the circumstances, I can place no reliance on them. She has had cruelty enough in her life and I will not add to it." He downed the last of his drink then said in an entirely different voice, "I've been out to the Cousins; Miss Rossiter has fractured her arm."

"So I've been told," Russell said, giving no indication of surprise in the change of subject; he considered the Cousins, two women of middle years who shared a small holding a short distance from Charity and were content to keep to themselves. "Well, better Miss Rossiter than Missus Bell," Russell went on. "I don't think Miss Rossiter could tend the stock by herself—that's Missus Bell's task."

Clayton went on in the same manner. "And Hiram Mattington says that his father is recovering from his apoplexy, although his speech is still not clear. I have said I would ride out to see him before the Sabbath." He looked around the room, as if searching for something else to talk about. "Missus Mattington is running the ranch for him."

Russell chuckled softly. "If you ask me, she's been doing that for years. That's not a word against Arthur Mattington—he is a fortunate man who has sense enough to know it. An indefatigable woman, Bess Mattington." He looked closely at Clayton. "Well, Henry, are you going to speak to Cora Vreeland, or are you going to let the matter drop?"

He did not answer directly. "Smilin' Jack has an order from me. If I use the abominable stuff, then I have no right to Cora Vreeland or any woman. I'm still a good enough physician to know that. Any woman contemplating marriage to someone who uses opium I would advise against the union. That includes myself."

"Setting yourself a quest, like one of the Knights of the Grail?" Russell suggested. "It's another excuse, another invitation to succumb. You set yourself a trial you know you cannot win, and wait for failure to overtake you, so that you can find solace in that vile pipe. What's the use of that, Henry? You are no Sir Lancelot—what man is?"

"You do not understand, Jason. I've tried to tell you: if I cannot turn from opium, if I succumb in spite of her, I will be no fit man for her, don't you see," Clayton said heatedly, though he spoke almost in a whisper. "What woman would be willing to have a man who was a slave to that foul poison? If I cannot give up those sweet, pernicious dreams for her, real as she is, then I am damned and I must accept that."

Russell ran his finger under his lower lip. "I do not know what more to say to you," he told the physician after a short silence.

"Then say nothing," Clayton snapped, adding almost at once, "I am grateful for your concern, Jason. I am. But it is my own affair."

"So long as you can do your work, is that it? Well, if you will not let yourself be aided, there is nothing more I can do." Russell said with a nod. He pulled his watch from his waistcoat pocket, peering at it in the gloom. "I must go," he said when he had made out the time by holding the watch at the length of his arm. "Luis is standing guard at the jail and I've said I would relieve him before nine." He was already on his feet. "If young Mister Frederick requires—

"I'll send Sun for you," said Clayton, sounding weary. "He can't keep on this way, you know. A few years of drink and other indulgences, and it will take its toll on him." His expression was cynical and contemptuous, but it changed as soon as the words were out of him. "I have no right to condemn him."

"You're his physician," Russell pointed out as he got to his feet.

Clayton shook his head and said nothing more as Russell pulled on his heavy coat.

"I met a man today," said Liam Cauliffe after he had been taken around Russell's half-built house. The preacher sat down on a barrel and removed his hat, slapping the dust out of it as he talked. "He and his...following have established themselves about seven, eight miles out on the Old North Road."

Russell leaned back against one of the door-frames, his arms folded. "Tell me about this man." It was a bright morning, the scent of grass and first flowers on the cool breeze.

"An imposing figure of a man, if I may say so. Most preachers don't look so much like Moses on the Mount." He clicked his tongue. "It is unchristian of me to speak this way of another of God's ministers, but there was something about the man that grated." His expression was apologetic. "I don't know quite why."

"Oh?" Russell was careful not to prod, for he knew the Scotsman well enough to realize that he would resist any pressure brought on him. "What happened?"

Cauliffe did not answer at once. He peered out through the frame of the house, his eyes on the roof of the barn. "You have some good stock in there."

"Yes; my half-brother has been punctilious in executing our father's wishes. I wish I had more room for the rest of the horses that are coming. As it is, they'll have to go into pasture first, and they may be a handful later on. I hope I can find a good man to help me with the horses, someone younger and spryer than I am." He pointed up the mountain to where the remaining snow was, first patches, then blanketing whiteness. "The passes will be open in a short while, or so I'm told. My stock will be here within days of that."

"You'll manage, with or without help," said Cauliffe. "This preacher," he went on as if there had been no digression, "struck me as...harsh, and unforgiving. I'm not one to pardon sin or excuse error or ignore the law of Scripture, but I don't see the worth of despising all humanity for Original Sin." Satisfied with his hat, he put it back on. "I have seen his kind before, and always they cause dissension, though they claim it is the sin of others, not their own pride, that brings dissension about."

"He doesn't sound promising," said Russell. "Where am I to find this paragon, then? Where is he on the Old North Road?"

Cauliffe sighed. "The second bridge? The one with the whole logs under the planking? You cross that, and then, on the right, there is a track leading down the slope. There's a lake in the hollow...you know where I mean?"

"Yes, approximately," said Russell. "The lake is long with a wide place at the north end, like a keyhole?"

"That's the one." He frowned and stroked his short beard. "They have put up tents on the south end."

"Tents?" Russell demanded incredulously. "In this weather? How long have they been there?"

"A month, a bit more," said Cauliffe. "The minister was emphatic about that."

"But tents," Russell said, frowning. "I have slept in tents when it was freezing, and I cursed the cold. You say he has followers, families with him. They are going to settle at the lake, I assume. If this man has not built houses, how are his followers surviving? And how many are there?" He decided that he would have to ride out to the lake in the next few days.

"He would not tell me, but I suspect there are more than twenty: men, women, and children." He paused, considering what he was going to say. "It is not as if they are poor. That would be another matter, if they were too poor to have anything but tents. They are surrounded by trees, and...something could have been done, it would not take much to get better shelter than tents. I saw that trees had been cut for lumber. They did have one building up—their church. According to Wachter the church is more important than houses."

"And you disagree?" Russell challenged with a quick smile.

"Where there is snow on the ground and children coughing, I most certainly do. It is the Word of God that is important, not the building where it is preached. I have given sermons in saloons and barns and wagons and sod houses and the Word was not lessened because of that." He flexed his long hands, then looked out at the barn again. "He is rigorous and severe, and he is pleased with being so."

"But you disagree?" Russell asked, knowing how strict Cauliffe was in his faith.

"Men come to God by many paths, and they serve Him in many ways. And do not tell me that you do not believe that because you have no faith yourself." He added the last with a shake of his head.

"There are times, Liam, when I suspect you pray for my conversion." He straightened up.

"Of course," said the Scot. "I would be lax if I did not." His mouth twitched. "It might even disappoint you if I did not pray for you."

"Possibly," was all Russell would concede. "Tell me more about this preacher...what was his name again?"

"Wachter. I did not learn his Christian name." He got up from the barrel. "There's another new farm in the same area, about a mile north of the turn-off to the lake."

"The widow with a boy about fourteen?" said Russell. "Yes, I have met her. Mayor Fletcher told me about her when she arrived last month. Apparently her husband secured the land and arranged for a house to be built last year. Then he died last November, and two of their children with him. This widow decided to come to the farm in spite of that." He made a gesture that showed his approval of this move. "She's not one to wear herself out griev- ing, I think."

"I haven't called there yet," said Cauliffe. "I am due to go out that way again."

"She will probably come into town in a week or so. She told the mayor that she intends to purchase more lamps for the house and supplies for her farm."

"You like her?" Cauliffe wondered aloud.

Russell gave him a startled glance. "Why, yes; I suppose so." Then he chuckled. "The trouble with you, Liam, is that since you have decided to marry Dorabelle Schmidt—and I recall that you warned me about her—you think that everyone is contemplating matrimony. Missus Lilhius has not had a year of mourning, and I have met her but once, and briefly at that."

Cauliffe took this in good nature. "You may be right, but I doubt it."

Russell pointed out across the big fenced pasture to the stand of timber beyond. "Look; a doe with two fawns."

"She's probably after the grain you keep for the horses," said Cauliffe. "They're as pesky as they are beautiful."

"I saw a stag last week, with six points." He strolled out through the place where a wall would soon be. "Once the chim- ney is ready, the rest of the house will go up quickly. I don't want to take any chances with fire."

"Wise precaution," said Cauliffe as he stopped to look at the fireplace made of smooth and rounded river stones cemented to form the traditional hearth. "It looks sound enough."

"We'll know next week." Russell walked across the muddy expanse between the house and the barn, saying as he went, "I have asked Smilin' Jack to bring me the latest bulletins from Denver and Saint Louis. I feel so isolated here; I want to know what is happening in the world. I want to know about the crimes and criminals who might come here."

"Charity is no different than a hundred other towns like it." Cauliffe thought about this. "I've seen places on the circuit that are more remote than this and have less contact with the rest of the world. Charity has a bank and two churches and a school, as well as a dairy and a tannery. Charity is on its way to becoming an important place."

"That's absurd," said Russell.

"No, it's not," Cauliffe said, so seriously that Russell stopped and looked at him. "You've been here only six months; you don't know how these things develop, how quickly they can change. Charity may be just eighty families now, but three years ago it was half the size it is now, and it is growing more rapidly each year. It has been a crossroads for the Spanish for almost a century; trappers have come here almost that long. In a decade this will be an important place."

"Unless another place becomes more important," said Russell. "I saw that happen in Australia more than once." His eyes clouded as they often did when he spoke of Australia.

"That is a different place," said Cauliffe in his most austere tone.

"You mean that it is a penal colony," said Russell flatly. "One enormous prison." He commenced walking again. "That's true enough, but the problems there are not so different than the problems here."

"They are different enough," Cauliffe insisted. "Are you going to get gravel for this yard?"

"Soon." He looked down at his mired boots. "One winter of this is sufficient."

They had reached the barn where their horses were tied, both with their heads down, munching the hay Russell had provided.

Cauliffe patted his raw-boned buckskin on the rump. "Good boy, Ezekiel."

Russell stroked the neck of his new grey mare, one of the horses sent by his half-brother. "Isn't she handsome?" he asked the preacher as both men mounted.

"A hunter, by the look of her," said Cauliffe.

"My brother prides himself on his hunters," said Russell as he pulled the mare's head around. "I have her papers."

"Are you going to keep records on your foals? Most ranchers around here don't bother with such niceties."

"Most ranchers around here are illiterate," Russell pointed out. "I most certainly shall keep records. I intend to have some of the finest horses west of the Mississippi before you bless my headstone." He set the mare trotting, watching the road ahead as their speed increased. "I hear that the Ramsey girl is getting married."

"In a month," said Cauliffe, keeping up with the sheriff.

"To the oldest Gall boy," said Russell with a shake of his head. "They're children."

"She's fourteen and he's sixteen; they're of age," said Cauliffe. "And they've known each other for five years."

As they rode by Lorinda Dooley's house, Cauliffe averted his eyes and murmured something Russell did not hear. "What's wrong, Liam?"

Cauliffe sighed with exasperation. "I know Our Lord forgave harlots, but this one is so obdurate in her sin."

Russell shook his head. "She's a woman alone with a child and nothing of value but her body," he said, as he had reminded the minister many times before.

"How can a just man tolerate that house, or that woman?" Cauliffe had argued this point with Russell often in the past, and so there was little condemnation in his question.

Rather than return to their continuing dispute, Russell said. "If it is not Lorinda Dooley, it will be another. It is the nature of men that keeps such houses in business. Better such a place than honest women ruined."

"But men can be improved," said Cauliffe, then reined in his buckskin as a rickety gig drawn by an old mule and driven by

Geraldine Bruder, the shoe-maker's wife, rattled up to them. "Good day, Missus Bruder."

"To you, Preacher," she said, then nodded to Russell without speaking; the gig continued on its way.

Cauliffe turned and looked after the gig. "Rather cool, Jason."

"She hasn't said much to me since she learned I'm illegitimate. The bar sinister matters more to her than the device. He had intended his words to be more flippant than they were, and he added hastily, "Not that most of the townspeople care one way or another."

"Missus Bruder is hardly entitled to cast the first stone," said Cauliffe darkly.

They had almost reach the branching of the road that would separate them. "For a man who condemns Lorinda Dooley, you are strangely tolerant, Liam." Russell brought his mare to a restless stop.

"Your mother was a mistress, not a whore. And whatever she was, your character is not in question," said Cauliffe, as if expecting Russell to argue the point.

He answered with a question instead. "Are you certain of that?" Russell held his mare still for a moment longer, then gave her her head; he went off down Caridad Road toward the jail, leaving Liam Cauliffe to continue into town alone.

Chapter Three

Spring was making headway; melting snow fed brooks and streams, and the freshets made little cascades on the flanks of the mountain that were almost as melodic as the birds. Along the banks the first wildflowers pushed above the earth. The wind was cold off the high, snow-draped peaks, but the sun was warm enough to make heavy coats unnecessary and to bring people out of their houses for nothing more than the pleasure of stepping into light.

Russell was walking up Charity Street, enjoying the weather and the returning activity he could see the length of the muddy street. He had stopped at the shipping office to hand over a packet of letters for the next mail and was on his way to Dorabelle Schmidt's hotel when he heard his name called out angrily by a dark-haired young woman riding a high-bred black horse side-saddle. "Missus Fletcher," he said, removing his hat and stopping to speak with her.

"There are people on my land!" stormed Elvira Fletcher, raising her riding crop as if to lash out at the sheriff. Every person on the street turned to stare at her. "Paco brought me word yesterday."

Russell's response was deliberately mild. "I take it you mean that there are people on your land who are there without your authorization." He paused, hoping she would not rage at him. "That is regrettable if it is true. Where are these people, Missus Fletcher?"

"At Cerradura Lago, my..."—she fumbled for the word in English—"my pond, my lake! Paco says there are twenty-three people there, claiming the land belongs to them. It is mine! Not theirs!"

"Missus Fletcher," Russell said evenly, nodding to indicate all the townspeople who had stopped to listen to this harangue, "I don't think you want to talk about this in the middle of the street. Why not come into the hotel; we can discuss this more privately. Missus Schmidt will permit us to use her parlor, I am sure." Ordinarily he would have taken the reins of the horse as he made this suggestion, but knew that Elvira Fletcher would not allow so great a liberty. "We may review this whole issue more thoroughly."

"There is nothing to discuss," announced Elvira Fletcher. "I want those people put off my land. You are the sheriff. You attend to it. I want them gone by tomorrow." Her dark eyes were glittering with anger. "Now! Now! Have them gone!" She pulled her horse around abruptly and pointed at Russell with her crop. "You will do this at once."

"I will ride out tomorrow, Missus Fletcher, and see what is going on at the lake. I can make no other assurances until I find out who these people are and what they are doing there."

"They are trespassing," screamed Elvira Fletcher. "If you will not see to it, I will order Paco and Andreas and the rest of the men at the rancho to arm themselves and put these...criminals off my land."

Russell realized that this exchange had attracted a small crowd of spectators, more than had heard the beginning of the exchange, and he wished for an instant that he could drag Elvira Fletcher into the hotel and force her to speak sensibly. That urge faded as quickly as it had risen and he said, "That would not be very wise, Missus Fletcher. If there were bloodshed, I would have to take your men into custody and hold them for the judge. It would not serve your purpose to have that happen. It would strengthen the sympathy felt for the newcomers, whoever they are." He watched her, waiting for the next outburst.

"They are stealing my land!" shouted Elvira Fletcher as she spurred her black so hard that the horse cantered up the street, his rider urging him to greater speed.

"Well, well," said Hosea Olfrant from the door to the hotel. "A fine show of Spanish temper. I wonder how young Frederick endures it?"

"She is right; the land is hers," said Russell as he turned to face one of the three members of the Town Council.

"According to what?" Olfrant countered. "Some parchment from the King of Spain? You aren't going to enforce the land grants, are you? The land grants given the Spanish mean nothing to the United States." He laughed to emphasize his ridicule.

"That isn't certain yet," said Russell, starting to pass Olfrant. "And for all her raving, she is within her rights to require me to see who has moved onto her land." He was not looking forward to the task, and his reluctance showed. "I will go to the lake tomorrow."

"Probably just a few settlers lying over on their way west," said Olfrant with a shrug. "If they were staying they would have come into town, wouldn't they? The only newcomer I've run into is that widow out on the Old North Road."

"Possibly you're right," said Russell. "But Liam Cauliffe mentioned them to me day before yesterday. I would have to check on them even if Missus Fletcher had said nothing to me." With that, he nodded to Olfrant as he entered the hotel.

A light rain was falling as Russell turned off the Old North Road at the place beyond the bridge that Liam Cauliffe had described. He noticed the new wagon tracks in the soil, the broken saplings along the way, and a few raw stumps where the trees had been recently cut down.

The lake covered just over four acres and was fed by two streams and a spring that came from the cold depths of the narrow, north end. At the south end, where the lake was the widest, there stood a cluster of tents and a single new building, topped with a cross on a short spire, and not yet completely whitewashed, though a number of men worked on the building, the only sound being the blows of their hammers and the hiss of their saws.

Russell approached the settlement slowly, keeping his horse to a walk. He took advantage of this little time to observe the improvised community, and what he saw made him frown. The tents were large, and each one had a cross painted on its side. The men and women Russell could see were dressed in conspicuously plain grey clothes, lacking both color and adornment; the children were all in garments of the same grey as their parents, and they moved quietly and attentively in the wake of their elders. As soon as one of the men working on the church saw Russell, the sheriff stopped his horse and dismounted, lifting his hand in greeting without going nearer.

A tall, heavily built man detached himself from the men working on the church and approached Russell. The man was bearded and dressed in heavy trousers and a European smock. He took a stance at the head of his followers and addressed Russell. "God be with you, stranger. Who are you and why are you here?" His voice was low and clipped, riding the pattern of English words without skill.

"Good morning," said Russell, touching his hat politely. "I'm Jason Russell. I'm the sheriff in Charity." He made a point of looking around. "And you are?"

"We are the Penitent Children of God's Wrath," said their leader, and several of those with him nodded their agreement. "This is Moab, our settlement. We will live here in penitence and Christian fellowship, to appease God. I am the Reverend Werner Wachter; I am charged with the care of this community of devout Christians."

"I see," said Russell, noticing how very light the man's blue eyes were, cold and hot at once. "Reverend Wachter, may I know by what authority you've claimed this land?"

"By God's authority," replied Wachter as if the answer were obvious. "This land is God's offer to us for our redemption." He turned around suddenly as a child started to whimper. Though he said nothing and made no gesture, nor spoke, the child fell silent at once.

"I see," Russell repeated, then smiled, though he brought his hand to rest on his baton, "I'm afraid that there may be some difficulty, Reverend Wachter. I am afraid you are not as much at liberty to occupy this place as you supposed. This land is part of the Arreba y Corre rancho, and the current owner has lodged a complaint about your presence."

"Owner? This land is not property of men, but of God. God guided us here," said Wachter. "There is no greater mandate than God's word. Surely it is said: 'Woe unto them that decree unrighteous decrees, and that write grievousness which they have prescribed.'"

This was going to be more awkward than he had anticipated; Russell folded his hands. "Reverend Wachter, I'm afraid that your arrangements with God are not in my purview. I am an officer of the law, and in this country, the law and the church are separate, and I must abide by the law and uphold it. Do you understand that?"

"You are an instrument of worldly men, of corrupt men," declared Wachter.

Russell felt a few drops of rain gather on his collar and slide down onto his neck. The sensation matched what he felt in the presence of the Reverend Wachter. He ignored both and began a patient explanation. "The owner of this land knows that you are here, and that you do not have the right to be here, under the law of the land. She has requested that you leave it. She is prepared to have her men escort you off her land if that is necessary. I would not advise resisting her request. She is within her rights to do this. Any arrangements you make must be with her. If you are determined to stay here, then you will have to come to some equitable settlement with—"

Wachter's cheeks and forehead darkened. "What man stands between us and the work God has set for us to do? And you say she? She? A woman seeks to destroy our work? 'I will stand upon my watch, and set me upon the tower.' No other has claim to this place, for God has led us here for His purpose."

This time there were murmurs of assent from the others, and a few of the men held their hammers and brushes a little higher.

"I'm afraid the law doesn't recognize your claim," Russell said, not giving ground, but now very much on guard.

"The law is the servant of God or it is unworthy to be law," said Wachter, motioning to the others. "'For strangers are risen up against me, and oppressors seek after my soul: they have not set God before them.'"

"I should warn you that you are apt to damage your cause if you do not make a reasonable effort to comply with the law, no matter what you think of it," said Russell, tightening his hands on the reins of his horse, for the animal was beginning to fret.

"'Now is the end come upon thee, and I will send mine anger upon thee, and I will judge thee according to thy ways, and will recompense upon thee all thine abominations.'" said Wachter, his voice tolling out like thunder. "Who is this woman who dares to rise up against us?"

A second and third drop went down Russell's neck. "Look, Reverend, it isn't my intention to impose on you or your group. But I have a duty to uphold the law, and just at present you are breaking the law. You and Missus Fletcher both seem to be under the assumption that there is open conflict between you already, and that you must fight to the finish for this land. At one time that may have been the way in this part of the country, but it is not anymore. I will not allow you or Missus Fletcher to work outside of the law. I was hoping that it would be possible for you and Missus Fletcher to settle this between you before it becomes unpleasant for everyone." He looked around him. "You wish to build a community here; Missus Fletcher owns the land. It was left to her by her father, who had it from his father and his father before him." He hoped that this long claim might make Elvira Fletcher's title to the land more established for the stern Reverend Wachter.

"You speak of this woman as married. What does her husband say? It is proper for a woman to follow the dictates of her husband." Again his sentiments were punctuated with nods from the others.

"She is married, but her inheritance predates her marriage; the exact status of the property has yet to be determined by the circuit judge," said Russell. "If you were to reach an agreement before he arrives—he is expected in about a month—there would be little he could do to complicate matters for you." He hoped that this consideration might possibly bring Reverend Wachter to his senses.

"I confess that I am a great sinner, but I am not so lost that I do not know abomination. I know that a woman labors for her family and is submissive to the will of her husband, who stands in the place of God in her life." This time he nodded along with the rest. "I will not sink so low to bargain with a female." He glowered at Russell. "'A virtuous woman is a crown to her husband: but she that maketh ashamed is as rottenness in his bones.'"

Russell rocked back on his heels and assumed the look of mild annoyance he was far from feeling. "There's something else in *Proverbs*, as I recall: that it's virtuous to sue for peace instead of war, and that a soft answer lessens anger but hard words increase it. I have that right, don't I? So long as we're invoking Scripture, that might apply as well."

Now Wachter's cheeks were ruddy, his beard shone with droplets of rain, and he was clearly prepared to attack Russell. He trembled with emotion, and though his lips worked, no sound came from them. He took one step toward Russell, then dropped the hammer he carried, let out a long, despairing howl, and dropped to his knees, his face pressed into his clasped hands. At his back, the rest knelt as well, heads bowed over their hands. "God, God, *God!*" he cried out. "Save me from the wickedness and sins of men." Then he began to pray in a rapid, low voice in another language.

Looking on this, Russell moved back, tugging on the reins to bring his horse with him. Only when he was at the edge of the trees did he risk mounting and turning away from Reverend Wachter and his followers. He made his horse walk away, though he would rather have gone faster. As he made for the Old North Road, he tried to decide if he should inform Lorinda Dooley that he thought he had found the man who had beaten her and stolen her money, for though he had no proof to offer, he hoped there were not two such men in that part of the Texas Territories—tall, strong men with light blue eyes and an ungroomed beard who had a fearsome temper and quoted Scripture.

"I'm afraid I haven't much to offer; a little venison stew and some biscuits," said Abigail Lilhius as Russell rode up to her house. She had come out at the first sound of his approach, a shotgun in her hands; she still carried the gun, but open and slung in the curve of her elbow. "I wasn't expecting company."

"Small wonder, this far from town," said Russell as he dismounted. "Perhaps I should have warned you that it's my practice to visit the various outlying farms and settlements as regularly as possible." He led his horse to the hitching rail. "It is a fine house," he said, nodding toward her home.

"Yes, it is. Mister Lilhius wanted us to have the best we could, since we were coming into the wilderness." Her voice was wistful, but she forced herself to a more hospitable manner. "Mister Fletcher, the mayor, did mention something about you making rounds. He said you were as bad as a constable that way. He laughed when he said it." She looked at him speculatively, as if gauging his reaction to the mayor's remark.

"I'm sure," said Russell dryly. "He makes jokes, does our mayor." He could not conceal his irritation, but he managed not to snap at her. He determined to put Mrs. Lilhius at ease and to mitigate the mayor's notion of humor. "Well, he was right in his way; I do make rounds. And since I was in this vicinity, I decided to see how you were settling in." He gestured to the large barn and the two-story house. "You seem prepared for everything."

"On the outside, at least for the moment. Eventually I will want proper coops and a sheepfold, but that is for later. As things stand now, we are well-launched," said Mrs. Lilhius. "The inside is another matter. Thank God I brought my iron pots or we would have difficulty getting meals. The stove Mister Lilhius bought has yet to be hauled from Denver."

"That's inconvenient," said Russell, looking once again at the house. "If it is a serious problem, perhaps I can be of assistance in some way." He thought perhaps he ought to speak with Smilin' Jack, to find out what drayage company would be given the task of delivering her stove.

She laughed. "No. But you can come in for a bite to eat. I was about to have dinner, and my boy won't be back for hours. I'd be pleased for your company. I've seen almost no one but Jonah since my last visit to town, and I admit it is wearing on me." As she started up the stairs to her house she looked back over her shoulder at him. "I am glad you have come, Sheriff. You may count yourself welcome any time." With that she opened the door and stood aside so that Russell could enter.

The ground floor consisted of three large rooms: the parlor with a massive fireplace and two leather-covered settees and a scattering of wooden chairs; the salon, where a large table stood flanked by eight more chairs, with an elaborate kerosene lantern suspended above, its brasswork shining; and the kitchen. Russell could just see the pump at the sink and part of a block table as he came through the door. Directly in front of him, dividing the parlor from the salon, were the stairs leading to the second floor and—presumably—the bedrooms and storage.

"A very comfortable place, Missus Lilhius," said Russell as he removed his hat.

"It is," she said as she closed the door and set her shotgun in the rack between the door and window. She indicated the iron pot suspended over the fire by a hook. "Though not as comfortable as it might be. Once the kitchen is finished, we'll do very well."

"Yes. When your stove arrives everything will be fine," said Russell.

"As fine as they can be," said Mrs. Lilhius softly, and turned to him before he could apologize. "Pay me no mind, Sheriff Russell. I fall into despondence, when I remember, but the times are over quickly and becoming less frequent. Mister Lilhius did all that he could to make our living here pleasant and productive, and I am determined that it shall be."

"An admirable tribute," said Russell, looking around once more. "You have had no intruders or unwelcome visitors?"

"That's part of the reason for your rounds, isn't it?" she asked as she started toward the kitchen. "Excuse me while I get a plate and fork for you, Sheriff. Sit down, do, and I will return."

Russell considered the two leather settees, then decided on one of the three chairs in the parlor. He put his hat on the rack and sat down, admiring the room and hoping that when his house was built it would be as nice as this one. "It isn't necessary for you to—" he called out to Mrs. Lilhius.

"I'm longing for company," she answered, and came from the kitchen almost at once, to set two places at the salon table and then to carry plates to the hearth. "For the first week I enjoyed this, cooking on the hearth as if we were camping out. Now it is a chore, but I believe I welcome it, for it gives me something to do. Oh, there are chores enough, but this is different. It does not remind me of how things were last year." Her hair, a soft color between amber and wheat, was knotted at the back of her neck in a neat bun; a few tendrils had come loose and hung by her face. She wiped them back before she began to ladle stew out of the deep pot. "I have chickens in the barn, so we have eggs enough for more than we eat. I do not need pin money at present, but I thought it might be possible"—she broke off as she handed one filled plate to Russell—"to arrange with someone in town to sell some of the eggs. I do not like seeing them go to waste."

Russell had risen and was waiting for her to finish serving herself. "I am certain that Missus Schmidt at the hotel would be delighted to buy eggs from you. Her cook is Chinese; he came from the Sandwich Islands, I believe. He is adept with eggs."

She rose, her own plate served, and nodded toward the table. "Either place will do," she said, indicating the two places laid across the table from each other.

"Thank you," said Russell as he set down his plate, then went to hold the chair for Mrs. Lilhius. "You're very kind."

"I have tea, as well. As soon as the water boils I'll make some." She joined her hands and lowered her head before she put her napkin in her lap. "You are not a religious man," she said when she had finished her private devotion, seeing that he did not do the same.

"No, I'm not. I intend to give no offense, but whatever faith I had I lost long, long ago. It's the despair of Liam Cauliffe. He's the circuit preacher in this region." He picked up his fork. "Truly, I do not mean to offend you, Missus Lilhius."

"I'm not offended," she said, and started to eat. "I wish I had some fresh carrots and cabbage, but that will have to wait a while. Jonah has just started to work the ground for our garden, and it will be a while before we have such treats."

"It is delicious," said Russell, with genuine enthusiasm.

"You're very kind," she said.

"I am also a bachelor who is tired of his own cooking," Russell answered, and wondered why he had said that.

Her smile was quick but guileless. "You haven't the look of a man wasting away," she observed.

"No; I do go to the hotel whenever I become too bored with my own fare." He listened to himself speaking and was baffled. What was it about this woman that brought him so much feeling?

He could not account for his response to her, unless it was the result of dealing with Reverend Wachter and his followers. Perhaps, he told himself, the encounter had troubled him more than he had realized and now he was caught up by the kindness of this fair-haired widow.

She looked at him, curiosity in her faded-green eyes. "You sound like an old Charity hand."

"Hardly that. I came here last October. They—that is, the Town Council—have given me a year to prove my worth." He had more of the stew to keep from speaking.

"But you are building a house, so I understand," said Missus Lilhius.

He looked at her a moment before he answered. "Yes. I like Charity, and I have decided to settle here whether they keep me on as sheriff or not." He was about to say something more when Abigail Lilhius got up suddenly, paying no attention as he rose.

"For Heaven's sake, stay seated," she said. "The biscuits. I'll bring them at once." With that, she bolted from the room to the kitchen.

Left alone, Russell stared down at his plate, at the stew she had served him. The fork, he noticed, was silver and polished to a glossy shine. The china she used was genuine, of Dutch manufacture, and elegant enough to bring back memories of the few times he had been at his father's main estate. With these obvious attributes of wealth, what had possessed Abigail Lilhius' late husband to come to the Texas Territories? He was determined to find out. His thoughts were interrupted as Mrs. Lilhius returned with a plate of biscuits, still warm and steaming. "They're wonderful," he said as she offered one to him, then held out a crock of fresh butter.

"You haven't tasted them," she said lightly.

"I can smell them; that's enough," said Russell as he pulled the biscuit apart.

Mrs. Lilhius took her seat once more. "I hope you do like them; I still tend to cook for six instead of two." Her eyes grew distant, but she did not permit herself to dwell on her grief. "I am learning, but biscuits and bread...well, that will take time, I suppose."

Luckily Russell had taken a first bite of biscuit, and so did not have to think of an answer.

Chapter Four

There were forty-two horses in the string, and six men to deliver them. They entered Charity from the south, coming up Charity Street, bringing people out to stare as they arrived. The leader of the drovers, a man in foreign clothes with an odd cap on his head, stopped the first passerby he came upon.

"Excuse me," he said, taking off his cap and bowing a little in the saddle. "Would you be good enough to direct me to the sheriff's office?" His accent was that of the English West Country, soft and burry.

"You want Sheriff Russell?" asked the wheelwright's half-grown son, his eyes widening as he looked at the horses.

"Yes. Sheriff Russell." The man put his cap back on, and indicated the horses and the men. "We're supposed to present these to him."

"More horses," marveled the young man. He collected his wits, and realized that a couple dozen citizens of Charity were watching. He drew himself up to his full, gangly height. "That first corner on the right? You turn there, and the building on the left is the jail. Sheriff Russell'll be there." He took a step back, so that the men and horses could pass more easily.

"Thank you, m'lad," said the leader, who rose in his stirrups and motioned to the others to follow him.

As the horses clattered by him, the wheelwright's son stared at them in admiration, for he fancied himself a good judge of horse-flesh, and these animals were as good as any he had seen.

At the jail, the leader dismounted, and shouted to the others, "Bring 'em to order, and get them out of the road. The sheriff will tell us where to take them, make no doubt." With that, he started up the steps to the door of the jail.

Luis Guerra was behind the desk; he sat abruptly upright as the door opened, his hand going to the Adams revolver he carried in his holster. "Madre de Dios!" he swore as he looked out the door to the long string of horses.

"Sheriff Russell?" asked the leader, his expression politely disbelieving.

"Momentito," said Guerra, his eyes coming back to the newcomer. He got up carefully, as if he expected to be attacked, then went toward the back of the jail, calling out, "Sheriff! Sheriff!"

The door connecting the cells to the office opened. "What's wrong?" Russell demanded, responding to the urgency in Guerra's voice. He had his baton in his hand.

"Horses," said Guerra, trying with that single word to convey what he saw outside.

Russell stopped the retort that rose in him, and looked to the newcomer. "I'm Jason Russell. I suppose you're looking for me." He slipped his baton back into its holster and held out his hand.

The man touched his cap respectfully before taking Russell's proffered hand. "The Earl of Mindenhall sent me," he said. "I'm Othery. My oldest brother's chief groom for the earl."

"A pleasure, Mister Othery," said Russell. "How many are with you?"

"I've five riders, three who came over with me, and forty-two horses. We had forty-five horses when we left, but—" he made a gesture as if he were embarrassed to admit that not all the horses had survived.

"To lose only three in—what? five thousand miles? five thousand miles, is quite an accomplishment. You must be very skilled, Mister Othery." He looked toward the door. "May I inspect them?"

Othery shifted on his feet. "I...the men have come a long way. They're tired and so are the horses. If you could tell us where to take them, you could inspect them at your leisure. Not that I mean to give you orders." The last was so deferential that Luis Guerra stared at the man.

"You'd be entitled to," said Russell. "And you're right, of course." He glanced toward Guerra. "I'll return in about an hour. If anyone asks for me, I will be at my ranch, and if you need me, send for me." He took a light jacket from a peg on the wall, pulling it on as he said, "You're in charge, Luis."

"Count on me, Sheriff," Guerra said boldly, as if anticipating the arrival of marauders.

As Russell stepped out of the office, Othery frowned and cocked his head. "What's a wog doing serving in your place, if you don't mind me asking."

"He's Mexican," said Russell. "Not many people call them wogs here." He looked up at the horses. "Gracious." He nodded to the other men. "My horse is across the way at the livery stable. If you'll wait a couple minutes, I'll be with you." He turned to Othery. "Come with me, if you will."

"Of course," said Othery, falling in beside Russell. He was about thirty, a bit taller than the sheriff, and long-headed. As he strode along, he said, "I hope I don't overstep myself, but you have the look of your father, sir."

Russell had expected some remark and was prepared for it. "I have often thought so, when I remember him. I have a miniature of him, but it was not considered a good likeness."

"Very much the look," said Othery, prepared to go on.

Russell changed the subject. "As you've probably noticed by now, this part of the world is filling up with all sorts of people, from all sorts of places. You will encounter a great deal of variety in this part of the west; almost everyone in this town, for example, has been here less than six years. It can give rise to difficulties, but it is also very…stimulating." He reached the side door to Calvin's smithy and livery stable. "If you care to come in, Mister Othery?"

"Thank you," he said, going through the door.

"My horses are on that side of the stable. One of them is saddled. I have taken to keeping one saddled and ready, on slack girths, in case I am called in an emergency. Minutes are precious at those times." He stepped into the open stall and backed the roan out. "This fellow was in the first lot my half-brother sent. He's a good, steady ride." As he spoke, he tightened the girths of the saddle and brought the reins over the gelding's head to lead him out of the livery stable.

"I remember him, sir," said Othery. "A shame he was not up to breeding standards. Looking at him, you can see his shoulder is too straight for hunting. Still, he's got a nice temperament—had it even when he was entire." They were on the street again, and waited for the pony-drawn dairy cart to pass them with its load of milk.

"In my estimation, temperament is as important in a horse as confirmation," said Russell. "A pity he wasn't bred, given his nature. And his confirmation"—they started across the street—"is satisfactory to me. If you could see some of the horses I've slung my leg over in my day, you'd understand. You might even agree."

Othery's face was very blank. "I have heard that you travel extensively."

"Used to," said Russell, paying no heed to the tone of Othery's comment. "But no more. This place suits me down to the ground, and it is time I found a home for myself. I'm nearing fifty, and if I don't settle soon, I never will."

"I was told you were planning to stay; that you wanted the horses because of staying."

Russell gave Othery an amused look. "What would I do with more than fifty horses, and more coming, if I were running about the world?"

"I can't guess," said Othery. He waved to his men and touched his cap as Russell mounted. "We'll just follow you, sir, if that's all right."

Russell offered him a salute as he started past the string of horses toward the Denver Road and his ranch.

He was no more than twenty, a slight, pale young man with flat, china eyes of light sandy brown. He stood uncertainly in the lobby of the hotel, his expression uncertain and his manner hesitant. There was a shotgun in his hands, two revolvers slung from crossed cartridge belts, and a hunting knife strapped at the top of his left boot.

"Is there anything I can do for you?" Martin Corley asked from his place behind the desk. Although Martin was not much older than the young stranger, he had a brash confidence that gave him the aura of age and experience, or so he liked to tell himself.

"I guess I'd like a room," said the young man, his voice as light and colorless as his lank hair.

"That's what you get at hotels: rooms," said Martin, pleased with his own wit.

The young man came a few steps nearer the registration counter, his air as uncertain as if Martin Corley were a wild animal. "How much is it?"

"Rooms are three-fifty and four dollars, in advance." He quoted the new, higher prices with authority. "If you want a bath, it's a half dollar for cold, a dollar for hot. If you want meals, it's another dollar a day, in advance. We serve breakfast at six, dinner at noon, and supper at seven. If you want anything else, you have to arrange it in advance and pay in advance." He trimmed the nib of a pen as he spoke and now dipped it in the inkwell. "Name and address?"

"Is there another hotel in this town?" the stranger asked.

"No," said Martin. "There's a tavern with a couple of upstairs rooms at the south end of town, and there's a road house about twelve miles out on the Denver Road. Otherwise, this is the only place to stay, unless you arrange to board with someone in town." He watched the stranger absorb this news. "Name and address," he repeated.

The young man took the pen as if he feared it would bite. "I don't have an address."

"Just write where you're from, that's all." He indicated the pen he had handed to the youngster. "You can write, can't you?"

"Enough," said the young man with what passed for dignity. His handwriting was a disorderly scrawl, leaning in spikes this way and that, but not completely illegible. *Silas Fitzroy,* he wrote, from *Pennsylvania.*

"Where about in Pennsylvania?" asked Martin, as much to satisfy his own curiosity as to be certain that he had read the word correctly.

"No place you ever heard of," said Fitzroy. "I left there five years ago. It's just a couple farms out in the hills."

"From hills to mountains, is that it?" Martin said, holding out his hand for payment. "How long you planning to stay?"

Again Fitzroy hesitated. "I don't have much money. I can give you twenty dollars. That's five nights, with meals. If I get the cheaper room, I can have a bath as well." He took the gold piece from a worn leather pouch. "Pretty costly. Three-fifty is a lot of money for a room, especially in a place like this."

"It was two dollars a year ago," said Corley. "But everything's costly in a place like this. We got to pay to bring in food and other things. Widow Schmidt orders sheets all the way from Baltimore. With more people coming, it costs more to run the hotel. Even the roadhouse raised prices last month, because the cost of hauling went up in Denver." He enjoyed this recitation, confident that it made him appear knowledgeable and experienced. "Missus Schmidt has dishes and glasses coming soon, to replace the ones that got broken during the winter."

"It's still a lot of money," said Fitzroy. "What about my horse, or does that cost, too?"

"Calvin's livery stable at the end of the street has stalls. Twenty cents a day if you want your horse fed; thirty if you feed grain as well as hay." He paused, and went on, "I'm with you, though, I think there should be a way to arrange for hotel guests to stable their horses for free. Missus Schmidt's for it, but Daniel Calvin isn't."

Fitzroy shook his head. "Is there work to be had in this town, or does everyone get rich off of strangers?"

Martin did not permit himself to argue with Fitzroy. "I think that we treat strangers well. We don't leave you on your own, and we got a nice quiet town. You won't get robbed and you won't get diddled here." He rocked back on his heels, the way he had seen the mayor do. "And there is work. We got people moving here, more and more of them. If you got any skill at building or painting, there's work for you."

"I see," said Fitzroy. "What room do I get?"

For a moment it seemed as if Martin wanted to pursue his point, but then he sighed. "Back of the parlor, there's a hall. This is the door at the end of it. There's a letter G on the door." He handed over the key. "You got anything you want me to carry?"

"For ten cents a bag, I bet," said Fitzroy, unwilling to face Martin; his tone was petulant. "I'll manage, and then I'll see to my horse."

"Fine. I'll tell the cook you'll be here at supper."

Henry Clayton stood in the cell door and shook his head in disbelief. "For God's sweet mercy, what happened?" he demanded as Russell eased his third prisoner back onto a cot.

"There was a fight," said Russell without emotion.

"I know that. I can see that. The Howes' boy was going on about it when he came for me. What on earth happened?" Before the sheriff could answer, Clayton went on, "If you say 'a fight' again, Jason, I will give you cause to regret it."

"Catty made a disparaging remark about the Dutch, and Ambruster's mother is Dutch. Watkins was drinking with Ambruster, so when the fight started—"

"—he sided with Ambruster," Clayton finished. He came into the cell and only then did he see Russell's face clearly. "You're hurt."

Russell put his hand to the blood that was scabbing over on his cheek and jaw. "Nothing drastic," he said. "These men need your services more than I do. I was forced to use the baton, and I think Ambruster has a broken arm. Catty's shoulder is very badly wrenched."

"You did that trick didn't you?" Clayton asked, not able to conceal his satisfaction. "You got him down, put your foot on the side of his chest and pulled his arm. Didn't you?"

"Of course," said Russell with a trace of irritation. "What else could I do?"

"I don't know; I didn't see the fight. But I do trust you, Jason, and you would not do such a thing if it were not truly necessary." He looked at the three men. "What about the other?"

"Catty knocked Watkins out: struck him with a bottle." He touched his face and winced. "Struck me, too."

"That Catty is a bad sort," said Clayton as he opened his bag and pulled out a roll of gauze. "Well, leave me to this. I'll tend to you when I'm finished here." He looked at the sheriff with a mixture of aggravation and concern. "I don't suppose you'd agree to let me tend to you first."

"No, I would not," said Russell as he went to the door. "I'm going to leave this open; I don't think these three will give you any trouble, but if they do...."

"I will call you," said Clayton. "I have no hesitation about guarding myself." He was already setting out his materials.

"If that was meant as an admonition, Doctor, it hardly applies." Russell was already stepping into his office, the door between the cells and the office left open. He pulled his chair out from the desk and sat down slowly. Now that he did not have to deal with the men and their pointless, violent argument, he felt sore and tired. A few minutes before his face had bothered him only slightly, now it ached like a rotten tooth. He closed his eyes and let out a long, slow sigh.

It was twenty minutes later when Clayton closed the cell door and turned the key. He had his bag in his hand, but it was still open. As he entered the office, he tossed the ring of keys onto Russell's desk, and said, "You're next, Sheriff."

Russell opened his eyes abruptly, startled to realize that he had been napping. "Finished already?" he asked, willing himself to alertness.

"Yes, though I'll want to see Ambruster in a day or so. He's going to be gruff as a bear when he wakes up, or you may call me a Chinaman." He placed his bag on the desk and pulled out his gauze again. Then he bent to inspect the damage to Russell's face. "Nasty. One or two blows?" he asked in a detached way.

"Two—one forehand and the other backhand. He's a canny fighter in his way." He looked up at Clayton. "Don't bother to tell me that this will hurt only a trifle. You and I both know better than that."

"All right, it is apt to be painful. Sit up straight, will you, Jason? It will be over sooner if you let me do my work." He pulled out a small bottle of spirits. "The cut on the cheek is going to leave a scar—not a large one, if you will permit me to stitch it closed. It needs two stitches, no more. Without the stitches, the scar will be wider." He was already reaching for the fine strings of catgut he used for such tasks. "It won't take long."

Russell sighed. "Go ahead," he said, wondering what he would do for the headache he had that would surely be worse by the time Henry Clayton was through with him. "But don't linger at it."

"As you wish," said Clayton as he chose a needle. "I'm going to clean the wound with spirits. It will sting."

"Yes; I know," said Russell.

William Red Pony arrived at Russell's half-finished house just as Russell was starting to tend to the morning feeding. He said nothing, but took the wheelbarrow and started down the aisle between the open stalls.

Othery, who was at the far end of the barn, stared. "Sheriff," he began. "What—"

"William is very good with horses," said Russell obliquely. It was two days since his face was cut and it hurt to talk.

"You need help, so here I am. I would have come yesterday if anyone had told me," said William, nodding to Russell before turning his attention to Othery. "You brought the new horses, didn't you. Nice stock, from what I can tell; bigger than we get around here most of the time."

"Yes," said Othery, still staring. "My lads and I brought the stock."

"In Charity, everyone knows everything about everyone else, sooner or later," said Russell, resisting the urge to smile. "William is no exception. In fact, working as he does at the livery stable, he is often the first with news."

William carried flakes of hay to the horses in the first two stalls. "That grey mare is looking better; she needs another fifty pounds and she'll be up to breeding weight."

Othery blinked. "That's less than she should carry to breed. She might not settle if she isn't heavier."

"At a fine, rich farm, perhaps," said William. He took two more flakes, and fed the next pair of horses in line.

In the barn the other horses were whickering in eager anticipation, a few of them making soft, chuckling neighs to bring their food sooner.

"Othery, will you tend to the horses in the pasture? A full flake for each horse. You and your men should be able to see them fed in the next half hour or forty minutes." Russell indicated the stalled horses. "William and I can tend to these. If you would be kind enough?" The last was to William.

"It's most irregular," said Othery. "Yesterday morning you left the feeding to my men and me."

"Yesterday morning I was still suffering from the fight I had been in, and was confined to my bed on the physician's orders. Today I am quite capable of tending my own stock, but I would be grateful for your assistance. You will be leaving soon, won't you? and I will have the task to myself; I might as well start it now. If this does not please you, then I recommend that you return to the hotel for your breakfast, and leave it for us to finish." He said this cordially enough, though his face was without expression.

"We will do as you ask, sir," said Othery, his back stiff and his eyes directed at a spot about two feet above Russell's head.

"Thank you," said Russell at his most bland.

As soon as Othery was out of the barn, William interrupted his task. "Why did you do that, Sheriff? You've offended him."

"That's unfortunate," said Russell with a marked lack of concern. "It is his way, I suppose. He is not at my half-brother's stud farm now, he is in the Texas Territories, and things are different here."

"He will lose respect for you if you show favor to me," warned Red Pony. "Most whites do now show favor to Indians if they wish to have the good opinion of other whites."

"I will lose respect for myself if I do not, for I do have a good opinion of you. Your advice has been very useful to me," said Russell in the same mild tone. "I'll get the scoops for the grain. They're on summer rations now—half a scoop for each horse."

William nodded but said nothing.

It took almost an hour to tend to the horses in the barn, and by the time he was finished with the work, Russell reluctantly admitted that he was tired. He pulled up the farrier's bench and dropped onto it, his thoughts far away, as William returned the wheelbarrow to the feed room. He was trying to make up his mind if he should send word to Luis Guerra that he would not be able to come to the office today when he saw Othery coming toward him.

"I don't mean to bother you, sir, seeing as how you're not entirely yourself," said Othery, as if to forestall any remark Russell might make.

"But you are going to," said Russell fatalistically, one hand going to the bandage on his face. "What is it?"

"Well, the flaxen dun, the mare? She's cut up around the hocks. It looks like something's been after her." He removed his cap. "She's not failing, or the like. She's moving well enough and she's eating, but the cuts are open, and it looks like they've been bleeding."

Russell got slowly to his feet. "Show me," he said.

"I had one of my men catch and tie her, sir, in case you wanted to see for yourself." He seemed pleased to have done the right thing. "She's active enough, and has mischief in her."

"I'll look for myself," said Russell. "Thank you for telling me." He called out, "William, I'm going out to check one of the mares. Come along when you can."

Othery grew visibly more rigid. "Why should he come?"

"Because he's the best at healing animals," said Russell, his irritation no longer concealed. "Ask anyone. Ask Daniel Calvin at the livery stable. If you have a sick animal or one that's been hurt, you bring it to William Red Pony, and he'll fix it if it can be fixed." He was walking between the stalls, listening to the sound of the horses eating. It was such a contented sound, he thought, comfortable as an old chair.

Outside the men were standing around the grey mare; they had tied her to the fence with enough rope for her to put her head down to eat the hay given her.

"On-side rear's the worst," said one of the men, a sallow-faced, undersized fellow whose Holborn accent stirred Russell's memories of being a Bow Street Runner every time the man spoke. "Bad cuts they are, sir."

"Bad cuts?" said Russell as he came up to the mare, patting her on the neck. "Oh, yes, I see." He bent to inspect the long rakings along her rump, and the shorter, more aggravated scratches above her hock. "Claws, by the look of it."

"I should say, sir," Othery agreed at once. "But what has such claws."

William had come up behind them, and answered Othery. "Bears. There's a mother and cubs on the hill, I think. They're hungry." He looked at the scratches closely. "Bear. No cat did this. The claws don't hook enough for cats. Bears swipe, cats hook. Two of them, I'd guess, one learning, perhaps."

Othery's face was skeptical, but Russell said, "Was this the mother and the cub?"

"The cub probably tried for her first. If the mother had caught her, the mare wouldn't be here." He leaned over and lifted the mare's rear hoof. "Nothing. Sometimes you can find fur, if she kicked hard enough. Too bad."

"I suppose the ranchers had better be warned," said Russell, not looking forward to a day in the saddle. He would carry willow-bark tea with him, that would help.

"Some of them must know already," said William. "But you might find out enough to help most of them take precautions, especially with young. That's what the mother bear will be after, the young ones. In a while all three will be hunting together." He looked away toward the flank of the mountain. "I don't envy those people at the lake. They still live in tents, and with bears out—"

"I'll do what I can to warn them. In the meantime, is there anything you can do for the mare?" asked Russell with real concern. He rested his hand on the mare's shoulder. "She seems all right."

William nodded. "If she doesn't take the fever from infection, I can make her better."

"Well enough," said Russell. "Put her in the barn then and—" He stopped as William held up his hand.

"Better to have her in the covered paddock during the day. She'll do better if she can move around." William glanced in the direction of Othery. "Wouldn't you say so, Mister Othery?"

Othery's amazement would have been amusing if he had not been so very serious. "It is what I would have recommended, yes," he admitted, as if he had seen water turn to wine.

"That's settled, then," said Russell, and gave William a direct look. "Do as you think best. I'm sure she can have no better care than what you give her."

William did not smile but the creases around his eyes grew deeper and he made a gesture of acceptance, apparently unaware of Othery's shocked expression.

Chapter Five

Mayor Fletcher was staring at the ceiling, doing his best to disassociate himself from the other two in his office. He sighed at the sound of his daughter-in-law's raised voice, thinking again that his son was a fool. These last several months he was beginning to suspect his mother had been right, and that late babies turn out badly.

"I expect these people to be put off my land," Elvira Fletcher said, each word crisp and precise. "You have been taking their part, Sheriff, and I intend to bring complaint to the circuit judge as soon as he arrives. I demand that justice be done."

Russell folded his arms and looked at the beautiful, furious young woman. "Missus Fletcher, you must do as you think right, of course. But so must I. As long as I have the obligation to obey the law, I cannot simply run these people off. They have what they claim to be a legal deed to their land. Reverend Wachter showed it to me when I went there yesterday. He was very reluctant to let me see it, but when I informed him that he and his followers would be removed, he produced the document. My hands are tied. It may be that the deed is provisionally valid, which—"

He got no further. "His deed is a fraud. It is a fake. He has no right. The *man* is a fraud. He is no priest. He is nothing more than a charlatan." Her pronunciation was not perfect but there was no mistaking her meaning even if her English had been much worse. "He is to go, and all those with him, or I will tell my men—"

Russell interrupted her as politely as he could. "Missus Fletcher, if you order your men to harass those people, it will be you who will have to answer to the law, and I will have the unpleasant duty of enforcing it. I've warned you before, Missus Fletcher." He waited, hoping he had her attention. "If you wish to know my personal assessment of the problem, I believe that the law ought to support the first claim and not the second. But it is a question of jurisdiction, and until that is settled, I must ask that all parties refrain from any action that might prejudice the case one way or another. And," he went on more pointedly, "Missus Fletcher, if you do anything to worsen the problem I will hold you answerable for it, as I will hold the Reverend Wachter answerable for any action he may take that is contrary to law."

"You will support him. You are a Protestant. He is a Protestant. You are both men." The last was the most damning epithet.

Russell was sorry that Mayor Fletcher would hear this, but he said, "You are mistaken. I am not a Protestant, nor would I support anyone whose religion is contrary to the laws of the land." He cleared his throat. "Missus Fletcher, I ask you to be patient. I understand how unfair this appears to you. It is difficult, I realize, to wait for the law to take its course, but it is necessary in cases of this sort, when there are so many unanswered questions." He saw the color heighten in her face and readied himself for her next outburst.

"Not only are you a liar, Sheriff, you are a coward. You must have contempt for me to say this. You would rather see these hypocrites take over land that is mine—mine!—than be seen to help a Spaniard." She paced the room, then turned on her father-in-law. "And you are worse than he is. You are a pompous fool. You are a worm, a toad. You have made my husband the same kind of weakling you are."

"Now, Elvira, see here—" Mayor Fletcher began, but was not allowed to go on.

"Listen to you! You dare address me like a wayward child! I am not a child, I am Elvira Carmen Isabel Arreba y Corre. I am not Missus Frederick Fletcher. He is my husband. You are his father. But I am not a Fletcher."

"Most certainly not," said George Fletcher. "We would not tolerate such behavior in our ladies."

"Ladies!" Elvira Fletcher laughed angrily. "What ladies? Your wives are not ladies, they are spoiled children, nothing more than shadows in petticoats. It is what you make them. You are afraid of women. You are afraid of me, father-of-my-husband. I have given you no reason to fear me, but if my land is taken from me, I will." She turned and marched up to Russell. "You are to get those trespassers off of my land, Sheriff, and you are to be sure they do not return to it, or I will bring you up on charges, if I have to go to Denver or Saint Louis to do it." She reached for her short, stylish, fur cape and flung it around her shoulders. "If my father were still alive, all those trespassers would be hanged."

"If your father were alive," Russell said with great cordiality, "you would still be in Mexico, and you would be wed to the man of his choice, and your husband would inherit your father's land, not you."

It was very still in the mayor's office.

"You are a vile person, Sheriff Russell," said Elvira Fletcher with acidic sweetness. "You throw that up to me, do you? It is wrong, very wrong, to do that."

"Why?" Russell asked. "Because it is true and you wish it were not?" He came up to her, favoring her with a nod that was not quite a bow. "Your father intended to carry on his family tradition, which required that he find a Spanish husband for you, another hidalgo—is that the right word?—who would carry on for him. You told me yourself this was not what you wanted. Yet now you claim that your father intended you to have the land. Your father intended that you have sons, not land, Missus Fletcher," Russell said with restraint. "If he had not died, you would not have inherited the land, and you would not have been permitted to marry Mister Frederick, which you said then was what you wanted most to do. Which is it, Missus Fletcher?"

Her dark eyes were bright as she looked him up and down once with the same appraising attitude she would use to examine a prize animal. "I will not underestimate you again, Sheriff." She ignored the mayor as she left the office.

"That was most regrettable," said Mayor Fletcher when he was certain that his daughter-in-law had left the bank.

"I'd have thought it was inevitable," said Russell, coming back to where the mayor sat at his wide desk. "Given the way that Wachter has been behaving, I'm relieved that the worst we have had to deal with is Missus Fletcher's outbursts."

"Please," said Mayor Fletcher. "She is right; she is no Missus Fletcher. What was Frederick thinking of when he married her? He is an impulsive boy." He hooked his meaty hands together. "He read *The Sorrows of Young Werther* when he was a lad, and it changed him, I'm sure of it. I was told it was a dangerous book, but I didn't believe it. Young Werther seemed a foolish malcontent to me, and I assumed that Frederick would benefit from seeing what such excesses brought. But he did not regard it that way." He sighed. "Missus Fletcher—my wife, not that Spanish creature—told me then that Frederick was the same sort of boy that the hero was. It is nonsense, of course, but she encouraged him in it. It is an infamous book."

"But surely," said Russell, trying to soothe the mayor, "he read other novels as well, not just Göethe."

"Of course, of course. I made sure he had copies of Swift and *The Last Days of Pompeii*. Missus Fletcher has a fondness for that scoundrel Dickens." He cleared his throat. "There are so many difficulties in educating a son."

"Certainly," said Russell, whose mother had been a teacher. He watched Fletcher with a trace of curiosity. "Tell me, do you suppose the circuit judge will be here within the month? I ask," he went on as the mayor gave him a quizzical look, "because I am reasonably certain I can keep your daughter-in-law from doing anything hasty for that length of time; beyond that, I cannot answer for what may happen."

"And that Reverend Wachter? What of him?" demanded Mayor Fletcher.

"I will speak with him. I doubt he will pay much heed to anything I say, since I don't quote Scripture to support myself, but I think that for a time he will have his hands full setting up the community for his followers." Russell cocked his head toward the window where a light spring drizzle turned the outside world a uniform blue-grey. "Housing must be their first concern. Once that is settled, well, things are apt to change."

"Yes, I see that," said Fletcher, his eyes narrowing. "What does Preacher Cauliffe think?" It was not unusual for the mayor to appeal to the Protestant circuit preacher in any matter of religion.

"I'll speak to him as soon as he returns," promised Russell, hoping that Cauliffe would be back soon.

Satisfied with Russell's answer, the mayor added, "I will have a word with Frederick."

"I appreciate that," said Russell, certain that anything Fletcher said to his youngest son would go unheeded.

Sister Mercedes looked completely out of place in the lobby of the hotel. Her voluminous habit, formal and archaic, made Martin Corley stare at her before he fled, calling for Dorabelle Schmidt.

"Good morning to you, Sister," said the Widow Schmidt as she came into the lobby from the back recesses of the building. "My assistant just brought me word you were here." The German woman indicated the parlor. "Perhaps you would like to sit down?"

"Muchas gracias," said the nun. *"Yo deseo una palabra, señora."*

Dorabelle Schmidt blinked. "I'm sorry. *Ich bedauere. Ich verstehe nicht.* I don't speak Spanish. Do you know English?"

"Ah," said Sister Mercedes. *"Sí, un poquito.* I...I must tell you." She turned toward the parlor. *"Puede parlar aquí?* You talk here?"

"Fine. Yes," said Mrs. Schmidt with relief as she went with the nun toward the parlor. "Take a seat, Sister," she said, speaking slowly and loudly, as if Sister Mercedes were a trifle deaf.

"Gracias," she said, choosing a small, unupholstered chair. "You are most nice."

"Danke," said Dorabelle Schmidt, taking her place on the settee, wondering what on earth the nun was doing here. What could she, the owner of the hotel, do for a nun?

"Another sister comes," said Sister Mercedes, choosing her words with great care. "Tomorrow or...another day."

"The day after?" asked Missus Schmidt. "Tomorrow or the next day?"

"Sí. Verdadamente." She took hold of the rosary that hung from her waist and rubbed at the polished wooden beads. "She comes. To Sagrada Caridad."

"To your church," said Mrs. Schmidt, wanting to be certain that it was the church, not the town, that was this new nun's destination.

"We are...not ready," said Sister Mercedes.

"Oh?" Mrs. Schmidt straightened on the settee. "Do you want her to have a room here, is that it? Until you are ready for her?"

Sister Mercedes looked relieved. "Yes. That is right." She smiled and bobbed her head to Mrs. Schmidt.

"Are you sure?" asked Dorabelle Schmidt, worried for the first time.

"We have money," said Sister Mercedes at once.

"Oh, no, no, no," said Dorabelle Schmidt, though she was glad to hear it. "It's not that." She folded her hands in her lap. "This is a hotel, Sister, and there are all sorts staying here. I can't...I am not able to promise that your sister would...like to be here." How was she supposed to explain about the men who drank every night, about the people who came to learn to read and write, about the fights that broke out from time to time? "All kinds stay here."

"*Sí. Lo siento,*" said Sister Mercedes.

"If that means what I think it means," said Dorabelle Schmidt, her face polite and her eyes shrewd, "it might be better if you found her another place to stay."

Sister Mercedes sat upright. "Oh, no, no. Please, señora. Please."

Dorabelle Schmidt had no idea how to calm her agitation. "If you have to have the room, Sister—" She made a gesture of compliance. "Four dollars the night. I'll see she has her meals in her room."

"No," said Sister Mercedes. "With us. She will not...be hard."

"It's not just her that worries me," said Missus Schmidt.

"*¿Como?*" said Sister Mercedes. "What is it?"

"Well, I don't like to say it," answered Dorabelle Schmidt, "but that sister might not take to the others here, even in her room. We got rough ones here, sometimes, and some of them don't like nuns, Sister." She coughed once, rather delicately, and to buy herself a little time, she rose and went to the parlor door, calling to Martin to send in some tea, with something to eat. That done, she turned back to her perplexing visitor. "I don't want her to do something that'll cause trouble. I already got trouble here most Saturday nights. If the sister's here, it could be worse for all of us."

"She keep in room," said Sister Mercedes. "And church."

"That's fine as far as it goes," said the hotel owner, coming back to the settee and resuming her place in a fussier manner. "But I don't want to be blamed if anything happens."

"What do you mean?" Sister Mercedes fingered her beads more insistently, as if the wood held an answer for her that it stubbornly refused to release.

This time Dorabelle Schmidt considered her answer with care. "I suppose I mean that I don't want it known there's a nun at the hotel. Some of the boys would not like that. It would be bad for her and bad for me. I can give her a room, that's sure. But I don't want her coming and going through the lobby. It would just make some of the men in town determined to prove—" She did not know how to go on.

Sister Mercedes nodded. "I know." She nodded. "It is good that...the sister not...show herself."

"It surely is," said Missus Schmidt emphatically. She got up and held out her hand. "Four dollars a night. Don't tell me it's too much. That's the rate, nun or no nun. You tell Padre Antonio that I can't let him have the room for nothing."

"De segura," said Sister Mercedes, nodding again. *"Tengo dinero."*

"I know dinero," said Missus Schmidt. "I picked up a few words." She smiled, looking up as Martin came in with a tray, doing best not to stare. He put the tray down on a side table and looked at his employer.

"Do you want me to do...anything?" he asked, glancing nervously at the nun.

"No. I'll pour. Thank you, Martin," said Dorabelle Schmidt, waving her young clerk away. "Go take care of inventorying what's left in the pantry and larder." She rose to pour the tea as Martin hastened out of the room. "I hope that Smilin' Jack gets here in a few days. I'm almost out of everything useful. We had a busy winter, and I wasn't prepared. I won't make that mistake again next year. Do you want sugar, Sister?"

Sister Mercedes, who followed about half of what Missus Schmidt was saying, shook her head. "Gracias, no."

"The English like lemon, but I never did. Do you want cream? I got it fresh this morning, right from the dairy. It's whipped." She indicated the bowl with the cloud-like mound in it. "It reminds me of home."

"No, gracias," said Sister Mercedes.

"I guess you don't have treats like whipped cream when you're a nun," said Mrs. Schmidt as she ladled out a generous portion of whipped cream on top of her tea. "And these things," she added, holding out a tray of strange little pastries. "Sun makes these out of God-knows-what—asking your pardon, Sister—but they sure taste good."

This time Sister Mercedes took what was offered, but after a short hesitation.

"Now, you try that," the Widow Schmidt went on. "You'll like it, Sister." She helped herself to two and went back to the settee. "It's settled, then?"

"I think," said Sister Mercedes. "The new sister...I come when she come."

Dorabelle Schmidt took a long sip of tea through the mass of whipped cream and smiled. "Good. She'll be glad to see you." As she sampled Sun's pastry, she hoped she would be able to get the nun into her hotel without anyone in Charity knowing about it. She did not want her hotel to be the site of any incident, and permitting a nun to stay here would court just such a catastrophe. From the recesses of her memory she heard her long-dead father's voice saying *Alles ist in Ordnung*. When she was a girl, that reassurance had calmed her, but now it served only to make her more apprehensive. "Would you like another cup of tea, Sister?" she asked as she saw her visitor put her cup down.

"No. It was good." She closed her eyes a moment, whispered something and crossed herself. "Gracias, señora." With that, she rose, and Dorabelle Schmidt hurried to set her cup aside and escort Sister Mercedes to the door.

When Hepsibah Mattington came to town, she made a point of stopping to speak to Sheriff Russell, saying as she got off her horse, "I'm tired of telling you I'm sorry about what that idiot Catty did, Jason, and that's a fact. Another fight like that last one, and I'm ordering him off my ranch." She stared at Russell's face. "He's been boasting that he marked you."

"He left a scar, if that's what he means," said Russell. "But what man reaches my age without a few scars?"

"I won't mention you said that; he'd want to try again." She came up the steps of the sheriff's office and jail, pulling her hat from her head and patting the iron-grey bun at the back of her neck. "The thing binds up on me," she explained. "Sit down, Jason, I got to have a talk with you."

Russell regarded her with curiosity. "Why? Because your hand did this?" He touched the new, still-red scar on his cheek.

"No, not entirely," she said. "I had a youngster out at the ranch the other day, looking for work. Tall, skinny fellow about twenty or so, calls himself Silas Fitzroy."

"Oh, yes," said Russell. "Martin Corley told me about him. I've seen him once or twice." He sat on the edge of his desk. "What about him?"

"That's what I can't figure out, and it bothers me," she said candidly. "He's got a soft-spoken manner—a lot better behaved than most of the hands we take on—and he can read and write some."

"Has he said or done anything—" Russell began only to have Mrs. Mattington interrupt him.

"There's not a thing about him that's troublesome, but he troubles me. I can't explain it. Something about him gives me the wobbles." She sighed once. "I'm not one of these women who have vapors or go off in tizzies. It's nothing like that."

Privately Russell thought he had met few women who were less likely to have vapors or go off in tizzies than Hepsibah Mattington, but kept that observation to himself. "What is it like?"

She considered her answer. "It's like hearing someone play a pretty tune on a bad piano," she said at last. "You know how it ought to sound, and everything's being done to make it sound that way, but it doesn't." She slapped her rough, strong hands on her thighs. "There's no reason for it, Jason."

"What are you going to do about it?" asked Russell, knowing

that she would not make such an effort to tell him about this man unless she had some reason to inform him of her plans.

"I want to find him work somewhere else—in town, where you can keep an eye on him." She squared her jaw. "I know that's not supposed to be done, but you mark me, Jason, this man needs watching." She flushed a little, and for an instant there was a faded reflection of her vanished girlhood on her weathered features. "You can call me a foolish old woman if you want, but you watch that young man, Jason."

"I haven't called you a foolish old woman yet, Bess," he said. "I wouldn't."

"Not where I can hear you, at least," she said. "You might have cause to when this is done."

Since Bess Mattington rarely admitted to any doubts whatever, the degree of uncertainty she displayed now was the more remarkable. "The young man has you spooked?"

"I suppose that's what it comes down to," she said, shaking her head in disbelief at her own state of mind. "I had it happen once or twice before, but not like this. I had the hair stand up on my neck, and that's the Good Lord's own truth, or I am a heathen and a liar."

"All right." He picked up his notepad and a pencil, going on as if this were the usual sort of information Missus Mattington provided. "Do you have any idea why you are bothered by this fellow? Anything specific or obvious that might give me something to look for?"

"You mean you're going to do it?" Bess Mattington asked, amazed that the sheriff was going along with her.

"To some extent," he said. "I have other duties to attend to, but I will keep an eye on him, the more so if you can point out to me something to watch for." He gave her an apologetic shrug. "I don't mean to question you, Bess. I trust your sense even if you do not. But with only Luis and myself to tend to the town, I haven't the time or manpower to do much about this Fitzroy."

She pushed out her lower lip. "I don't know what to tell you. It's something in the eyes. You know what I mean—you can see something not right in his eyes. Not like Catty or McPhee, not wild like them, or mean like Tuck, but something else. He won't look you in the eye much, that's the start of it. But..." She let the thought fade.

Russell waited, then put his notepad down. "That's not much to go on, Bess."

"You think I don't know that?" she demanded, her voice roughened by her doubts. "I almost didn't stop to see you. I knew it was foolish. I told myself all the way in that I had no call to talk to you about this. I know there's no law about making someone feel strange; I know you can't do something because I got a bad feeling about someone. But it was such a bad feeling." At that, she relented. "Well, Sheriff. You do what you think's the right thing, and I'll side with you no matter what that is."

"Bess—"

She stopped him. "If you see your way clear to keeping a lookout for that boy, well and good, but I won't ask it of you." She headed for the door with her characteristically long stride.

"Bess," Russell said after her, "I'm glad you told me. And I will see what the fellow does, all right?"

She smiled at him, a little abashed, over her shoulder. "Whatever you do is fine by me, Sheriff." She was almost out the door when she turned back. "One more thing. I want to have a look at these new horses I keep hearing about. Mind if I stop off at your place on my way home?"

Russell recognized the gesture for what it was. "Well, if you don't mind it being out of your way, I don't mind you stopping off."

Chapter Six

Smilin' Jack came back to Charity two days later, his big wagon pulled by an eight-mule hitch; behind him, his brother Jesse drove a smaller, six-mule version of the first. Their arrival was greeted with whoops and applause, and by the time the two big wagons drew up in front of the general store and shipping office, they were followed by an enthusiastic, impromptu parade.

"I hear there's more'n ten families fixing to head up this way before summer," Smilin' Jack told Russell as they sat over a deep plate of Sun Fan-Li's soup.

"Where did you hear that?" Russell asked.

"Denver mostly. That's not saying they're coming right to Charity, or that they'll get here at all. But I hope the town is ready to do some serious growing." He broke open one of the biscuits that were piled in a basket at the center of the table.

"I thought that's what we had been doing already," said Russell, making light of it, but clearly not joking.

"Oh, you've just been practicing a little. You been going up the easy side of the mountain, and now there's the hard side. The whole country's coming west. You wait and see. In three, four years, five years at the most, yep, this place'll be at least twice the size it is right now, maybe more." He handed the basket of biscuits to his brother. "For Lord's sake, Jesse, have some of this. No reason to be shy. Soup's just soup without biscuits." He gave Jesse a gesture of encouragement.

"Are you certain? About doubling in size, that is?" asked Russell, feeling troubled.

"Well, it's done it already, hasn't it? What was here ten years ago, or five? It's doubled and doubled again." said Smilin' Jack through a mouthful of food.

"But it was so small. Two new families were enough to double the size, five years ago." Russell shook his head in doubt. "No. I don't see how you can be right. The area around here has more than four hundred souls. Are you so certain—"

"Certain as a tracking hound dog. Eight hundred easy," said Smilin' Jack confidently. "Why, I heard that there's more people coming over from Europe, too, getting away from everything. I hear that Irish are coming in whole families." He poked his brother in the arm. "And look, Widow Schmidt comes from somewhere in Germany. That shows you."

Jesse took a biscuit and broke it into four sections, then dropped it into his soup. "Jack's right. At the freight office they say they got more than twice as much to ship up here over the same time last year. That counts for something."

"See?" Smilin' Jack said triumphantly, his argument supported. "There's new people coming all the time." He leaned back in his chair. "In a couple of years I'm going to settle down here myself, like you done, Sheriff. I'll get my own company, and I'll have my own wagons and drivers. By then, we can go down to Denver and bring our own freight back. We'll make more money and we can carry for all the farmers and the rest hereabouts. Maybe we'll take the Howes' cheeses and sell 'em in Denver." He chuckled at the notion. "The Howes'll have to get more cows." His chuckles turned to laughter.

Jesse laughed along with his brother, and while they laughed they looked very much alike. Jesse was the first to notice that the sheriff had not laughed with him. "No offense, Sheriff," he said, giving all his attention to his soup.

"Oh, Jason Russell's not that sort, Jesse," Smilin' Jack explained. "He's from England, don't you know, and he doesn't laugh much. And maybe he's worried what he's going to do with eight hundred people to look after. That's a lot of work, eight hundred people, a lot harder than four hundred." He grinned, knowing he had guessed right. "So, Sheriff, you better plan to hire a few more deputies. A town of eight hundred, you'll need three or four at least, so you'll have someone at the jail around the clock and the others can tend to the trouble."

"Not a bad plan," said Russell, but with less enthusiasm than Smilin' Jack was demonstrating. "But I will have to ask myself if I want to be in office then, too. I'll be fifty in less than four years." He reached for the big white mug Sun Fan-Li brought to him, fragrant with fresh-ground, fresh-brewed coffee. "I've missed my coffee, and that's the truth."

"I bring coffee for rest?" Sun asked, indicating the Johnson brothers. He bowed to Sheriff Russell to show courtesy, and paid no heed to the stare Jesse Johnson gave him.

"Certainly. Have Missus Schmidt put it on my bill." He watched the cook go back toward the kitchen. "Tell me," he went on, knowing that if he did not ask now, he would not have the courage or the gall to ask again, "did you bring a package...anything...to Henry Clayton?"

"Yep," said Smilin' Jack grimly. "Worse luck. Good sized, too. I told him if he uses it for himself and not his patients, he's a bigger fool than the rest of us, because he knows what that poison is for." He glanced at his brother. "You stay away from that, you hear me?"

"O'course," said Jesse, who knew only that opium would knock you out faster than whiskey and leave you thin as a rake to boot.

"Well, see that you do," said Smilin' Jack. "I don't want you messing with it. And don't let anyone but doctors and dentists buy it. They're the only ones got any call to have it on hand." Satisfied that he had warned his brother sufficiently, he turned back to Russell. "Now that you got so many horses, what else are you supposed to get?"

"How do you mean?" Russell asked, not following the change of subject.

"We got word that there's another shipment coming to you from England for you. Maybe not next time, but the time after we'll be bringing more from your brother, harness and such."

"Oh, dear. Yes, he would do that. I've written to him to say that it isn't necessary, but the provision is part of our father's will, so..." He made a gesture of acceptance. "I'll have to talk to

Linus Cooke before the shipment arrives or he'll think I want to undercut his business, when in fact, I need his help. I'll have to hire hands, as well."

"Speaking of Linus Cooke, he's got new goods, too. We brought Linus a load of tacks and leather tools. Seems he wants to fancy up his saddles." Smilin' Jack took another biscuit as Sun came back from the kitchen with more coffee. "You know, sometimes think I got lucky, back then, getting this route while I was new and got the longest runs to the smallest places. Then, that was what happened to the new men, and everyone thought it was a waste of time, just a way to learn how to handle yourself and the wagons. But finding a place like Charity, or Benson's Mill, you know you're onto something. I know more'n the rest of the drivers about these places, and they're not so little anymore, or so out-of-the-way. Now it's Los Osos that seems small and far away."

Russell heard him out, not sure he was as convinced as Smilin' Jack was. "I don't doubt we're growing," he said when he realized that the brothers were waiting for him to speak. "I don't know that we're growing as fast as you think we are."

"Could be." His eyes narrowed, a burlesque of craftiness. "Would you want to put some money on it, Sheriff? Say, twenty dollars?"

"Twenty dollars?" It was a sizable amount, and both men knew it. "You must be very sure of yourself to be willing to lose that much money. If you have it to lose." Russell drank some of his coffee. "Twenty dollars that we will not have eight hundred people living within five miles of Charity in five years' time? Is that the wager?"

"That's it. Five miles gives you an advantage. If I'd said ten, I'd win for sure," said Smilin' Jack with gusto. "Well?"

Russell held out his hand. "Done. I will accept Liam Cauliffe as the judge of the numbers, if he is acceptable to you," Russell added. "Neither of us should be the ones to keep the toll, should we?"

"Liam's fine by me," said Smilin' Jack, ignoring the expression of dismay that spread over Jesse's face.

"Jack, you're not doin' it, for real?" he protested, his voice higher than before.

"It'll be the easiest twenty dollars I ever made. That'll get me another mule or two for hauling, won't it." He picked up his spoon and went at his soup again.

"Five years, then, on the—shall we round it off and say May first?—" Russell took his notepad from his pocket, and pulled the stub of a pencil from the side of his baton holster.

"Right you are: May first, 1854. I say there will be at least eight hundred people living within five miles of the center of Charity." Smilin' Jack grinned merrily. "You want to put up the money now, Sheriff, or do you want to wait to settle then?"

"Whichever you prefer," said Russell as he finished writing. "I'll give this to Liam to hold. He doesn't approve of gambling, but theres no more honest man in all of the Texas Territories."

"Fine by me," said Smilin' Jack. "I'll figure you'll pay then. I know you got money in the bank, and I know you got horses. I'll get my twenty dollars."

"But we can't spare twenty," Jesse objected, his face darkening with emotion.

"We won't have to," said Smilin' Jack, turning to soothe his brother. "We'll get gold or horseflesh, don't you worry about it."

Jesse heaved a sigh, shaking his head as he remarked to the ceiling, "We're never goin' get this business goin', not if this keeps up."

"You think I'd get us in trouble, Jesse? Not me, not any way." He looked at Russell. "The sheriff's an honorable man, and he'll stand by his wager, and do the right thing when he loses."

"You are certain, aren't you," said Russell, amused. He finished his coffee, and said, in a different tone of voice. "Which way are you heading when you leave?"

"Upslope," said Smilin' Jack. "We got another four days out before we start back. Why?"

"Because I thought you might be willing to have some company back to Denver," said Russell, his thoughts working swiftly.

"You going to Denver?" Jesse asked in surprise.

"No; but the men who brought my horses to me are. Mister Othery has instructions to return as soon as is convenient. Now that the horses are here and the smaller pastures fenced, there's no reason for them to stay."

Smilin' Jack beamed. "My pleasure, Jason, and make no doubt about it. I'll see those men down the mountain and on their way to Boston or wherever they take ship." He patted the table with his free hand. "Happy to oblige, Sheriff. It'll be a pleasure."

"A couple more men with us is fine," said Jesse. "We know all each other's jokes."

Russell nodded as he started to get up from the table. "You'll be here, then?" He gestured, indicating the hotel.

"Or delivering. We'll be here at supper, that's for sure," said Smilin' Jack. "Send the men over. We'll arrange it all."

"Thank you," said Russell, and he went in search of Henry Clayton with dread in his heart.

"What did you expect to find?" the physician asked, sneering, as he let Russell into his office. "Or is the pretense that you want me to look at that scar, to make sure it's healing properly?"

"I want you to do that, certainly," said Russell, "but I was concerned for you."

"Because Jack Johnson told you what he brought, didn't he?" Clayton looked around his little office. "You wanted to be here before I lost myself in the smoke."

"Yes," said Russell without apology.

"At least you have courage enough to admit it." He indicated his battered desk. "It's in the bottom drawer, locked. I locked it up as soon as I got it."

"And where is the key?" Russell asked with unusual severity.

"On my chain, of course," said Clayton, bringing his head up sharply. "I am not going to take any. I am going to save it for those who need it."

"You could give the key to me," said Russell, making the offer conversational.

"And have you miles out of town when a man comes to me with blood pumping out of him and I have to cut off his arm?" Clayton challenged. "Isn't that too great a risk, Sheriff?"

"Oh, stop it, Henry," said Russell, taking off his wide-brimmed hat and sitting down on the edge of the examination table. "I do not doubt your skill as a physician, but you know yourself that your judgment about opium isn't very good." He directed his gaze to a place on the floor where two side-by-side knots in the planking gave the appearance of enormous eyes. "You've said that you are worried about what you do when you are influenced by that pernicious pipe. You want to prove you can avoid the temptation of the smoke. Fine. But help yourself, why don't you? There is no reason you have to do this alone."

Clayton's face darkened. "There's every reason. You know there is. You aren't prepared to watch me for the rest of my life, Jason. If I cannot turn away from opium of my own volition, then I have not turned away from it at all." He came over to Russell. "I might as well look at that scar while you're here," he said grudgingly.

While Clayton peered at the raspberry-colored crescent, Russell went on, "I can arrange for the key to be left at the jail, with Luis, or at the hotel with Widow Schmidt. You could have the opium in a matter of moments, if that is your true fear." He winced as the physician pressed the skin on either side of the half-healed scar.

"Good. It hasn't disrupted your sensation." Clayton stepped back. "Blows like that one do, sometimes." He moved back. "I thank you, Jason; little as I want to, I thank you. But I ask you not to make such a suggestion to me again if you value our friendship, for…" He shook his head and would not go on.

Russell continued to stare at the knots in the floor. "If ever you change your mind, Henry, you have only to say it." He got off the table. "Well. I will not linger, since you are supposed to dine with the Fletchers tonight."

Clayton's laughter was without mirth. "How do you contrive to know all these things? You must have an ability to hear whispers on the wind."

"No, but I do listen. Mister Frederick was bringing that high-bred dun of his for shoeing while I was checking my waiting horse, and he was…remarking that—"

"Complaining, you mean," said Clayton bluntly.

"Everything Mister Frederick says seems a complaint," Russell said, with considerable truth. "He mentioned that it was inconvenient for him to dine with his parents and his wife this evening— he was supposed to meet one of his drinking cronies and play cards."

"At the tavern, no doubt," said Henry Clayton. "How does that boy contrive to be so cod-headed? You'd think Dona Elvira would not tolerate it."

Russell shrugged. "Well, what else is there for him to do? He wants to be one of those break-of-day boys, roistering about the town, swilling champagne at the brothels or slumming at the music halls. And the best that Charity can offer him is the hotel and the tavern. A pity he cannot visit New York or New Orleans, or London, since that is what he longs for, and they know how to deal with wild coves like him in those places. Here, he is only able to carouse until midnight, and everyone is disgusted if he tries his pranks." His smile was not sympathetic.

"Uhn," muttered Clayton, then said abruptly. "His wife's in an interesting condition. She should start to show in another month at the most."

"Pregnant?" Russell said, startled, and surprised to be startled. "Are you certain?"

"It's not unusual," said Clayton. "New wives often become pregnant. That is what they married for, as I understand it." He shook his head. "She was not pleased with the news. I thought that she would be, but she behaved as if I had inconvenienced her."

"Perhaps you did," said Russell seriously. "She may not want to take the time away from her land to raise a child."

"She may not want to do any number of things," said Clayton, "but I say it is unnatural for such a young woman not to want a child. She is not in ill health, she has money and position, she is secure in her holdings—there is no reason that a child should be anything other than a joy and fulfillment to her. It does not bode well that she is not happy about the child." His face darkened. "I do not want to have to explain to the mayor how his daughter-in-law comes to hate her own child."

"Well, it's early days yet," said Russell, adding in a distant way, "Are you satisfied I have not contracted blood poisoning?"

"It does not appear that you have," said Clayton, then returned to the matter at hand. "I am afraid for Dona Elvira's child, Jason. I have tried to convince myself that there is nothing to fear, but every time the thought of her crosses my mind, I am filled with dread for her child." He lowered his head. "I know you think I am raving, and I have no—"

"I never said you were raving," Russell interrupted. "I understand your fears, and I share your worry about her. If you believe that she is unhappy with the coming child, I must listen to what you say, because you are her physician and…well, there are things a physician knows that no husband suspects, aren't there?"

"I wish we had a reliable midwife in Charity," said Clayton softly. "I have never been skilled at dealing with new mothers. A midwife, now, that would be different, for it would be another woman, and she would be able to understand what women feel. What can I tell them?" He made a gesture of surrender. "But I must see this one to the end, for the sake of the child."

"And if there were a midwife in Charity, it would not matter, since the Fletchers would not permit Dona Elvira to use her. You are the physician, and you are the one they will permit to treat her; no other. And if we are to mention what we need in Charity," Russell went on with more vigor, "then let us mention a schoolmaster and a dentist and a maker of eyeglasses." He picked up his hat. "Let me know how it fares with Dona Elvira."

"I shall," said Clayton. "Indeed I shall." He was about to wave the sheriff away when something more occurred to him. "Jason? Have you been out to the Cousins recently?"

"Not for more than a week," said Russell, his brows lowering. "Why? Is something wrong?"

Clayton shook his head. "I truly do not know. It is possible, but…" He tapped his leather-bound notebook. "I have been reviewing Miss Rossiter's progress since she broke her arm. I don't know how to describe my sense about her, but I cannot rid myself of the worry that she is not faring well."

"And?" Russell asked, waiting in the door. "Is there anything there in your records that troubles you?"

"Nothing specific. I have a notion, however, that she is not regaining her strength." He tapped the page. "The bones in her arm are almost knit, but I don't like the feel of them. She seems fragile, as if anything could break her arm again." He looked at Russell. "If you are going out that way, will you stop to see them? Will you see how Miss Rossiter gets on?"

Russell had planned to ride out to Reverend Wachter's settlement the next day; the Cousins were less than an hour away from the lake, so he said, "All right. I will see how they are, and I will report back to you upon my return. If that is satisfactory."

"That's kindly of you, Jason," said Clayton with an expression that was almost a smile.

"It is, isn't it?" Russell countered as he closed the door behind him.

There were now four flimsy houses standing around the church, with the sound of sawing and hammering cluttering up the bright spring morning. Russell got off his blood bay gelding and led him down the track that was supposed to be a street. Under the noise of construction he could hear a few children's voices singing a ponderous hymn.

"Who are you, Brother, and where are you going?" One of the men, a leather-headed mallet in his hands, stepped around the side of the cook tent and confronted Russell.

"I'm here to see Reverend Wachter. I'm Sheriff Russell from Charity." He said it calmly, but his senses were on the alert. He felt his horse respond, bringing his head up, ears pricked.

"The Reverend is occupied. You will have to come back later," said the man with the mallet.

"I'm afraid that's not convenient," said Russell with stern politeness. "Please tell me where I can find him."

"He cannot be disturbed," said the man, and Russell saw that there were others coming to join him.

"Then be good enough to tell him I'm here and that I need to have a few words with him." He looked around. "Is there anywhere I can tie my horse?"

"You cannot wait for the reverend. You will have to come back later," the man with the mallet insisted.

Russell made sure he could get his baton out of its holster quickly if it was necessary. "You have that wrong, don't you know." He straightened up. "I am not here to annoy you; I have duties to perform, just as the reverend has, and I am obliged to discharge my duties." He tightened his hold on the blood bay's reins. "Where, please, is Reverend Wachter?"

"He is leading prayers with the women," said one of the men. "They cannot be interrupted, and no man can enter."

"Save Reverend Wachter?" said Russell. "How long does he keep at these prayers?"

"As long as the women need it to be rid of their sins," said one of the younger men, a rangy youngster with a newly grown beard. The other men nodded, and a man with a long saw added, "He knows their sins, and he helps them to be rid of the weakness Eve gave them. Amen." This last was echoed by the rest.

Russell knew that these men would not tolerate any questioning of his purpose, so he said, "You see, I am an officer of the court—that is part of being a sheriff. I have to deliver certain messages and documents to Reverend Wachter."

"We will present them," one of the men promptly offered.

"No, thank you," Russell said, shaking his head. "I must see him receive them with his own hands, and sign a receipt for them; I will be derelict in my duty if I do otherwise. Surely you understand why I cannot—"

The man with the mallet looked around at the others. "Reverend Wachter is not to be disturbed and we do not want disbelievers in our midst."

"Then we have an impasse, it appears," said Russell without any trace of apology.

One of the other men spoke up. "Reverend Wachter does not welcome disobedience, for it leads to waywardness and sin. We must abide by his will, or risk damning our souls."

"Ah, well you see," said Russell with more cordiality, "that is something of the same fix I am in, for if I leave here, I will be disobeying the ruling of the court. That may mean little to you, but it is my calling, and I am its sworn officer." He indicated his saddlebags. "It will not take long."

"Come back later," said the man with the mallet, his tone now belligerent.

Russell shook his head. "And when I come back later, there will be another reason why I cannot speak with Reverend Wachter, and you will say that I will have to return another day, when we will play the same farce again. No, gentlemen. I must speak with Reverend Wachter or I will have to turn the matter over to the district marshals, and they will come with guns." He let this sink in. "You will have to interrupt him, I fear."

"It isn't possible," said the man with the saw. "We are not permitted."

"Surely there is some way," said Russell, doing his best to keep his tone of good sense and reason. "If there were an emergency, what would you do then?"

"We would pray," said the man with the mallet. "What else should a good Christian do?"

Russell held back the three answers that came most quickly to his mind, and he coughed once. "You may tell the good reverend I insisted. Or you may stand aside and I will tend to the task myself."

"You cannot go into the church," said the youngest man. "You are not of our faith."

Russell had already taken a step in the direction of the church. "Is your faith so weak that the doubts of one man can shake it?" He looped his blood bay's rein around the nearest upright of the cook tent and went to unbuckle his saddlebags. "I will ask for forgiveness, but this must be attended to." He slung the saddlebags over his shoulder and started again toward the church, walking with a purposeful stride, his baton loose in its holster.

"You are not to enter," shouted one of the men.

"I'm sorry to offend you, but I must," said Russell as he went up the two shallow steps of the church and rapped on the door. "Reverend Wachter," he said in a loud, distinct voice, "this is Sheriff Russell. I have some documents I need to present to you; I require your signature as proof you have received the documents. And I will explain them, if that is what you wish me to do, so you may comply with the law." He stood and listened, hearing soft voices and rustlings in the church; from the corner of his eye, he watched the men in the narrow street, hoping they would remain where they were.

Suddenly the church door was tugged open, and Reverend Wachter, his face flushed, blocked the entrance. "What do you mean by this? You are impious."

"True enough," said Russell, and took the saddlebags from his shoulder. "I am sorry to interrupt your devotions, Reverend

Wachter, but I have to obtain your signature on this"—he held out an official-looking sheet of parchment—"and I have these documents to leave with you, stating that you have been informed that you are building on land of disputed ownership." He saw Reverend Wachter's face darken. "Please do not read me more lessons from Scripture. I am only doing what the court requires of me; your argument is not with me, but with the court and the law. Anything you say to me will not help you, and I cannot change the law." He offered the documents another time. "The Fletchers have filed a petition with the court to find for their claim. While the court reviews the case, you are not to put up any more buildings on this site." He sensed more than saw the fury hidden in Reverend Wachter.

"That woman is filled with the wiles of the Devil." He turned back into the church. "Take a lesson and fill your hearts with sub-mission, so that you will not offend God as this idol-worshipping Spanish whore does."

Russell shook his head. "Reverend, it is not wise to call Missus Fletcher a whore. If you do that where you might be overheard, it would not help your case, and could lead to other actions against you." He put the papers into Reverend Wachter's hands. "There. You have copies of the writs, and I have informed you of the contents in the presence of witnesses." Privately he doubted that any of Wachter's followers would speak out against him in open court, but he wanted to make the warning in any case. "I must have your mark or your signature on this receipt, and then I will leave you to your...worship."

"The chastisement of wives is not worship, it is a duty," said Wachter, his voice sounding thick with emotion. "I will sign your paper, but only that I may battle this affront in court. 'In the day when the keepers of the house shall tremble, and the strong men shall bow themselves, and the grinders cease because they are few, and those that look out of the windows shall be darkened.' Tell those sin-infested pagans that I am no swinish back-slider wallowing in liberality, but a staunch and righteous defender of God, unafraid to keep the strictest of His laws." He laughed once. "My followers know well that I do not permit sentiment to conta-minate this community, and I will not be swayed by worldly claims and the venality of the laws of men. Laws that uphold the will of a foolish and Popish woman. You do not ask a man of my position to respect those laws."

"Certainly not," said Russell, making no effort to disguise the sarcasm of his remark. "Nonetheless, I must have your signature, as proof that you have been given the documents. There is nothing that compels you to abide by them but the law of the land." He produced a grease-pencil from the inner pocket of his jacket and offered it to Reverend Wachter. "If you will sign with this, I will not trouble you any longer."

Wachter took the pencil and scrawled his large, irregular signature. "You do not trouble me at all; you are less than a gnat, or a flea. You are a slave to the ungodly, who mask their perfidy in legal tricks." He all but flung the pencil at Russell. "The women— our virtuous women—require my aid and correction," he said, more to his followers than to Russell. With a single nod of his large head, he went back into the church and slammed the door.

Russell folded the paper carefully and put it into his saddlebag before going back to where his blood bay waited. He buckled his saddlebags into place, then took the reins and swung into the saddle. "Thank you for your help," he said to the men who stood watching him. Since there seemed to be nothing more to say, he clapped his heels to the horse's sides and set him cantering away.

Chapter Seven

Henry Clayton's face was grey and his eyes had taken on a haunted stare. "It's not what you think," he said as he came into the sheriff's office and faced Russell. "It's not the opium."

"What is it, then?" Russell asked, indicating the chair by the stove. "You look…"

"Dreadful," said Clayton when Russell did not go on.

"Dreadful," Russell agreed. "Are you ill?"

"Yes, in a way." He leaned over, his head in his hands. "That new family just sent for me…Grover's their name, and they're putting up a house beyond the dairy." He stopped, swallowing convulsively.

"I know who they are, Henry," said Russell, beginning to worry. "Is there something the matter?"

"The oldest daughter." He had to stop again. "I just came from there. She…"

"Dead?" asked Russell, trying to imagine what might bring about this misery in the doctor.

"Oh, yes," said Clayton, rubbing his face. "They found her, and they sent for me, though why.… There was nothing I could do for her, and they must have known it." He took a long, shuddering breath. "I've told them not to move her, Jason. I don't know if they can bear it, but I told them."

Russell was already moving, taking his notebook and his baton as he went to the door. "Tell me the rest on the way," he said, motioning to Clayton to rise.

"I don't want to look at her again," said Clayton softly.

They were outside now, walking along the side of the road toward Charity Street. As they crossed this central roadway, Russell noticed that a small carriage had pulled up in front of the hotel. He had a fleeting question in his mind, then gave his attention to Henry Clayton. "What's wrong?" He had rarely seen Clayton so shaken, or so distressed.

"She died hard," said Clayton, and went on slowly, the words coming out in little clumps as if that made their import more bearable. "It happened last night. Probably late. Maybe she went to the outhouse. Outside, anyway. Someone caught her. She's been violated. And cut." This last was the most difficult thing of all, and his voice dropped to a whisper.

"Stabbed?" Russell asked, motioning Clayton to the side so that one of the Cooke children could rush by pulling a wagon.

"Cut," said Clayton more emphatically.

"More than once?" Russell asked, noticing the physician was still the color of whey.

"More than twenty times," he said, his voice suddenly very harsh. "Both breasts are gone. So is her nose. And lips." He fell abruptly silent.

"Gone?" Russell repeated. "Cut or...or missing?"

"Missing," said Clayton, and motioned Russell to silence.

This time Russell was willing to comply. He steeled himself to face the corpse, for it had been a long time since he had dealt with death from mutilation. He tried to bring the girl to mind, and could only picture a rather plain, pallid child with light-green eyes, yellow hair, and skin that burnt easily.

"It's the next turning," said Clayton, jarring Russell out of his thoughts.

"Yes," he said, going toward the newly framed house, doing his best to school his features to neutrality and his manner to dutiful sympathy.

Marcus Grover stood beside his wife, his face set in stony wrath. He nodded once to the sheriff, indicating the side of the house. "She's over there."

Russell stopped, turning his eyes on the outraged father. "I am very sorry, Mister Grover. I am."

"Just look at her if you must so we can get her decently into the ground before anyone learns what happened to her." He glared at Clayton. "He's looked at her already. She's a modest girl, she ought not to have this done."

"No girl should have this done," muttered Clayton, not looking at the Grovers. "No person anywhere."

"Hush, Henry," said Russell as he pulled the physician away by the arm. "They're only trying to preserve their dignity. It's the decent thing to do." He saw the blanket-covered form lying just beyond the outhouse. "Is that—?"

"Yes," said Clayton. "I asked the boy to keep an eye on it, to keep curious people away. And dogs." He coughed once. "I don't want to look at her again."

"But you must," said Russell with determination. "I have need of your opinion."

"Why? You've seen stabbings and mutilations and all the rest of it. I can't tell you—" He was silent, seeing the ten-year-old brother of the girl coming toward them. "You've done well, young man."

Russell saw that the brown blanket had several large, wet patches on it, and knew them for blood. "You've been very brave for your sister."

"She got killed," said the boy as if he were reciting a lesson. "Ma wants to go to church, but Pa won't have it, not until she's ready to bury." He took care to avoid getting too near the covered figure.

"That will take a little while," said Russell. "It might be just as well to send for Preacher Cauliffe. He'll come if you ask him." He put his hand on the boy's shoulder. "Your Pa wouldn't mind if Preacher came here, would he?"

"I don't know," said the boy, and hurried away from them, calling out to his mother.

"Did he see her?" asked Russell in a hushed voice.

"He found her," answered Clayton heavily.

"I see," said Russell. He removed his hat out of respect and knelt down to lift the blanket. Even though he had prepared himself for the sight, he was shocked by the condition of the body. The murders committed by the Mayhew gang were not nearly so savage as this. The gaping wounds and deep slashes were awful testimony to the rage that had consumed the killer. White bone showed where the killer had hacked away her breasts, and her left arm was nearly severed from her body.

"She's bled a lot," said Clayton. "But there are bruises." He was still on his feet, but he pointed to her hips and thighs. "You can see them. She fought the man."

"Yes," said Russell quietly. "Her clothes—"

"Just the scraps under her," said Clayton abruptly. "Nothing else." He took two steps back, as if distance would make the murder more bearable.

"I'll have to start a search for them. The killer might have taken them." He stood up and let the blanket fall once more. "Is there anyone else who can prepare the body for burial? It seems to be—"

Clayton interrupted him. "There's no one and you know it. And I will do it properly, you need not worry yourself about that." He folded his arms, and went on in a whisper. "And you'll want to make your damned sketches, won't you?"

"Yes," admitted Russell. "I must have some record."

"In case it happens again, isn't that right?" challenged Clayton, his face like a mask.

"Sadly, yes." Russell turned away from the body and started back toward the girl's family. "Mister Grover," he said as he drew nearer, "I would like your permission to have your daughter's body carried to the doctor's office so that it can be prepared for proper burial."

"My wife's going to do that," said Marcus Grover. "It's her duty, and she'll tend to it." He moved a step nearer to his wife, his manner all but threatening.

Mrs. Grover stifled a sob and shook her head. "God give me strength, husband."

Russell hesitated. "I hope you will permit the doctor to do this task," he said, and continued as tactfully as he could. "He has experience in sewing up wounds of all kinds, and surely you would prefer that be done?"

At this offer, Clayton added, "I might find something that would lead to her killer. I mean no disrespect for the dead, or for your family, Mister Grover, but I know medicine, and if there is something suspicious, I will find it." It was a struggle for him to say this, and it came out badly, angrily.

"There's no reason for you to trouble yourself over her," said Mr. Grover. "It's our lot."

This time Russell was more emphatic. "Mister Grover, I hope you will change your mind. I will do all in my power to see that your daughter's murderer is caught, but I need all the assistance I can get if I am to succeed. Please give me that chance. I swear that I will not touch your daughter. You have my word as a gentleman. But I need to learn everything the doctor can discover in order to know what I must about her killer." He studied the furious, grieving man. "Help me, Mister Grover."

"Help you? By desecrating my child?" Marcus Grove was ready to unleash his wrath on anyone; he roared at the sheriff. "You monster, you fiend to ask this. You are as evil as the wretch who killed her."

"Mister Grover," said his wife, her red, swollen eyes filling again with tears, "no more. I beg you, Mister Grover."

He was silenced by her words. The rage was gone as quickly as it had risen. "Forgive me," he said to his wife, then said to Russell, "I will consider your request. Now leave us alone."

This time it was Clayton who pulled Russell away from the half-built house and the stricken family. "Leave them alone, Jason. There's nothing more you can do now, not without their permission. And they will not give it to accommodate you. Think what you're asking of them, man. You can't expect them to agree."

Russell put his hat back on, his thoughts in turmoil as long-buried recollections returned. He made himself block out the past in order to concentrate on the current problem. "I want to find out everything we can about the Grovers, especially the girl. Everything. And quickly." He was speaking quietly and rapidly. "Did she have a suitor before they left Ohio—was it Ohio? or Iowa?—and was there difficulty about it?"

"I don't know, Jason," said Clayton, increasing the length of his stride to keep up with the sheriff. "And I don't imagine they'll tell you, not now, not if there was trouble before they left. They will not want to have that known."

"Possibly not," said Russell. "But if I write to the town they left, someone might know. Once I learn where they came from."

He stopped walking suddenly, making Clayton halt beside him. "I hope they decide to let you have the body."

"I can't say I share your wish," said Clayton darkly.

"I want to know..." He faltered.

"How she died?" suggested Clayton.

"We can see that. No. I want to know why it was she." He raised his head, squinting into the bright sky.

"Misfortune," said Clayton, and started to walk again.

"Misfortune," echoed Russell as he started after Clayton; his apprehension increased with every step he took, blighting the spring day and filling the sheriff's mind with memories that were the stuff of his nightmares. It would not happen again, not now, not here. He had failed before in India. If he failed again now, he would not know how to endure that failure.

Before he drank his tea, Liam Cauliffe looked across the desk at Russell. "It was a bad business," he said, referring to the burial of Evangeline Grover. "The way that father is conducting himself, you'd think that Henry Clayton was the criminal, not the man who killed the girl."

"I'm afraid that's my fault," said Russell, indulging in the luxury of coffee. "I asked him to examine the body properly, and I sketched the wounds."

Cauliffe shook his head slowly. "A terrible thing. With such killings, what can we expect?"

"Killings?" Russell repeated. His pulse hammered at his temples. "What do you mean?"

The circuit preacher did not answer at once, and when he did, he went carefully. "Well, you see, when I went out in early spring— you remember that?"

"Yes," said Russell shortly.

"I stopped at the Wilson–Blackthorn mine. There's a couple hundred miners there, some with their families. During the winter there'd been two girls killed, stabbed, and the other—"

"Raped," said Russell bluntly.

"Yes," Cauliffe admitted. "A very bad business. I saw one of the bodies. She was a sweet young thing, not more than twenty, and her husband left with two children to raise. I hate to think what was done to that poor woman." He stopped to clear his throat. "They never caught anyone. And this one was similar, so—"

Russell put his elbows on his desk and looked hard at Cauliffe. "Why didn't you mention this to me sooner?"

Cauliffe blinked. "Why should I? The Wilson–Blackthorn mine is forty miles away. It's not properly speaking a town, but it's like to turn into one." He sighed. "Perhaps I should have said something to you. It might have been a good precaution. But it was so far, and what connection is there between those two women and this child we put in the ground today?"

"I don't know," said Russell, his light blue eyes fading to grey. "But I don't know that there is no connection."

"You don't seriously imagine…" Cauliffe was so aghast that he could not continue. He took a long sip of tea. "Jason, you are mistaken."

"I hope you're right," said Russell after a short pause. He got up and refilled his cup, then went to the door and called out, "Luis! *Veng' aquí*!"

As he poured out the last of his tea, Cauliffe said, "What are you going to do?"

"I'm going to get some information," said Russell, and stood aside as his deputy came bounding into the office.

"Is it urgent, Sheriff?" His face was alight with eager anticipation. "What do you wish me to do?"

Russell motioned to Guerra to close the door. "In private, please. I don't want the whole town privy to my request." He watched his young deputy comply, then indicated the circuit preacher. "Reverend Cauliffe tells me that there were two women murdered down at the Wilson–Blackthorn mine in early spring. I want to find out more about the murders, and the victims. And I want you to ride to every town within a fifty-mile radius of Charity to see if there have been any more murders of women like the Grover girl. If you find anything, I want to have details on it. I want specific information."

"Do you believe you'll find something?" Cauliffe asked as Guerra stared at Russell.

"I hope I will not." In his mind Russell once again saw the bodies, and his very soul flinched.

"What is it?" Guerra asked, seeing the haunted look in Russell's eyes.

Russell did not answer; instead he gave his attention to Cauliffe. "And you. While you're on the circuit this time, ask questions for me. It's probably awkward, but there is a chance that people will talk to you when they might not speak to Luis or to me. You're a man of the cloth, and that means they are more apt to trust you."

"About such matters? Do you think so?" asked Cauliffe. He gave a gesture of resignation. "Well, if that is what you will have, I suppose I must honor it. You do your work well, Jason, and I am certain you would not make such a request unless you were convinced it was necessary." He made a sign to Guerra. "You might as well do as he tells you, for he will not relent."

"No, I will not," said Russell, his face growing more stern. "Pray, if you want, that I am wrong, and that what I fear is only the bad dreams from my past. Because if it is other than that, this town, and those around it, are in great danger."

Guerra could not disguise his amazement. "What is this, Sheriff? What do you think will happen?" He shook his head to show the extent of his bewilderment. "I am to find out about dead girls. You do not say why, but I am to find out about them. Why do you think this is necessary?"

Russell put his hand on his baton. "I would not ask if I did not believe there might be more." He waited a moment, then said, "It may be that others will die if we do not act."

"Other women?" suggested Cauliffe. "Is that what this is about? You think that there is a madman hunting women? Don't be absurd. That is the stuff of the theater."

"It would not be the first time women have been hunted. There have been other times," said Russell; he changed the subject. "When have you and Missus Schmidt decided to marry, Liam? Or have you not agreed on a day?"

He accepted this change of direction in their conversation, and answered, "It will depend on when I return. I must bring another preacher with me, for we cannot go to Padre Antonio, and I will not ask such a service of that Reverend Wachter. Preacher Dunne has said he will come and say the words for us. If he is able to accompany me, then we will be married before the end of June. It will be August at the latest." He gave one of his rare smiles. "And I will establish myself here in Charity, and leave the circuit to a younger man. Charity is of a size to require a minister in residence now."

"I wish you both very happy, whatever day it is," said Russell, with a lessening of his unapproachability. "You warned me about the Widow Schmidt when I first came here; do you remember?"

"You will not let me forget it," said Cauliffe pleasantly. "As to our happiness God will tend to that," he went on, setting his cup aside and rising. "I will be leaving in a day or two, and you have my promise that I will find out what I can, and report what I learn faithfully to you unless it requires that I violate a confidence, which I cannot do."

"I won't ask that of you," said Russell, adding to Guerra, "And I won't ask you to investigate anything that puts you at hazard. You do not need to endanger yourself to obtain this information for me." He could not make himself smile, but he tried to appear less forbidding. "I don't mean to impose on you."

"But I am an officer of the law, and I have sworn to undertake things that are dangerous," Guerra protested. "This is no imposition. It is my duty to do dangerous things, and to pursue dangerous men."

Russell saw the amusement in Cauliffe's eyes at Guerra's outburst. "Yes, but let us discover who the dangerous man is before you undertake to go after him." He paused. "You like that roan mare of mine, don't you? The new one, about six years old?" He did not need to hear Guerra's response to know the answer. "I'm willing to let you take her for this journey, if you will not push her too hard."

"Oh, of course not," said Guerra, his face brightening. "Never would I abuse such a horse. I will treat her as if she is going to her first Communion."

"Make sure she is properly fed and she does not hurt her legs and I will be satisfied," said Russell, adding to Cauliffe, "Before you go, tell Luis where you will be. You will be able to work out the most effective way for the both of you to deal with these tasks I have set you."

"And you are determined that we will do this," said Cauliffe. "In that case, Guerra, come to the hotel this evening and I will discuss my route with you." At the door he paused and looked long and thoughtfully at Russell. "Perhaps one day you will tell me why you are so caught up in this case."

"I am sheriff here and a young woman has been violently murdered. Do I need more reason than that?" His tone did not invite more comments.

"No; but there is more," said Cauliffe, with a subtle emphasis on *is.* "Well, I will see you later." With that and a nod he was gone, leaving Guerra to give voice to all the questions that roiled in his mind.

Every eye in Lorinda Dooley's parlor was turned toward the woman in the door.

"God's peace on you all," said Sister Angelica as she came through the door, her green eyes snapping as she looked around.

One of the men swore softly and colorfully, and another spat, not willing to look at the nun. Three of Lorinda Dooley's girls were all but frozen with amazement, and Lorinda herself was appalled. "What the Devil are you doing here?" she demanded, hating the weak, apologetic whine she heard in her own voice.

"The Devil is what *you* are doing," said Sister Angelica in her most forthright way. "It is God's work that should occupy man." She looked around the parlor. "As we see, these do not labor in the Lord's vineyards."

One of the women giggled, her voice high and nervous.

"What right do you have—" began Lorinda Dooley, trying to find courage enough to face Sister Angelica with the same aplomb the nun displayed.

"The right given by the vows I've made to God and Jesus Christ," said Sister Angelica, now standing in the center of the parlor. "I have promised God that I would uphold His work, His commandments, and I must do this if I am not to be ashamed to see His face on Judgment Day."

Hiram Mattington, Hepsibah's son, came up to Sister Angelica and stared down at her. He was not insolent, and nothing in his stance was threatening. "Lady, you're making a joke out of that rig you're wearing. If we come to you, you got every right to tell us just what you think, but here, it's not the same as in your church. Here, you got to do things by Miz Dooley's rules, and they aren't your style, Sister, and that's a fact."

Sister Angelica glared at him. "I could have taken an easier path. I could have remained in my convent. But I asked to be allowed to go into the world for God."

"Well," said Hiram with half a smile, "you're rightly doing that." The others chuckled with him.

"Hiram," said Lorinda, who had composed herself, "let me handle this. I am a Catholic and you're not." She came and took Hiram's arm. "I go to Confession, Sister, and I do penance for my sins. Padre Antonio has talked about my way of life to me, and has told me that I need not continue to earn my living this way. But since I have been robbed, I must make money while I may, to provide for myself and my daughter. I do the things I know to do. You are not doing God's work if you stop me at mine."

"This is not work—" began Sister Angelica.

"That's what you think," one of the girls declared.

"This is not work," the nun said again. "This is the triumph of sin."

Hiram looked around. "Will one of you fellows go get the sheriff? He'll take care of this."

At his suggestion, a portly man recently arrived in Charity left the room through the rear door.

"No man sworn to enforce the law should permit the existence of this establishment," said Sister Angelica. "Bring him, if you must, but I will smile when I see the use he makes of you, for the law will be the defense of God."

"We'll see," said Hiram, and walked over to the largest chair, where he sat, regarding Sister Angelica politely.

Lorinda gave a defiant toss to her head and went behind the little bar at the far corner of the room. "I'm pouring whiskey; first round on the house."

"Another sin," said Sister Angelica.

Hiram raised his voice, "Slip a glass of that over this way, will you, Lorinda?"

"Fine," said Lorinda. She was generous in her drinks, not wanting the men to be embarrassed, for then she feared they might want to leave her house, which she could not afford. "You all go on with what you were doing. This is my house, and when the sheriff gets here, we'll see what he has to say about this."

"So we will," agreed Sister Angelica. "I will dutifully report all that I witness."

"Excellent," said Lorinda, her voice sharp. "By all means tell him. In detail."

For a moment Sister Angelica felt uneasy, then she straightened her back and stood as if on guard. As she watched the men drinking with the casually dressed women, she began to pray.

"You can do that as well in your church," observed Hiram. He took a sip of whiskey and whistled his approval. "Your best, Lorinda, bless your heart."

An uneasy quiet settled over the room. What few words were spoken were in whispers and Sister Angelica directed the full weight of her eyes on those who dared to break the calm. Lorinda continued to pour drinks as if there was nothing unusual in having her customers say nothing, and her girls stand about with their peignoirs clutched tightly closed.

"You know, Sister," said Hiram a little while later, "I don't know if you thought this through. You can't stay here every minute; you got services to attend. As soon as you're gone, we'll carry on like before."

"Not if I stay long enough," declared Sister Angelica, her face set with intent. "If I stay long enough you will have to leave, most of you, and you will leave without what you came for. Next time you won't be so hasty." She crossed herself and began to pray softly in Latin.

"Papist nonsense," said one of the men, loudly enough to be heard but not so loudly that it was a deliberate offense.

"Leave her alone," said Lorinda. "Leave her be. She'll just offer it up if you're rude to her." She drank some of the whiskey she had poured for the rest, coughing once. "That goes for the rest of you."

"If that's what you want," said Hiram pleasantly. He rubbed at the stubble on his chin. "I hope you can spare soap and a razor before long. I don't want to scratch the merchandise."

"Glad to," said Lorinda, and was surprised to see Susanne blush at the remark.

Sister Angelica stopped praying long enough to say, "You wish to shock me, but you cannot succeed."

"I wish to shave," Hiram corrected her. "Sorry, Sister. If you want me to shock you, I'll have to think of something else.

The chuckle this comment evoked truly irritated the nun. "You are no fit person, young man."

Hiram started to say something but thought better of it, shrugging instead. He finished off his whiskey and set his glass aside, making no effort to get more. Lorinda Dooley sighed loudly and signaled to one of the girls to take her place behind the bar.

"I'll get something from the kitchen," said Lorinda as she hurried out of the parlor, wondering what there was that she could serve quickly.

Sister Angelica continued to recite her prayers, her voice growing louder and louder, as if by volume alone the Latin words would become comprehensible to the rest waiting in the parlor. While she prayed she raked her glance over the others, her eyes bright and piercing. Her cheeks were flushed with triumph.

Aaron Gall, the wheelwright's younger brother, began to slap the bar with the flat of his hand in strong, irregular rhythm, making the tension in the room much greater. He had a set grin on his face as he did this, knowing how much it goaded the nun.

"Don't press her, Aaron, said Hiram in a lazy voice. "You just encourage her."

"Let's see if it does," said Aaron, hitting the bar with almost enough force to drown out the drone of Sister Angelica's prayers.

In the kitchen Lorinda Dooley almost dropped the tray she had filled with sweet biscuits. She saw that her hands were shaking and she stared at them in shame; it was an effort not to cry with vexation. Bracing the tray against the chopping block, she tried to calm herself, and succeeded only in starting to weep. She cursed herself for being a fool.

"Is it that bad?" asked Russell from the rear door. He came into the kitchen and approached Lorinda as he might a skittish young horse. "I'll take the tray."

"I didn't think you'd come." She looked at him, green eyes brimming. "You aren't going to make me leave town, are you?"

"Why should I?" Russell asked. "You know I would not require that; indeed, I haven't the authority. Technically you aren't in the town at all. According to the Town Council the boundary is two fields west of here, remember?" He put his hand on her shoulder. "Compose yourself, girl. It's going to be difficult enough without you in pieces."

She wiped at her eyes. "Of course," she said, trying her best to sound businesslike. "You know the situation?" There were still tears on her face, but she did her best to ignore them. "The sister came and has not left."

"She's still in the parlor?" asked Russell, deliberately making no show of sympathy so that Lorinda could keep her dignity intact. "Well?"

"As far as I know," said Lorinda, and gave Russell her report, taking comfort in reciting the problem. "Praying. Thank God Hiram Mattington's here—he's been wonderful. Aaron Gall's been making it worse, as you might expect."

"Not a sensible fellow, our Aaron," mused Russell. "Anyone else I should consider? other than the nun?"

"Well, there's Susanne. She's acting strangely, too quiet by half. I think she's afraid that Sister will do something to her. Susanne's not Catholic, and she thinks they eat babies for breakfast." She cleared her throat. "She worries about having so many Catholics near her."

"All right, I'll keep that in mind." Russell pulled his baton from the holster and held it out. "Give me the tray. I'll take care of serving. I want you to remain back here, and call your girls when I tell you to. There's no reason for there to be a fight, but it could happen."

"Not here," protested Lorinda. "I've had two dozen glasses smashed in the last month. I can't afford another fight."

"Don't worry about that now," said Russell as he took the tray and balanced it. "It won't be long, Miz Dooley. And I don't want to fight any more than you want me to." With that he was off down the hall to the parlor.

The air all but crackled with tension, and Russell saw at once that Aaron Gall was ruddy with anger. Only Hiram seemed at ease, raising his hand in greeting.

"Good you could come, Sheriff," he said, indicating the sister. "We have a guest."

"So I see," said Russell, keeping the tray and moving around the room, letting everybody help themselves. "Here," he said at last as he stopped in front of Sister Angelica. "Have a sweet biscuit, Sister."

"I am not here to eat." She would not face him, blocking the sight of him with the restrictions of veil and wimple.

"Well, I can't think of any other reason you might have come. Sister Mercedes takes care of Miz Dooley's daughter, and the… entertainment offered here is not what you are said to like." He lifted the tray a little higher. "They're very good sweet biscuits."

Sister Angelica stamped her foot. "You have no right to do this. I demand you do your duty and arrest everyone, lock them up for public indecency and fornication." Her voice was harsh now, and she was breathing quickly. "They are not saved."

Carefully Russell put the tray down on the nearest occasional table. "Sister, it is not your place to come here, and it is not your task to exhort these people, no matter what you think of them; it is your obligation to pray for them, as I understand it."

"I do pray for them," she said stubbornly. "And I pray where they may see I do it, where they can know that I am begging the Virgin to intercede for them."

Russell moved a little closer. "You are being very diligent, certainly." His voice was even and low, steady without too much power. "But it is not proper for you to be here. You do not aid your mission if you intrude here in this way. You can serve your calling and your God better if you do not subject yourself to this. Believe me, Sister, you do not need to prove your faith to these people." It was a guess, but he saw from the sudden furious look she gave him that he was right. "You show your faith in obedience, don't you?"

"I show my faith in every act of my life!" Her demeanor had changed; now she was truly angry and the veneer of unctuousness was gone. "What perfidy is this, that—"

Russell did not permit her to finish, for he saw that Aaron Gall was rising, his wrath matching that of the nun. "We can sort this out at the church. I have to take you back, Sister. Then you and Padre Antonio will have to determine what is to be done. Please." He moved so that he was between Sister Angelica and Aaron Gall. "Hiram," he said in his most conversational manner, "let's not have any trouble."

Hiram Mattington got to his feet. "Right you are, Sheriff."

"Thank you, Hiram," said Russell as he began, with great skill, to force Sister Angelica to move back toward the vestibule and the door. "So far this has been just an embarrassment. Let us be patient and that is all it will be."

"Just say the word, Sheriff." Hiram stationed himself near the bar; he bent to take his knife from his boot. "Let the Sheriff handle this," he said to the others. "That includes you, Aaron."

Sister Angelica knew what was happening, but short of physically resisting the sheriff could do nothing to stop him. She continued to back away from him. "I must be worthy of my calling," she said, anger giving way to desperation. "If I do not succeed, I will fail my vows to the Virgin. Don't you see?"

"Yes," said Russell with compassion. "But I can't allow you to do this, vows or no vows, Sister." He had her almost to the vestibule, and he was beginning to hope that he would get her away from Lorinda Dooley's without incident.

Then Aaron Gall threw his knife, missing Sister Angelica, but catching Russell on the arm. As he saw he had missed his target, he yelled in frustration.

"Lorinda! Call your girls!" yelled Russell, for an instant all but paralyzed by the pain of the cut.

The girls did not need to hear anything more; shrieking they bolted from the room, pressing together and struggling down the narrow hallway toward the kitchen.

Bellowing, Aaron charged at Sister Angelica, trying to shove Russell aside, and deflecting the starting arc of Russell's baton so that it fell from his hand. As Aaron struck Russell's shoulder, Hiram Mattington grabbed him around the waist and pulled him over with a resounding crash.

Russell thrust Sister Angelica against the door and shielded her with his body while she screamed and struck out at him with her nails, calling on God to save her from humiliation.

"Stop it!" Russell ordered her. "Hold still." Behind him Aaron and Hiram were thrashing about on the floor. One of them had knocked over the table where Russell had set the tray and there were sweet biscuits everywhere.

Hiram hollered an oath as Aaron bit his hand, then made a

club of his other fist and pounded Aaron twice on the side of his neck, his jaw set against the hurt of the blows. As Aaron stopped resisting, Hiram flexed his hand to relieve the worst of the pain.

"Are you all right?" Russell asked over his shoulder.

"My hand's sore," said Hiram. "But I'm better than Aaron." He got to his knees. "He's got another knife in his belt. Want me to take it?"

"No, leave it. Keep watch on him, though." Russell stepped back, and looked down at Sister Angelica, who was making an odd, whimpering noise. "Well, are you pleased with your accomplishment, Sister?" he asked, finally letting himself touch the cut on his sleeve. There was blood but not enough to warrant more than a simple bandage.

"I have a task," Sister Angelica said in a small voice.

Russell nodded grimly. "And so have I." He turned to Hiram. "Bring Aaron along to the jail, will you? Have Luis lock him up until he comes to his sense."

"Pleasure, sheriff." Hiram ran his fingers through his hair and hitched his belt. "What about you?"

With a cocked head, Russell indicated the sister. "I have to attend to this." He looked back at the nun. "I hope you don't intend to make a practice of this, Sister," he said wearily as he retrieved his fallen baton and reached to open the door.

Chapter Eight

Maude Rossiter climbed down from her seat in the wagon with great care. She smiled apologetically at Henry Clayton and at her cousin, saying, "I'm sorry to be so much trouble."

"No trouble, I assure you," said Henry Clayton as he held out his hand to assist her the last of the way. "Good afternoon to you, too, Miz Bell."

"Doctor Clayton," said Cloris Bell, her curtness—more than her expression—revealing how worried she was for her cousin.

"I've told Cloris that she is being too cautious," said Miss Rossiter, "but she insists that I consult you. I am afraid my arm has weakened me. I do not mean to be so tiresome."

"You are not being tiresome," said Clayton, noticing how pale she was, and how translucent her skin appeared. "I must say, I can understand why Miz Bell is concerned; you are—"

"She's not in her best looks," Cloris said for him. "That's why I brought her. And we don't want any mealy-mouthed answers from you, Henry Clayton. We want to be told what is the matter and what we are to do about it."

Clayton looked from Maude Rossiter to Cloris Bell. "I will do what I can, ladies, I assure you. But there is only so much I can achieve, especially here. If we were in a great city like Boston or Philadelphia there might be newer, better treatments to hand. Here, I am hampered." He indicated the door to his office and the short flight of steps that led to it. "Do you want my arm?"

Miss Rossiter's face grew rosy. "That is not necessary. My cousin will look after me." She turned to wait while Cloris Bell climbed down from the wagon and tied the horse to the nearest rail. "Thank you, Cousin," she said, and took Cloris' arm.

Clayton followed them up the stairs, shaking his head as he saw how quickly Maude tired; only nine steps and she was breathing deeply, coughing a little. He did not like the look of it at all.

In his office, he sat Maude on his table and took her pulse, smelled her breath and put his ear to her back to listen to her lungs. He made notes in his book, and then drew up a chair. "Have you ever suffered from jaundice?" he asked.

Maude stared at him, smiling a little. "Jaundice? Oh, dear, no, not for years and years." She glanced at her cousin and nodded. "You recall?"

"You were no more than fifteen," said Cloris, her manner more suspicious than Maude's. "What does this have to do with jaundice?"

"I don't know," said Clayton heavily. "But there are times when those who have suffered from jaundice in youth later develop these symptoms. Many go into a decline." He looked from one cousin to the other. "You told me to be direct, and I am trying to be. I do not say that Miss Rossiter will go into a decline, I only tell you that it has happened to others."

"She will not go into a decline," said Cloris sharply.

"Certainly not," agreed Maude.

"It is what I want, as well," said Clayton, clearing his throat. "Nevertheless, it is best to take precautions." He straightened up. "I believe that for the next two months Miss Rossiter should avoid all strenuous chores."

"It is Cousin Bell who does the strenuous chores," said Maude. "I tend the house."

"For the time being, it would be wise not to do even that," said Clayton. "For the time being, if you can afford it, it would be best if you hired that work done." He saw the two women exchange glances. "This need not be for a long time," he went on in a hurry, "but I think you will improve if you are permitted to rest."

"But we have a farm," Maude protested, laughing a little breathlessly. "I am not one of these die-away creatures who has to loosen her stays when she walks a mile, doctor. It's true that

Cousin Bell does all the more strenuous work, but both find it more convenient." She favored Clayton with a warm smile. "You are like most physicians, aren't you, impressing us by asking more than you expect and thereby causing us to take those measures you believe are necessary."

Clayton shook his head, feeling helpless. "I am not trying to frighten you, Miss Rossiter. I do not want to deceive you. But it is my opinion as a physician that you require a period of rest. There are a few measures I want you to take, as well, if you want to speed your recovery."

"If the requests are reasonable, of course I will comply," said Maude Rossiter in her comfortable way. "Tell me."

"You are to have blood pudding every day, a full serving. One of the reasons you are so faint of breath is that you are suffering from weakened blood. This is slowing your return to health." He cleared his throat. "Once a week, you are to soak your feet in fresh blood, pig's or deer's or sheep's or cattle's. You will have to leave your feet in the blood until it cools and begins to clot.

"But I don't have gout," Maude pointed out in her most reasonable way. "Why should I soak my feet in fresh blood if I don't have gout?"

"You have a similar condition, though your foot does not pain you." He decided to take advantage of her knowledge. "And if you take care now, there is a good chance that you never will develop gout. I believe that you will be able to keep the gout from becoming stronger if you will but follow my instructions." He folded his arms. "I want you to go to Hosea Olfrant's place and order a case of port wine, as well. Each evening you are to have a glass of port before you retire." He turned to the other cousin. "You, too, Miz Bell. It wouldn't hurt you to have a glass of port of an evening."

"I'm sound as a horse," said Cloris Bell scornfully.

"And, God willing, you will remain so," said Clayton. "But if you are to aid your Cousin, then you will do well to see that you suffer no ills while she is recovering her health." Inwardly he was not certain that Maude Rossiter would improve. He did not like the color of her fair, fair skin; even with blood pudding every day he was not convinced she would be robust again. "How is your arm, Miss Rossiter?"

"Well enough," she said, smiling as she swung it in demon-
stration. "A trifle weak still, but not at all painful. There is no
knot where the bone knit. I am more fortunate than most." She
wiggled her fingers. "You made sure that my hand would not suffer from the break. I am delighted."

"Very good," Clayton approved, aware that Maude's arm was
not as strong as it ought to be. "I think you will want to continue
to have your cousin massage your arm in the evening, so that the
fingers will not stiffen. Is that agreeable to you, Miz Bell?"

"Certainly," said Cloris Bell. "Her grip is improving, but her
progress is slow."

"That is not unexpected," said Clayton, leaving his meaning
obscure. "You might use a little rosewater-and-glycerine for the
massage. Have Olfrant include that in the order you place."

"Fripperies like that have no place in farm life," said Cloris at
once. "They're expensive and do nothing but increase vanity."
She looked to her cousin for endorsement.

"That is often very true," said Clayton patiently, "but in this
instance, there are advantages to using the rosewater-and-glycerine
as part of the massage, in that it softens the skin and helps
develop pliancy." He lowered his head. "Ladies, please, in this
instance there is no fault in using it."

Maude Rossiter spoke for them both. "If you have good reason to require this, I will do it. And Cousin Bell will use it for the
massage."

"That I will," said Cloris Bell, then added, "We don't slaugh-
ter every week, doctor. Often as not, two weeks or three go by
between the times we kill animals. Is that often enough for Cousin
Rossiter, or must we make other arrangements?"

"Once a week is most advisable. I will speak to some of the
people in town—Missus Mattington, too. There will be someone
who will be pleased to help you."

Cloris Bell did not concur. "Doctor, most people in Charity pay
no attention to us because they don't approve of how we live—
not that they know how we live. What makes you think that any
of them would be willing to assist us, given how they feel?"

"Because we all live here," Clayton said with a sigh. "We have
a little community, and we are very isolated. No matter what we

think of one another, we must act together or we will fail, without doubt." He stood up. "I will make the arrangements and I will expect you to follow the instructions I give you." He offered Maude Rossiter his hand so that she could get down from the table. "I will send you word in the next day or so; Luis will bring instructions for me."

"Well enough," said Cloris Bell. "We'll be waiting."

"And in the meantime, rest for Miss Rossiter," Clayton reminded them.

"Can I at least get on with my weaving?" Maude asked.

"Not if you are tired," said Clayton. "Knitting and sewing are acceptable, but not weaving unless you are in better frame than you are today." He glanced at Cloris Bell. "I depend upon you, Miz Bell, to use your good sense in looking after your cousin. Err on the side of caution, for her sake."

"I will," she said, holding out her hand to Maude to aid her out the door and down the stairs.

Clayton closed the door behind them, then went to his desk and sat down, staring blankly at the far wall. He had not moved from that position when Jason Russell came into the room almost an hour later.

"Henry?" said Russell, seeing the physician's expression. "What is it?"

Clayton rubbed his face and turned to the sheriff. "Maude Rossiter. She's ailing."

"Trouble with her arm?" Russell asked as he dropped into the wooden chair between the desk and examination table.

"No. I think it's a factor, but..." He made a gesture of helplessness. "She has the look of a woman going into a decline. She's too pale and too tired and she gets short of breath too easily." He shook his head. "I don't know what more I can do but recommend ways to slow down the condition."

"She's not the sort to surrender her health, Henry," said Russell with unexpected gentleness. "If you help her, she'll improve. She will."

"I hope you're right," said Clayton, then regarded Russell distantly. "Why are you here? Is this more than a friendship call?" He straightened up.

"Partly," said Russell. He fell silent and frowned, then went on. "I had word yesterday from the managers of the Wilson–Blackthorn mine. You remember what Liam Cauliffe told me about the women there?"

"Two girls killed like the Grover girl was?" said Clayton, speaking disinterestedly in order to preserve his composure.

"Yes; according to the manager, there were actually three. The same kind of mutilation, as well. He has asked for more information about Evangeline Grover, as part of his records."

"Be damned to him," said Clayton just above a whisper.

"He sent me a copy of a letter from Denver. There have been killings near Denver as well. Women. Violated and disfigured." He closed his eyes. "God, I thought I had left that behind me."

Clayton looked at Russell. "What is it, Jason? Something has been troubling you from the first. What is it?"

Russell shook his head and got up, pacing the room in slow deliberation. "After the Runners were disbanded, I went to work for the East India Company—"

"So you've said," Clayton reminded him.

"We were not like the army, we were there to investigate and to protect." This bitterness of his smile was new to Clayton. "We were, in fact, very like police; Company Peelers, in fact." He rested his hand on the top of his baton as he continued to move. "I'd been out there for over three years when the killings started. Women—Indian women—working for the English were being killed. Most of them were…were like victims at a ritual." Again he was silent.

Clayton looked at him, aware that he was seeing a part of Jason Everard Nicholas Russell that was so private that Russell himself was not often aware of it. "How many?"

He stood quite still, his eyes fixed beyond the walls, deep in his past. "In two years, thirty-seven that we knew of."

"Thirty-seven," Clayton repeated.

"Probably more, or that's what the chief investigator for the Company thought likely." He looked at Clayton. "I was certain there were more."

"Dear God," said Clayton. "And you were one of those who investigated?"

"There were four of us. One died in a landslide, one was poisoned, and one broke his neck when his horse threw him. All the deaths were accidental—"

"Poison?" Clayton asked incredulously.

"Tainted meat according to the physician. If the other two were not dead no one would have been suspicious. Such things happen in India." He crossed his arms, holding his elbows tightly. "I was sent away. The case...I never knew what happened in the end. The Company paid reparation to some of the women's families, I think, and that was the end of it."

Clayton stared at him. "The end of it?"

"Yes." Russell took a deep breath. "I think I was getting close. We all were. That was the trouble."

"Trouble?" echoed Clayton, more confused than before. "How can that be trouble?"

Russell gave Clayton a direct look. "The man we suspected was English; an officer, well connected and popular in the mess. The dead women were wogs."

"Oh." Clayton hitched his shoulder. "What else would you expect?"

"I expected to catch the murderer, no matter who he was or who he killed." There was a quiet, intense passion in Russell's voice now. "If you had seen what he did to those women, you would know how I felt." His voice grew louder. "That poor Grover child was nothing. These women were...gutted and skinned when he was through having his pleasure of them." He was white around the mouth and his eyes, usually cool, were now as hot as the blue at the center of a flame.

"But an Englishman—" Clayton began, then stopped as he saw the set of Russell's features. "They did not permit you to catch him, is that what you are saying?"

"Yes," said Russell. "Before I left the Company they admitted as much to me. It was too late then. The man was back in England." His manner grew more sardonic. "He's something of a crony now of my half-brother, this murderer. He took his seat in the Lords a few years ago."

"You've kept track of him?" Clayton asked with surprise.

"I have," was Russell's grim answer. "All the while he was in

India, and later when he returned home." He swung around as if expecting to confront an adversary. "I can do nothing about that man. He will never face justice. But this murderer, the one who killed Evangeline Grover and those women at the mine, will not get away."

"Jason, you cannot—" Clayton began, only to be cut off.

"I cannot what? vow that I will bring the killer to the bench? I will do it because if I cannot, I will not be worthy of my office." He came and stood squarely in front of the physician's desk. "I will do it because I must, Henry."

Clayton frowned with worry. "It might not be possible."

"Only if both he and I are dead," Russell told Clayton, the words tight as banjo wires.

Clayton could think of nothing else to say.

On the north side of Charity, beyond the Protestant cemetery, the Houghton family pitched their tents and announced that they would build two houses and a barn before autumn, and offered good pay for those who were willing and able to work for them. All nine of the children—who ranged in age from seventeen to four—were busy with the building, working steadily to frame the house and get the walls up.

"The Grovers, the Houghtons, the Balzas, the Lindens, the Miekelmanns, the Twyfords, the Smiths, the Rivertons, the Challisers, the Bergers, the Lilhius woman and her son, and Wachter's crew. I told you the place was growing," said Smilin' Jack as he got onto the box of the wagon. "I'm going to win my bet, Sheriff, and long before the years are up."

"You may," said Russell, still holding the packet of letters Smilin' Jack had brought to him. "Have a safe journey."

"At this time of year, there's no trouble at all. The snows are gone and it isn't so hot that the horses don't want to move." He paused. "That fellow who came up with us from Denver—you met him yet?"

"I don't think so," said Russell. "I have been away for two days."

"He's putting up at the hotel, I think. He said he knew you from Australia. He talked kind of like you do." He touched the brim of his hat. "I'll be back in two weeks."

"We'll look for you then," said Russell, moving back onto the wooden sidewalk as Smilin' Jack started his wagon down the middle of Charity Street, raising dust as he went.

Russell watched a moment, then turned and crossed the street, going toward the hotel.

"Sheriff," said Martin Corley as Russell came into the lobby.

"Good morning to you," Russell said to the clerk. "Is Frau... Missus Schmidt free to give me a little of her time?"

"A little? I suppose so," said Martin, going to one of the two hallways leading to the back of the building. "Missus Schmidt, sheriff's here."

Dorabelle Schmidt joined Russell at the reception desk, leaning over to speak to him quietly. "I wanted to thank you for what you did with that Sister Angelica. She hasn't been down to pray for us during supper since you did that."

"She is a little overwhelming, isn't she," said Russell.

"Yes. I have told Padre Antonio that I do not want to have her here much longer. I know I agreed, but it is not what I was expecting. Perhaps you would be willing to have a word with him for me?" The request was asked easily enough but there was a tightness in her face that belied her words.

"I don't suppose it would be wrong to speak with him," said Russell. "Very well. In return, you might tell me if there have been any more newcomers here in the last few days."

"Well, there's the man who came up from Denver, but he's not suspicious, being an old friend of yours."

"An old friend of mine?" Russell repeated. "What old friend?"

Missus Schmidt consulted the registry. "A Robert Spaulding. He gives his address as Australia."

Russell's face froze. "Robert Spaulding. Here." He saw Missus Schmidt nod in confirmation. "Now what in the name of all the green devils in hell is he doing here?"

"He is not your friend?" Missus Schmidt asked, watching Russell with surprise. "He claimed he knew you."

"He knew me, if it is the man I assume it is. But he is not my friend and never was." He looked around the lobby. "Is he here now?"

"I don't believe so," said Missus Schmidt; suddenly she smiled and her rather plain face became charming. "I had word from Preacher Cauliffe," she announced.

Russell did not object to this change in their conversation. "He's coming back soon?"

"A week at the most," said Missus Schmidt. "And he will bring another preacher with him. So we will be married before we expected to be." Her smile widened. "He has said we will have our own house, other than the hotel, so that we may be a proper man and wife, and not always at the beck and call of guests."

"A preacher has plenty of calls on his time," Russell warned.

"But if he has his own house many will not disturb him unless it is necessary. If he is here, they will come to him for everything." She sighed. "I have seen how they flock to him while he stays here."

Russell's expression changed. "And do they flock to Sister Angelica?"

"No, that I say they do not," said Missus Schmidt. "Only once did someone come for her, and that was Missus Fletcher."

"Dona Elvira?" Russell said, certain that was the Missus Fletcher Dorabelle Schmidt intended.

"That creature, yes." She made a disapproving sound. "She is a very grand lady, but she is too volatile, and it will be to her disadvantage one day."

"Have you said as much to her?" Russell asked, trying to picture such an encounter.

"No, but I fear for the baby she carries. Oh, yes," she went on. "I can see that she is going to have one. Any woman can see that in another. It makes me fear for her when I see her ride down the street like an impulsive boy, or hear her upbraiding someone who has displeased her. All these humors are part of what shapes the baby. My own mother warned me that it was best to hear only pleasant things while…pregnant. She herself listened to sermons and good religious music while she carried her children, and none of us have gone too far astray."

"Unless you count the miles you have come from Hannover," said Russell mildly.

"You understand my meaning," said Missus Schmidt. "That Spanish woman is endangering her child with her wild escapades.

I have spoken to Preacher Cauliffe about it." Her brows flicked and she gave a little nod in the direction of the door. "I think Mister Spaulding is returning, Sheriff."

Russell glanced toward the door, being as unobvious as he knew how. "Which one is he?" The light was in his eyes and the men coming through the door were little more than dark shapes.

"In the middle, about the same size as Mister Olfrant." She closed the register and put it away on its shelf beneath the desk. "Do you wish to speak with him."

"No. Not yet." Russell moved a little to the side so that the shadow of the door fell across his eyes; he looked at the men without appearing to study them. He grew tense as he watched. "You right sodding bastard," he said under his breath as he recognized Robert Spaulding.

Something Spaulding said must have been amusing, for Hosea Olfrant burst out laughing, shaking his head repeatedly. "Ripe, very ripe, sir. I should blush to repeat the story."

"But it is amusing, repeated or not," said the other man with them, the saddler Linus Cooke.

"Well, I would not tell it where ladies or the clergy would hear," said Spaulding, his chuckle just as Russell remembered it. He looked around the lobby, going toward the bar without noticing Russell where he stood to the side of the front desk. "I think, gentlemen," Spaulding went on as he parted the curtain that separated the bar from the lobby, "that you might like to hear about the pretty little doxy your sheriff had in his keeping when I knew him. As pretty as you please and soft-spoken, but vicious enough to be transported."

"I cannot imagine our sheriff keeping such a woman," said Olfrant. "He seems very nice in his manner."

Spaulding's answer was lost as the men moved out of earshot. For more than a minute Russell remained where he was, silent in his anger. Then he made himself speak to Dorabelle Schmidt again. "Do you mind having the classes being given in the hotel?"

"No, not at all," said Missus Schmidt pleasantly. "It is very good to have so much to learn. My English is much better, and I can read many more words. Poor Martin has complained, but he is improving, too."

"You think we ought to continue the classes?" He found it hard to concentrate, for he had to fight the desire to follow Spaulding and demand an apology.

"Yes, definitely. It is one of the best things about Charity, that we teach everyone to read and write." She waited, and when Russell said nothing, she asked, "Is something the matter, Mister Russell?"

He made himself give his attention to her. "No, nothing. An irritation, nothing more." He managed a quick, tight smile. "Well, with your permission I will inform the Town Council of what you've said. They are scheduled to consider enlarging the classes. I wish they would hire a schoolmaster and be done with it, but that would mean spending money, I suppose."

Dorabelle Schmidt regarded Russell evenly. "You spoke the truth: you truly do not like that man, do you?"

"Which man?" asked Russell, knowing precisely what man she meant.

"The one in the other room, who has said he is your friend. You do not consider him a friend, do you?" Her tone was concerned without being prying. "You were not pleased when you learned he was here. You did not try to speak to him when he came in. Now you avoid talk of him."

Russell offered her an indirect answer. "I have not seen him in many years."

"And would have preferred it to continue, I'd wager," she said. "Your eyes give you away, Sheriff. Your eyes turn to ice, grey ice."

"Do they?" He glanced toward the bar. "Well, perhaps you're right; Mister Spaulding and I did not part on the best of terms when he left Australia."

Missus Schmidt gave him a gesture of encouragement. "He is a stranger. You are the sheriff."

"And I have been here only since last October," Russell reminded her. "My first year of probationary employment will not be up before then. This is June, and that is some time to go."

"You are the sheriff," she repeated. "Everyone knows you. He is a newcomer—there are so many newcomers—and there is no reason to suppose that he will cause you problems if you are careful." She indicated the stairs. "I wish I felt as sure of that nun. Sister Angelica may be the death of me. She's a wild girl under those clothes."

Russell met her eyes. "You are a good woman, Missus Schmidt. I hope that Liam Cauliffe knows how very fortunate he is." Some of the chill that had overtaken him faded.

There was rare mischief in her face. "I hope so, as well."

Chapter Nine

Her horse had thrown her just a quarter mile from the main road; she heard the sound of his hooves fading as she slipped from raw pain to unconsciousness. She did not recover when Abigail Lilhius found her, half an hour later, and realized what was happening. Even the bumpy, hurried ride to the Lilhius house was wiped from her mind: there was only the haze of pain between the welcome, muffling darkness.

"Jonah!" his mother shouted as she turned the mule-drawn trap toward the front of her house. "Jonah!"

There was no response from the house. Abigail Lilhius scrambled off the driving box and ran toward the barn, shouting her son's name, and was distressed when she found the barn deserted. She hitched up her skirts and ran back to the trap, struggling to take Elvira Fletcher out of it and get her into the house. She swore as she attempted to carry the unconscious woman up the steps and into the house. With a quiet exclamation of dismay, she saw the blood on Elvira's skirt clearly for the first time. "Dear God," she whispered, and put the young Spanish woman down on the rug as gently as she was able.

At the door she called for her son twice more, then rushed back to Elvira Fletcher, noticing with horror that the young woman was breathing with difficulty and there was a sheen of cold sweat on her forehead. "I am going for help," she said as she smoothed the abundant black hair back from her pale face. "I'll get Doctor Clayton, and I'll be back. I'm going to get the doctor. I won't be more than an hour. Hang on, Missus Fletcher. Don't move." She reached up and pulled a pillow from one of the chairs, which she put behind Elvira's head. Then she got to her feet, rubbing her hands on her skirt to clean the blood off as she hurried back to the trap, climbing to the box and giving her horse a smart slap of the reins in almost the same movement. She used the whip to keep the little mare at a smart trot almost all the way into Charity, while praying that nothing more would happen to Elvira Fletcher while she was gone.

Doctor Clayton's office was empty, and a note tacked to the door said that he was at the Mattington Ranch. Mrs. Lilhius cursed again, and after the shortest of pauses to think, she raced off to the sheriff's office, forcing her way across the busy street in her determination to reach the jail quickly.

"You must help me," she said as she flung the door open.

Russell looked up from the letter he was reading, and, seeing Abigail Lilhius, put the letter down. "Missus Lilhius. What is the matter."

"At my house," she said, and then without warning started to cry. "Oh, pay no mind," she said, infuriated at herself for this weakness. "It is Missus Fletcher. She has had a fall."

"Mister Frederick's wife?" Russell demanded, hoping he was mistaken.

"The young lady," said Missus Lilhius, waving away the assistance he attempted to offer. "There is no time. She was on the road, and I...I fear it is very bad for her." She wiped her face with shaking fingers. "Doctor Clayton is gone. Someone must help."

Russell was already reaching for his jacket. "You are correct, of course." He went to the door separating the cells from the office at the jail. "McPhee, I have a task for you. Do it well and you will be rewarded. Fail to do it and you will spend most of the next month in there. Do you understand me?" He turned back to Mrs. Lilhius. "My deputy is not here at present, or I would send him." He went to unlock the cell door and let out a scruffy-looking ranch hand. "Pay attention, McPhee. I am going to write a note and you will take it to Mister Fletcher at the bank. You will give it to him and only to him. You will tell him, and anyone who questions you, that you are acting for me. I am going to authorize a reward for doing this. You will be paid for the service you do. And you may be certain I will not forgive your failure to do this, nor will the Fletchers." As he spoke he went back to his desk and began to write hastily in the notebook he always carried. "This note," he said, holding it out to McPhee, "is for Mayor Fletcher. No one else. Tend to this at once."

McPhee looked at the paper narrowly. "I don't know."

"Refuse and I will extend your sentence by three days." Russell said this bluntly, making no other effort to persuade the man. "Choose."

"All right," McPhee said when he had considered it. "I'll give the note to Mayor Fletcher, but there better be a reward like you said, or I'll break your skull for you."

"You've tried that before," said Russell, "and have yet to do it."

"Well, I will," said McPhee, more sullenly. "I can do it, Sheriff." He took the note and shoved it into his breast pocket. "You sure the mayor'll talk to the likes of me?"

"If you say that you have a message for the mayor from me, you may be certain that he will admit you. Collect your reward and go back to the Mattington Ranch. I don't want to find out that you went to drink at the hotel or the tavern. Is that clear to you?"

Mrs. Lilhius plucked at Russell's sleeve. "Sheriff, it is imperative that we leave at once."

"As you say," said Russell, reaching for his hat and going toward the door. "My horse is at the livery stable. I will join you very shortly." He called back, "McPhee, I will be very interested in your success. If you do well, it might be useful to you in the future. If you do not discharge your task in a timely way, the next stay in jail will be longer." Then he was out of the door and rushing toward Calvin's Livery Stable.

By the time he returned on the blood bay, Mrs. Lilhius had brought her trap around, the little mare fretting at the bit as the nervousness of her driver communicated itself to the animal. "If you will accompany me, Sheriff?" she said as she put the trap into motion.

They set off at a smart pace, the sheriff riding beside the trap. "How seriously is Missus Fletcher hurt, do you know?"

"She was unconscious when I left her," said Mrs. Lilhius. "And unless I am mistaken, she may have miscarried."

Russell looked down at her. "How unfortunate," he said carefully, not knowing what was expected of him. "Are you certain?"

"I am no physician, but there was more than enough blood," she said as she used the whip to make the mare pick up speed. "My son...was not to be found. I trust he has returned and kept watch over the woman."

"What was she doing so far from town?" Russell asked of the air. "Why was she there?"

"She was coming from that new settlement, by the lake." Mrs. Lilhius said it without inflection.

"Oh, no," muttered Russell. "She was supposed to keep away from that place. If she went there, who knows what trouble she might have..." He stopped, knowing it was not correct for Mrs. Lilhius to hear this.

"She does not want Reverend Wachter on that land, or so I have heard," she said. "She claims the land and so do they."

"Yes," the sheriff allowed as they passed the newest building going up. "It is part of the land grant, but it is not known if the Spanish land grants will be honored by Congress."

Mrs. Lilhius handled her horse with skill as they passed one of the outlying farms where sheep were being clipped for the summer. The noise of the animals and the confusion around the house distracted the mare pulling the trap, but Mrs. Lilhius was able to keep the mare moving forward with minimum fuss. "Why must Congress decide?"

"Because this part of the country no longer belongs to Spain, and the grants of the Spanish King have no bearing on the United States unless the United States is willing to have it so." He looked down at her, admiring the way the sun shone on her fair hair. She had dragged it back into a neat, sensible bun at the back of her neck, which did little to show the color and sheen that Russell liked so well. "How long have you been gone from Missus Fletcher?"

"Not quite an hour, as I reckon. She might be much worse." This was the most difficult thing for her to say, and the words were forced and unnatural.

"Let us hope that is not the case," he said evenly, his tone giving no indication of his feelings; if Elvira Fletcher died because of her fall, there was no telling what Frederick might decide to do, and for once have his father's approval.

"What is it, Sheriff? Is there something you're not telling me?" She had read his misgivings in the narrowing of his eyes and the hard line of his mouth. "Will you—"

"I am borrowing trouble," he said, interrupting her without apology. "I have considered the problems we face and I am determined to take every precaution for Missus Fletcher's benefit. We are near the turn-off, aren't we?"

"The other side of the bridge," she said, nodding to a bend in the road. "Ten minutes more."

"Excellent," he said, then added, "Is that pony all you have to pull your trap?"

"Yes," she said. "We have two draft horses—yellow Belgians, very sturdy. But this is our only driving animal." She watched the little mare. "And she is tiring, I admit that without question. She will not be much use if we have to carry Missus Fletcher back to town ourselves."

"Let us trust that Doctor Clayton will arrive, or someone he appoints in his place." They were almost to the bridge. "You go first, Missus Lilhius."

"Thank you, Sheriff," she said, glad that he did not insist on taking the lead and giving her pony the office to fall behind. Once across the bridge, the pony moved more quickly, sensing the end of her journey.

"I don't know if Jonah is here or not," said Mrs. Lilhius as she took the turn away from the road toward her house. "This morning he tended to the milking and then...well, he is of an age, I suppose, when he has no desire to account for all his actions to me."

Russell held his tongue, giving his blood bay his head so that he could canter up the last stretch of road. He brought the horse to a halt at the rail below the porch and swung out of the saddle, already preparing to tie the gelding. He hoped that he would not find Elvira Fletcher dead.

Mrs. Lilhius' trap rattled up behind him. "I must put the horse in the barn; I will be with you directly. Call Jonah, if you would."

As Mrs. Lilhius went on toward the barn, Russell shouted once, twice for Jonah as he went up the steps two at a time.

There was no answer, and as he pushed through the door, he half expected to see the young man standing guard over Missus Fletcher.

But Elvira Fletcher was alone, lying in a puddle of blood that soaked her skirts. Her face was pale as bleached linen, but there was enough motion in the rise and fall of her chest to assure Russell that she was alive for the moment. He tossed his hat and jacket aside and knelt down next to her, lifting her gently, trying to ignore the blood around her. "Missus Fletcher, Dona Elvira. Can you hear me? Missus Fletcher?"

Elvira Fletcher gave a soft groan and her eyelids fluttered.

Russell decided to be encouraged by this. "We're bringing help to you, Missus Fletcher. You won't have to lie here much longer. You will be better shortly. Do you understand me? We're bringing you help."

Although she said nothing, Elvira Fletcher sighed, or so Russell wanted to believe. One hand rose a little, fluttered, and dropped again.

"You will be home in a little while. You've had…an accident, Missus Fletcher. You fell from your horse. You have been… hurt." He wished he did not feel so ill-equipped to deal with her trouble; it was not correct for him to lift her skirt, or to try to loosen her bodice. As soon as Mrs. Lilhius returned he would have to ask those things of her. He wiped her brow, saying as he did, "Do not be afraid; everything will be fine." He called himself a fool as he spoke.

Elvira Fletcher murmured something, but Russell could not make out the words, which seemed to be in Spanish.

The kitchen door opened and Abigail Lilhius hurried in, her face flushed. "The pony will have to wait for grooming later. I see that Jonah is not here." She came to Russell's side. "Oh, dear. She is so white."

"Yes," said Russell in as calm a manner as he could. "I think if you have some spirits that would help."

"My wits have gone wool-gathering," she said as an apology. "I have brandy, of course, and port."

"The brandy, I think," said Russell.

"Yes," she agreed, and went into the dining room to open the cabinet there. "A small glass should be enough, don't you think, Sheriff?"

"I doubt she is much used to spirits," said Russell carefully, "but I know that she often has served wine, or so her father-in-law informs me." He wondered if he dared move her. Now that she was in his arms, was there anything more he ought to do for her?

Mrs. Lilhius brought a small glass filled with brandy. "I don't know…how much to give her."

He took the glass and held it to Elvira Fletcher's lips. "If she can swallow a little, it should help," he said, looking from Mrs. Fletcher to Mrs. Lilhius. "Thank you. You have been most generous."

"There is nothing to thank me for," said Abigail Lilhius as she went down on one knee, the better to tend to Elvira Fletcher."She needs my help, and as a good Christian, I am obliged to give it." She took Mrs. Fletcher's hand and chafed at it. "Drink a little more of the spirits, Missus Fletcher," she urged.

As Russell fretted over the stricken Elvira Fletcher, he found himself watching Mrs. Lilhius, and liking what he saw.

Frederick Fletcher and Jonah Lilhius arrived at the house within five minutes of each other. Frederick had just hurtled through the door demanding to know what had become of his wife when Jonah hurried in from the kitchen, his youthful features sullen and dismayed.

Russell was trying to explain to Frederick Fletcher what had happened to his wife when Jonah interrupted them.

"She came to Reverend Wachter's settlement, that's what happened," he announced, his face flushing. "I was there and I saw it all. She ordered him about as if he were nothing more than a ranch hand."

"She went to Reverend Wachter?" Frederick said, eyes narrowing.

"She said he could not stay there, that he was on her land. Her land! The land is the Lord's, to bestow on His people, not the plaything of a Popish woman." He glared at Elvira Fletcher.

"Jonah!" his mother remonstrated.

"I saw her!" Jonah insisted.

"It is her land," Frederick said, more calmly than Russell had ever heard him speak. "Reverend Wachter, whatever he may think, is trespassing. It has nothing to do with my wife's religion, it has to do with the law of the country, and so the courts will prove. She has not released her claim to Reverend Wachter, and he is breaking the law to be there." He took Russell's place supporting her; he held her carefully.

"She has no right to the land," Jonah announced.

"She has every right to it," Frederick informed the youngster. "It was left to her by her father, who had it from his father. She has documents to prove it."

"Spanish documents, from a Papist king!" Jonah scoffed. "They mean nothing. You'll see. The law will not stand by those foreigners."

Now Abigail Lilhius was on her feet again, paying no heed to Elvira Fletcher's blood on her skirt. "What possesses you, young man? The Fletchers are here at my offer. How dare you speak to guests in our house that way, guests who have need of our help?"

Jonah turned away from his mother. "We have no need to render aid to them."

"You have need to do as your mother bids you, sir," said Russell, wishing he could banish the distress from Abigail Lilhius' eyes.

"My mother is a woman, and there is no older man here to guide her. I am the man of this house, and it is for me to decide what we ought to do." He folded his arms but took a step backward as well. "She needs me to take care of her."

"We're agreed on the last," said Russell. "But the rest you've learned from Reverend Wachter, and it has no place in this house." He turned to Mrs. Lilhius. "It isn't my right to correct your boy, but it galls me to listen to him—"

"I would say the same thing," said Mrs. Lilhius.

Frederick Fletcher had been whispering to his wife, holding her with a tenderness that Russell found as surprising as it was revealing. He looked up long enough to give Jonah a direct stare. "You tell your Reverend Wachter that as Dona Elvira's husband I make claim to the land, as is my right, and if he wants to pursue the matter in court, I will see that he regrets his temerity every day of his life. Tell him also that if any harm comes to my wife from this fall, I will hold him responsible and answerable for it."

Jonah sulked, but moved a little distance, muttering something about the blood. He looked angrily at his mother, then stared out the window toward the barn. "Godless," he said, not so loudly that he could be heard, but loudly enough to satisfy his own pride.

"There is a wagon coming," said Frederick, with more decision than Russell had thought him capable of. "I will take her back to Charity. One of the servants is waiting for Doctor Clayton to return, and he will be brought to the house as soon as it is possible." He stared at the blood. "She has miscarried, hasn't she?"

Missus Lilhius nodded once. "I am very sorry."

"Yes," said Frederick. "We must take care that the infant is the only thing lost today." He looked at Russell. "Tomorrow I want a proper order served on Reverend Wachter, Sheriff, and I want it served in front of witnesses from town."

"The circuit judge won't be back for a month," said Russell, who had thought that the skinny, pursed-lipped old man was hardly worthy of the title and power the court bestowed upon him. He had argued with the judge on three of his sentences and the judge had threatened to bar Russell from the Protestant church where court was convened.

"Then we will arrange something ourselves. Father will know how to do it. Bankers are always preparing documents of one sort and another." Heedless of the blood and frowning at her moan, he lifted his wife into his arms and started with her toward the door. "I hear the wagon. At last." He looked at Russell. "Thank you, Sheriff."

"Thank Missus Lilhius. She's the one who found Missus Fletcher and who brought her here, and fetched me." Russell indicated the widow with some gallantry as well as sincerity, for he knew that Frederick Fletcher would pay no heed otherwise. "She, more than I, deserves your thanks."

Frederick gave her an even stare. "I am grateful, Missus Lilhius. You have very probably saved my wife's life. I am in your debt." He struggled out of the door and was down the front steps when the wagon pulled up, four sweating horses pulling it and Daniel Calvin himself driving.

"Do you think she will be all right?" asked Mrs. Lilhius as she and Russell watched Frederick Fletcher place Elvira in the bed of the wagon, enveloping her in pillows and blankets.

"If she is it will be because of you," said Russell, his voice blunt. "I meant what I told Mister Frederick. If anyone deserves credit for Missus Fletcher being alive, it is you." He stared out at the wagon. "I hope she will be all right; she hasn't the temperament for poor health."

"No," said Mrs. Lilhius as Calvin swung the wagon around in the curve of the drive. "I suppose not."

Robert Spaulding regarded Sheriff Russell with amusement. "I know you're busy, Jason, but after so long, I thought you could spare me a little more time. I've had less than two hours of your attention and I have been in this town for well over a week Charity's too small to require that much looking after." He waved toward the bar. "What's your pleasure?"

"You would not like to hear my answer to that question," said Russell, not bothering to take the proffered seat.

"What do you mean?" Spaulding asked, making no attempt to disguise his dislike since only Sun Fan-Li could overhear them. "Or ought I to guess."

"I am wondering," said Russell, pointedly ignoring the challenge, "how it is that you arrived here. America is a long way from Australia, and Charity is a long way from anything. So you did not happen up these mountains by accident, did you?"

"Well, no," admitted Spaulding. "I have been at some pains to find you, I will tell you that much. It has taken time and cost a few bribes."

"Was it worth it?" Russell asked without expecting an answer. He kept his hand on his baton.

"That remains to be seen." He sighed. "I found out from a clerk in the Inns of Chancery—never mind how—that you had asked for your inheritance. Forty horses are conspicuous, especially coming so great a distance and to a place like this."

"Why did you bother?" He was fascinated by Spaulding, though it distressed him to recognize that fascination.

"After what you did to me?" countered Spaulding, venom in his question, and for the first time with color in his thin lips.

"I did nothing to you, not against you. You were breaking the law," said Russell directly. "If you believe otherwise, you are deceiving yourself."

Spaulding laughed, then spat. "More of that upright pap."

Russell kept his voice low with an effort. "You were forcing women to whore for you, Spaulding, and you maimed two men who tried to stop you."

"Criminals," he said with a gesture of dismissal. "For Lord Harry's sake, Jason, they were in Australia for whoring and pandering. What could they expect."

Russell shook his head, still disbelieving after all the intervening years. "They were entitled to expect that the Governor General's men would not use them in that fashion. We were sworn to uphold the law, yet you did not."

"Uphold the law!" Spaulding jeered. "What law? There were ten, twenty criminals for every one of us. If we didn't control them, if we weren't masters, we weren't safe." He slammed his hand down. "You betrayed us all when you reported me."

Sun Fan-Li looked up, his face impassive but his bright eyes alive with curiosity.

Spaulding swore at him and yelled, "Get out of here. Filthy Chink." He directed his glare at Russell. "You thought you got away with it, didn't you? Must have cost you a night's sleep to see me here."

"Not for the reason you suppose," said Russell slowly.

"It will get worse, Jason; my word on it." His smile was all teeth, like a snarl.

"Your word?" Russell said, bluntly incredulous.

"You will answer for what you have done to me." Spaulding announced this with satisfaction. "Before I am through, this whole town will know about your doxy and what happened to her."

"She died," Russell said quietly.

Spaulding laughed angrily. "How neatly you put it, Jason." He pushed his chair back and got to his feet. "You won't mind if I fill in the details for the people of your little town, will you?" He waited a moment, as if expecting Russell to respond in some way. When the sheriff was silent, he shrugged. "They think a lot of you now—but in a month, who knows?"

For once Russell was unwilling to cavil. "If you are convinced that it was my action and not your conduct that ended your... enterprise, then you are doubtless within your rights, pursuing me in this way. But if you are incorrect, then it is another matter entirely, and you are nothing more than a bully trying to exact vengeance for being challenged. But if you decide to drag Miss Leyton's name into it, I will put an end to the problem at once." He coughed. "I hope you come to your senses and leave before there are any more misunderstandings between us."

Spaulding overturned the glass that held his drink. "It is worse than I thought."

"There's no reason to despise Missus Schmidt's whiskey because you want to insult me," said Russell, taking a step away from the bar.

"You cannot provoke me, Jason," said Spaulding in a voice of ill-concealed wrath. When Russell said nothing, Spaulding went on, "You should have paid for this long ago. You ought to have been put on trial and shown for the hypocrite you were, calling down the law on me when you were breaking it yourself."

Russell stared down at the floor. "I did not want to break the law. If it had been allowed, I would have married her. It was what I wanted to do."

"Marry a whore!" Spaulding's voice cracked with laughter. "No man marries a whore, Jason. No man is such a fool."

"This man was, and would be still if the lady were alive."

With that, he left Spaulding to his whiskey.

Chapter Ten

"Not another one," said Russell as Padre Antonio stammered out what he had discovered behind the Lady Chapel of Sagrada Caridad. It was after ten, and few lights burned in Charity; at his house Russell had been occupied with fitting shutter hinges to the outside of his windows.

"She has been...she is very bloody," said the priest, his hands closing on his rosary beads.

"Young, fair, violated, and stabbed?" Russell ventured, needing no answer.

Padre Antonio lowered his head and crossed himself. "I pray for her soul, and for the soul of the man who killed her, who has fallen so far from God."

"That he has, " said Russell with a sigh. He set his tool belt aside. "Come in, Padre. I'll be with you shortly. And I'll send word to Doctor Clayton." He held the door so that Padre Antonio could enter the house ahead of him.

"Gracias," said the priest, looking around the front room with curiosity. "It is a pleasant place."

"Ta. It'll be pleasanter when it's finished. They tell me that another six weeks should do most of it. I have a range being brought up from Denver, for the kitchen, and there's furniture on its way from Boston." He looked around before he left his tool belt draped over a straight-backed chair. "I'll be with you," he said as he went up the bannisterless stairs to retrieve his notebook and his baton.

Padre Antonio had not moved by the time Russell returned three minutes later. "I like the fireplace."

"I remembered how the fireplaces were in my father's hunting lodge in the Cotswolds." As he buckled on his baton holster, he continued in a gentle tone, "There were two branching chimneys, one at either end of the lodge. Each supported three fireplaces. This one has only two, and the kitchen range will heat the water for the bath as well." He shrugged. "I was told that in his principle seat, there were much more elaborate chimneys, but I never saw it." He held the door for Padre Antonio, saying as he closed the door, "I am looking for a cook and housekeeper. If there is anyone you can recommend?"

Padre Antonio answered no so quickly that he felt moved to explain. "There have been rumors, Sheriff, but it would not be good for an honest woman to…to spend too much time in your employ. I am sorry."

Russell started toward the barn, then saw that Padre Antonio was in his gig. "It'll save time if I ride with you."

"*Vamanos*," said the priest, unhitching a single rein from the rail at the front of Russell's porch. He indicated the other side of the driver's box. "Here, Sheriff."

The two lanterns on either side of the gig threw little useful light on the dark road, but the way was familiar enough that it was not difficult to find the track in the night. There were three lights on in the upstairs windows of Lorinda Dooley's house, but the rest of the side of the mountain seemed to be made of shades of black. Russell rubbed his jaw and said, "These rumors, the ones that make it impossible for a virtuous woman to work for me; what are they?"

"It is not for a priest to gossip," said Padre Antonio as he brought the team to the left-branching street that led to his church. "It is not fitting."

"But if I don't know about this, how am I to combat it, and how am I to find a woman to serve as my housekeeper?" He folded his arms. "There are older women in Charity, women with grandchildren. Would that be satisfactory?"

"If you were a very young man, perhaps, Sheriff. But as you are not, there would be talk." He guided his little horse around a small obstacle in the road, then went on, "It is always thus with rumors, sheriff—they create suspicion more than they answer questions, and for that reason, they are more dangerous than questions, for without questions there can be no answers."

The looming square of the Sagrada Caridad school blocked their way, and beyond it the bulk of the church. Padre Antonio brought his horse to a stop. "Please get down, Sheriff. I must take this to my stable—"

Russell was off the driver's box, but he reached up to restrain the horse. "It may be that we will need the gig, Padre." His face caught the edge of the feeble beam of the off-side headlight, showing the worry etched into his face.

"Ah. Of course. I did not think...." He got down and led the horse to the hitching rail at the side of the church. "The...thing we are looking for is around on the side of the church," said Padre Antonio, growing more obviously nervous. "I have Sister Mercedes keeping watch. There are dogs and...and other animals...." He looked away.

"Yes; I understand. Very sensible of you, Padre," said Russell as he followed the priest.

"The other two nuns are in the chapel, praying." He raised his voice a little. "Sister Mercedes! It is Padre Antonio. The sheriff is with me."

"*Deo gratias*," came back the nun's voice. She was illumed by two candles placed beside something that looked like a sack of discarded clothes. As she rose to her feet, she crossed herself, looking away from what she guarded. "An animal came near, but I don't know what it was."

"You have done well," said Padre Antonio as he came up to Sister Mercedes. "This is a trial from God, my child."

"More for that sad girl than for me, I fear," Sister Mercedes answered. "Sister Angelica was distraught when she saw the body, but even her faith is strong enough to tend to this poor creature."

"I doubt that will be necessary," said Russell quickly, not wanting to deal with the zealous young nun. "I will tend to my work, and if you, Padre, are willing to wake Doctor Clayton and bring him to me, we can release you from this unpleasant task." He indicated the candles. "Do you need these?"

"They are for the dead," Padre Antonio said, trying not to be offended by what was so clearly an innocent question.

"It would be helpful to keep them here, and to have a lantern as well, if you can spare one." Russell looked at the body, noticing how pale the flesh was. "Have you looked? Is there blood on the ground?"

"We found her after dark," said Padre Antonio. "Were it not for a dog whining, we might not have discovered her until the morning, and who can say what mischief might have befallen her by then?" He indicated the body. "There is much blood on the clothes. What does it matter if it is on the ground?"

"If there is a great deal of blood on the ground, then it is likely that she died here. If there is not, then she may well have been killed somewhere else and brought here," said Russell in as emotionless a voice as he could achieve.

"I see," said Padre Antonio. He was silent, trying to swallow against the nausea rising in him. "Well," he went on when he was more certain that it was safe to continue, "we made no search. When we discovered her, we...brought the candles, I anointed her, for the protection of her soul, and we lit the candles. You have said that it is best not to move a...a body when it is found." He crossed himself.

"You are a man of excellent sense, Padre. Thank you. Please wake Doctor Clayton, see that we have light enough, and then you may leave us to our work, unless you have some objection to what we must do." He did his best to be encouraging.

Padre Antonio hesitated, then said something that had been building within him for some little time. "If this poor child were Catholic, I could not permit the things you are doing. But she is one of the newcomers who goes to the Protestant church at the far end of the street, and I cannot do more than bless her at her passing." He stared down at the body. "A knife did that?"

"Yes, or most of it," said Russell flatly.

"Poor girl," said Padre Antonio, and went off in the direction of Charity Street.

"Shall I stay with you, Sheriff?" asked Sister Mercedes from her place near the wall of the church. She had been watching all that passed between the priest and the sheriff.

"If you believe it's necessary, Sister; certainly. If you would prefer to return to your quarters, then do so." He had already dropped onto his knee, the better to examine the corpse. He took his notebook from his pocket, pulled out his pencil, and started to sketch.

"It might be wisest if I remain here," said Sister Mercedes. "I would not like it known that we left this sad girl alone here...." Her voice faded.

"You mean it would not be correct to leave a man of my reputation alone with a mutilated body?" Russell asked, his tone level. "It may be useless to say this, but I am not so depraved, Sister. Whatever the rumors are, they are not true. But stay, by all means, so that there can be no question about my conduct." He sighed as he resumed sketching. "How does it happen?" he asked of the girl a little later. "How did he get you to come with him? Or did he trap you? What were you doing here?"

Sister Mercedes cleared her throat. "I think," she said at her most tentative, "that the poor child came here to see Sister Angelica."

"Sister Angelica?" Russell repeated, turning to look at the nun. "Why on earth?"

"It is...it is—" Sister Mercedes looked away in confusion, then steeled herself to go on. "Sister Angelica has great fervor."

"True," said Russell, his pencil still as he listened.

"She has...she has taken it upon herself to address many of the younger people in Charity.... She is convinced that it is her mission to convert the world to our faith. It is her most abiding... passion."

"That is an apt word for it," said Russell. Then he looked directly at Sister Mercedes. "Are you saying to me that she was trying to convert this young woman?"

"Well," Sister Mercedes hesitated, "I have seen her twice at the meetings Sister Angelica has held in the school, after the close of the day. This girl and half a dozen like her have attended the...the talks that Sister Angelica gives."

"And there was such a meeting tonight?" Russell asked, puzzled that he knew nothing about it.

"It was impromptu. Three or four of the young people came to get the study materials Sister Angelica wished them to read, and it became something of a class in itself." She looked down at her hands. "Sheriff, it is not my place to speak against my sister in Christ."

"Nor would you—you answer your conscience, Sister," said Russell, who had finished his general sketch of the body as it lay in the shadow of the church.

"Yes. And if I err, I will offer up that error and do any penance that is given me." She crossed herself. "I think that Sister Angelica is...too ardent in her ways. For all the good she wishes to do, I fear that she does harm in its place. I hear how she exhorts others and I am troubled by her implacable dictates, for we do not live in the Dark Ages, Sheriff, and in a place like this, we do our faith a disservice if we become too divisive." She raised her head, her gorget and wimple making her head appear to float in the blackness.

"I applaud your judgment, Sister," said Russell as he turned the page of his notebook and started to make a record of the wounds to the young woman's face.

"Oh, not my judgment," said Sister Mercedes hastily. "It is all for the glory of God."

"If that is what you wish," said Russell, finding it difficult to be disinterested in what he was drawing. Both nostrils slit up almost to the eyes, so that the skin was two bloody tatters with the white of bone and cartilage showing. The eyelids had been cut off, and the eyebrows above them. There were stab wounds in the cheeks that revealed teeth. Four deep thrusts into the neck had all but severed her head from her body.

"Sheriff," said Padre Antonio as he came up, a bit out of breath from his run. "Doctor Clayton tells me he will be here in fifteen minutes at the most."

"Fifteen minutes," Russell echoed, wondering what the good doctor had been doing that it would take him so long to attend this new investigation.

"Miss Rossiter was in his house, along with Missus Bell, of course. He said he had to assure himself that they were all right before he left them." Padre Antonio glanced at Sister Mercedes. "Do you want to go into the chapel with your sisters?"

Sister Mercedes nodded. "Yes, Padre, if you are willing."

"God go with you and bless you, Sister Mercedes," he said, giving her a hasty blessing.

"Thank you for your help, Sister," Russell called after her without raising his voice much above a whisper. He turned to Padre Antonio. "And thanks to you, Padre. I have been remiss in letting you know how much I appreciate your work here."

"It is for God," said Padre Antonio simply. He stood beside the body while Russell knelt down and went back to sketching. "What do you know of the man who killed her."

"We know that he used a knife," said Russell. "We can assume he was stronger than she or that he rendered her unconscious. If she was violated, then…"

"If?" Padre Antonio asked.

"Doctor Clayton will confirm that, if it can be confirmed." He rocked back on his heels. "Whoever did this will probably do it again. And again and again until he is stopped."

Padre Antonio took an involuntary step backward. "But how can he continue?"

"Easily," Russell said, letting the word out reluctantly. "He will not remain anywhere very long. In each place, there will be one or two murders, and they will end as mysteriously as they began." He looked at the supine girl and shook his head. "And no one will know, because no one will bother to learn of other killings, at other times. In every place the people will think that they are the only ones to have this misfortune, and they will be…ashamed"—he looked up and caught this odd expression in Padre Antonio's eyes—"oh, yes, ashamed. What family wants it known that their daughter was defiled and slaughtered? What father or brother wishes anyone to know how a young girl dies, when the death is like this?"

Padre Antonio nodded.

"And that is all the aid that the murderer requires, that no one speak of what he has done, that they remain silent about the means and mode of death. So when it happens later, somewhere else, there is no reason to link one death with another. If the murderer is skillful, he can continue for years." He reached for one of the candles to move it, but Padre Antonio stopped him.

"No, Sheriff, that is not acceptable."

"Oh. Very well." He got to his feet and dusted off his knees. "As soon as Doctor Clayton is here, we'll get on with it. You did ask him to bring his lantern, didn't you?"

"Yes," said Padre Antonio. "And I can provide one more, if that will be useful."

"Very," said Russell, and watched as the priest hurried away, thinking once he was alone that he would be hard-put to discover the murderer if his own reputation was under fire.

George Fletcher rocked back on his heels, but for once did not begin to orate. He stared up at the ceiling of the sheriff's office, thumbs sunk in his waistcoat pockets, and grew rosy with embarrassment. "I want to…to thank you, Russell."

"Mayor Fletcher," said Russell, non-plussed at this announcement. "For what reason?" He was aware how this must sound, and so he added, "I can think of nothing deserving of thanks."

"You are a modest man," said Fletcher. "Unassuming." He directed his eyes at Russell without actually looking at him. "I have just come from my home. We have arranged for my daughter-in-law to be taken to Denver for treatment. Even she has accepted the wisdom in this." He cleared his throat. "My son Frederick has been most generous in his praise of you. If you had not acted quickly, he might have lost his wife as well as his heir." This last made him flush, for they were topics no man wanted to discuss. "That my daughter-in-law is alive is due to you, and that is—"

Russell held up his hand. "Excuse me, Mayor Fletcher, but such thanks are far better directed to Widow Lilhius. It was she who found Missus Frederick and it was she who cared for her."

"Well, women understand these things," said George Fletcher, intensely uncomfortable. "It is not surprising that she would realize the…gravity of the situation."

"She did more than that. She carried Missus Frederick back to her house and then brought her help. It is my job to answer a summons of that sort, and not requiring of thanks." He leaned back, feeling the warmth of the day in the walls. "You have no cause to do this, Mayor Fletcher, unless you wish to give your thanks to Widow Lilhius."

"I will see that she is sent a note. As you say, it is proper." He nodded ponderously.

Russell wondered if yelling would do it, would penetrate the rind of indifference that insulated George Fletcher from all the things he did not want to know. He tried snobbery. "I think it would be more fitting, more appropriate, for a personal call; you and your good wife, perhaps, might visit her farm, or offer her tea when she is next in town. For a widow alone, these gestures are especially significant."

"You can be a stickler for form, Sheriff, and that's a fact," said Fletcher. "I will discuss it with Missus Fletcher, and determine what is to be done. I feel I should warn you that while he is in Denver, it is my son's intention to file suit against the Reverend Wachter and all his community. He wants them off the land no matter what the final disposition of the Spanish land grants may be. He claims that as her husband, her property passes to him—quite right—and that as a citizen of the United States, her holdings are no longer simply a Spanish land grant but the property of a United States citizen and therefore Reverend Wachter is trespassing." He gave a smug little smile. "Not that I wish any harm on Dona Elvira, but I cannot help but think her...misfortune is the making of my son." He cocked his head, waiting for Russell to agree.

"It is a pity that he needed such an...inspiration in order to come into his own," said Russell carefully.

George Fletcher pursed his lips. "Yes, of course. To lose a child is always regrettable. But under the circumstances, it is not surprising. In future, she may take more care and not go careering over the hills in that ramshackle fashion." He took a turn about the office. "There is another reason I have come, Sheriff."

"Yes?" said Russell, becoming wary.

"Your agreement with the Town Council, your year of trial employment, will not be concluded until October. However, I think, given all you have done, that it might be best if we agree that the terms have been met. We will make your employment official and continuous from this date." He placed his meaty hands together. "It would be most appropriate, given current circumstances...."

"Do you refer to your family or to the rumors that have been circulating about me?" asked Russell directly.

Again Fletcher reddened. "Well, for your work, naturally. It is not correct for you to be employed simply because you have done your work for my family. No. And as to the rumors—phuff!—no sensible man gives them credence."

"I see," said Russell. He rose from his chair and went to pour himself more of his precious coffee. "Will you have some with me, Mayor Fletcher?"

"No; I do not take coffee before luncheon." He appeared ill at ease now, and his manner was cautious.

When his mug was filled, Russell regarded Mayor Fletcher. "I think it would be best if we kept to the original terms of our agreement. This position was offered me with a one-year period of trial. I am willing to serve that full year before final decisions are made. Whatever the Town Council decides, I will be here, raising horses if not keeping the peace." He smiled once at Fletcher. "As to the rumors, bring me any concrete statement and I will answer it. You have my word."

Fletcher stared down at the floor. "No man would ask that."

"Oh, I hope one will, at least one," said Russell, becoming more affable. "I do not want these questions hanging over me for any length of time, for they will become more dreadful the longer they are unanswered. Speculation and elaboration has ruined more than one reputation, Mayor."

"Do you say that these rumors are that?" His expression was intended to intimidate, but had no impact on Russell.

"Since I have not heard any of them directly, I do not know what they are. I have suspicions, but that means nothing. If you wish to assist me, Mayor, discover what is being said and who is saying it so that I can put an end to them." He strolled back the few paces to his desk. "Please keep me informed as to your daughter-in-law's progress and your son's activities. If I am to enforce his actions, I will need to know what they are."

"Certainly," said George Fletcher, once again thrusting his thumbs into his waistcoat pockets.

Russell reached for the letters he had written the night before. "When is Hosea Olfrant expecting the post?"

"In the next three days," said Fletcher.

"Good; then I have time to write a few more of these." He

tapped the envelopes.

"What are they? More inquiries about killings?" His face showed disgust.

"Well, between Liam Cauliffe and Luis Guerra, I now have information on seventeen killings in the last year and a half, all stabbings, all violations, all mutilations, all of girls with fair hair. I think that this is enough to alert other towns and settlements, don't you?"

"But if the murderer is still here?" said George Fletcher.

"He may be. He may have moved on." Russell tapped the letters again. "I hope this will assist other lawmen if the criminal leaves Charity."

"I pray God every night that he will," said George Fletcher with more fervor than Russell had heard him express before. "I do not like to think of this town so sullied."

"If I prayed, I would pray to bring him to justice," said Russell quietly, then leaned back and had a long sip of coffee.

Hepsibah Mattington stumped into the hotel, her new bonnet askew on her iron-grey hair. "A fine thing, when a new preacher won't listen to the old," she said as she surged into the parlor. "Missus Cauliffe!" she called out in a voice made loud and rough handling drovers. "I've come for that tea!"

Dorabelle Cauliffe, twenty-three days after her marriage to Liam Cauliffe, was rosy and bouncing. She sailed into the parlor and favored Mrs. Mattington with a wide smile. "Good afternoon to you, Missus Mattington."

"Cut line and call me Bess." She patted the place beside her on the settee. "I have to talk to you, Missus Sch—Cauliffe. About the reading and writing taught here."

"We are making good progress. Even Sun has learned to write in English a little. Everything he does in his own tongue is chicken scratching to me." She beamed at her guest. "What is it you want?"

"I want to start a proper school here. I want to see that the little ones coming up have a decent schoolmaster, so that the Catholics are not the only ones with educations in this town." She folded her big arms. "I want to get up a bunch of people,

people with influence, and I want to convince the Town Council to make the arrangements. We got to do it now or another year will go by without one." She gave a single, emphatic shake of her head. "It's not right. We got to have a proper school."

"Preacher Cauliffe is not on the circuit now. He would be willing to serve as schoolmaster until a proper one is found," said his recent bride. "Everyone knows him. They would send their children to him. Some of the people here might not want to have a stranger teaching their youngsters."

"Better a stranger than no teacher at all." She glowered at the embroidered pillow on the chair opposite the settee. "If Preacher Cauliffe started teaching, he'd have to get paid for it. Otherwise George Fletcher would not agree to hire a proper schoolmaster, nor get money for a school if Preacher Cauliffe uses the church for his classroom." She mulled this over a little longer and added, "How's Preacher at numbers and figuring?"

"I don't know," said Dorabelle Cauliffe, surprised at her own answer. "He reads and writes and knows geography. I suppose he can figure well enough." She would have to find out from him, later, what his skills were with numbers.

"Geography. I don't know as that's important, but we'd best have it taught," said Bess Mattington with her usual ferocity. "I told my boy Hiram that he would have to do something about learning more about the Texas Territories. I suppose that's good geography. Can Preacher teach proper handwriting, too?"

"He writes well," said Dorabelle Cauliffe, remembering the fine copperplate script her new husband used when signing his name. "I suppose he can show children how."

"Good enough." She looked up as Sun Fan-Li came into the parlor with a tray of tea and little cakes. "Is that China tea?"

"From India, Missus," said Sun. He placed the tray properly, bowed in the Chinese fashion, and withdrew.

"Let me pour," said Missus Cauliffe. "I have a little sugar."

"I don't believe in mauling my insides with sweets. It puts the humors off. Just tea, thank you, strong." She accepted the cup and admired it. "Never could see the sense in pretty things like this, not out on the ranch, but now and again it does me good to have a little tea in a fancy china cup."

Mrs. Cauliffe added sugar to her tea. "When I was a child, still in Hannover, I used to have little sweet peppermints in tea, for special times. I wish I could find some of those little sweet peppermints again."

"Well, ask the sheriff. He probably knows someone in England who can find them." Mrs. Mattington finished her first cup in two energetic swallows. "Now, I want to arrange a meeting for after the next class. I want you to talk to your husband and find out if he's willing to aid us in our work. If he is, I want him to attend the meeting. It won't do us any good to go before George Fletcher unless we're all ready for him. We got to make our plans in advance, so he can't upset us." She watched as Mrs. Cauliffe refilled her cup. "Is it hard, being new-married and still running the hotel?"

"It is awkward, sometimes," said Dorabelle Cauliffe, flushing. "But once we have our own house, things will be easier, I think."

"Well, I know I wouldn't want every newcomer trampling through my living room during my honeymoon, but it's your business, I suppose." She smiled gruffly. "I'm counting on you to talk to Preacher. Will you do it?"

"Of course. And I will talk to Sheriff Russell."

"I'll tend to that," said Mrs. Mattington as she set about demolishing a tea cake. "It's a pleasure to have a chance to speak to a gentleman now and again. Especially now that my Arthur has the apoplexy and is more like a baby than a man, it's good to spend a few minutes with Jason Russell from time to time. These tea cakes are wonderful, Missus Cauliffe."

"Sun makes them. He will not let me know how." She smiled, amused at her Chinese assistant's stubbornness. "It is his secret."

"Well, you got a few secrets of your own, or so I recall." She started to get up. "By the way, I noticed that there were two big wagons pulled in here. Another family coming?"

"A man and two sons. His wife and their daughters will arrive later. His name is Smithers." She giggled. "Such a funny name."

"Smithers. What does Mister Smithers do? Or does he do anything?" She was adjusting her bonnet and retying it with the same steady strength as she hog-tied calves.

"He is going to set up his shop, or so he says. He went yesterday to speak to Mayor Fletcher about the location and to deposit money so that he can get a shop and house built." She let herself have a second tea cake, though she knew it was bad manners to continue to eat after her guest had stopped.

Hepsibah Mattington thought about what she had been told. "Well, at least he has some money; that's good news. But what is it he does?"

"He is a gunsmith," said Mrs. Cauliffe as she bit into a third tea cake.

Chapter Eleven

"Well, I can tend to your stock," said Silas Fitzroy to Sheriff Russell. "You only got that Indian to help you half-days, and there's over forty horses out there."

"We're managing so far, Mister Fitzroy," said Russell quietly, interrupting his work cleaning tack. The afternoon was very warm and turning close, and he had left the hammering to the four-man crew who had raised the walls of his house.

"But I need a job, Sheriff. I thought it would be good to work for you." His soft face, screwed up now, looked more like that of a ten-year-old than a young man.

"Sheriffs make poor bosses, Mister Fitzroy. You'd do better signing on to build houses in town. I'm not ready to hire on anyone else right now." He studied Fitzroy as he spoke, trying to find what it was that made him hesitate to deal with the newcomer. "If you haven't found a proper position in a month, talk to me again."

"A month?" burst out Fitzroy. "In a month I won't have more than twenty cents to my name."

"Only if you take no work in the meantime." Russell fished in his pocket and pulled out a dollar. "Here. You can pay me back when you have found proper employment."

Fitzroy's expression was contemptuous, but his voice continued to plead. "I don't want just any work, Sheriff. I want to do something important. I don't want to work for the mayor—there's nothing for me to do. Mister Olfrant has all the help he needs. Mister Purvis has his own help now that he's feeling poorly.

He says he won't stay on the Town Council, not sick as he is; he wants Preacher Cauliffe to take his place." He offered these bits of information as if they were proof of his value as an employee. "I tell you, Sheriff, I can do things for you. I could earn my way for sure."

"And I repeat, if you have found nothing in a month, speak to me again." He disliked giving this sort of answer, for he knew that he had no intention of hiring Silas Fitzroy. He added, as a sop to his conscience, "I might have learned about a position for you by then. That is, assuming you have not discovered one on your own."

"Dogdang it, Sheriff," said Fitzroy, taking off his hat and dragging his forearm across his brow. "What do I got to do to show you I can help you? You can put me in charge of ten horses, just ten, and I'll do the feeding and watering and all the rest of it. I can do it, Sheriff. I can make sure that they're all fine. Give me a chance."

Russell sighed. "Mister Fitzroy, I am not yet in a position to bring in another employee. Do you understand that?" He dropped the waxing rag in his hand over the pommel of the hussar's saddle. "I will try to learn who can offer you reasonable employment, if you cannot find it for yourself."

"But I want to work for you." He turned away, then looked back at the sheriff. "What about around the jail? I could take care of things there—you know, bringing food to the prisoners and making sure they're locked in at night."

"I have a deputy for that," said Russell, disliking this too-accommodating young man more with every word he spoke.

"Well, but think about it. He could do more deputying if he didn't have to take care of the jail. I'd be good at it, Sheriff, real good." The urgent expression was back in his eyes and he waited for Russell's answer.

This time Russell made himself speak calmly and slowly. "I am not going to employ you, Mister Fitzroy. I have made arrangements for my horses, and I do not expect to need another deputy for more than a year. If you are as much in need of money as you say you are, then it would be more prudent for you to look elsewhere. There are many new people in Charity, most of them needing help in building their houses so that they will not have to face the winter without a proper roof over their heads. Any one of them would be glad of your work." He looked down at Fitzroy. "I have certain requirements, and I am afraid you cannot meet them."

Fitzroy's cheeks grew ruddy and his eyes darkened. "You can't speak to me this way. You can't refuse to take me on."

The lack of quiet Russell had been feeling became acute. "Yes, I can, Mister Fitzroy. And the more you comport yourself in this manner, the more I believe I am correct to refuse you." He started once more with his cleaning.

"Be damned to you, then," Fitzroy said through clenched teeth. "I came to you in good faith, but you, you'd rather have Mexicans and Indians around you. You want savages." He turned on his heels and started away, but he stopped before he was more than a dozen paces down the drive. "You're just show, Russell. You're nothing but an old man with a fancy accent."

"True enough," said Russell, watching Fitzroy narrowly as he continued to work the cloth over the saddle.

"An old man!" Fitzroy shouted before he sprinted away toward the Denver Road.

Mr. Morton Smithers had obtained a little space from Barton Purvis and had started to set up his shop. With his thick spectacles perched on his nose, he had something of the look of an ancient elf. As he heard the door open, he set the stock he was sanding aside and said politely, "Good morning; may I help you?" to the middle-aged man.

"To you, as well," said Russell, noticing as he approached that in spite of the eyeglasses, Mr. Smithers could not see clearly much further than the length of his arm. He held out his hand. "I'm Jason Russell. I'm the sheriff here in Charity."

"Ah, yes." Mr. Smithers' manner trod the fine line between extreme politeness and obsequiousness. He shook Russell's hand as if they were long-lost friends, then peered at him. "May I be of help, Sheriff?"

"Well, yes," said Russell. "I rather think you may." He looked around the little shop. "How is your business, Mister Smithers? Going well?"

"Oh, excellent, excellent," said Smithers, all but rubbing his hands together. "I've had several inquiries, as you would expect, and most of my present stock is all but exhausted. I assume that guns have been a luxury in this place."

"That is not far from the truth," said Russell, glancing over the shelves. "I see you are stocking a great deal of ammunition."

"Well, yes," said Smithers, laughing faintly. "What would be the point of guns if there were no ammunition to fire?"

"Precisely," said Russell. He once again allowed his gaze to roam over the shelves. "And that is selling well, too? The ammunition?"

"Yes, yes. Very well indeed. I have sent Roland—my oldest boy—back to Denver for more, and for other items. I understand that there is no other gunsmith between here and Boulder." He was plainly impressed by this information. "That is astonishing, quite astonishing."

"That may be one way to think of it," said Russell. "I do not mean to intrude, but I hope you are willing to keep careful records of the purchase of guns and ammunition."

Mr. Smithers looked aghast. "What is the purpose of that, sir? Every man needs to arm himself."

"I don't dispute that," said Russell, and went on in a quiet way, "We all need our weapons. Every man must be prepared to form a local militia if such is needed. We all pray it will never be required, but every family must have means to contribute to the defense of the town."

"Quite right, quite right," said Smithers, nodding several times. "It's part of the Constitution. Have you established such a militia, Sheriff?"

"It hasn't been necessary until now. Until a few years ago Charity was little more than a few farms and a mission. Today it is growing so quickly that it may soon outrun its limits and have to vote to expand them, assuming Missus Fletcher permits it."

"The mayor's wife?" asked Smithers, baffled.

"His daughter-in-law. She inherited the land grant that pertains to most of the land in this area. We expand at her sufferance." He did not elaborate. "So it appears that a militia may well be in order, and that requires that the people of the town be armed."

"Most laudable, Sheriff." Smithers beamed, since the militia boded well for business. "I'm prepared to fill all the demands the militia may have."

"Thank you. I'm pleased to know I can rely on you." He looked at the little gunsmith. "I am concerned: you see, Mister Smithers, before you arrived, most men carried guns for hunting, and used them sparingly. If they were going to get up to something, they did that with knives. I've seen few deaths by shooting in this place. Most of the killings have been done with knives. That's bad, but not as bad as using guns." He gave a faint, cynical smile. "For hunting and for defense I am delighted you are here. It is good to know that there can be a local militia. But for keeping the peace, I shudder at what may come now that ammunition and guns are so handy." He saw the skepticism in Smithers' face. "You don't believe me, do you?"

"Not entirely, no, not entirely." He pointed to the shelves. "Guns are not inexpensive, Sheriff, and ammunition is not so valueless that most can afford to waste it on mischief. I assume you are sincere, but I am afraid I do not share your concern." He gave a little bow. "Still, I suppose it would be good business to keep records of who has purchased what, as well as what was purchased. There are towns in the east that require those records, for the militia, as you say. If a man does not have a gun recorded, he may be fined. That is the law. If I do decide to make such a record, it will be for my own use, for the sake of the militia."

"Fair enough. I would only want to see it if it had direct bearing on the defense of Charity or the investigation of a crime." He was not wholly convinced by Smithers' appearance of cooperation.

"Certainly," said Smithers. "Yes, certainly."

Russell watched him a little longer. "Tell me, Mister Smithers, has anyone yet ordered new or special guns from you?"

"Well, before we came here, yes, of course. I had the privilege of making several pistols for distinguished men. One set was especially beautiful, with grips of rosewood and mother-of-pearl." His eyes, behind his glasses, gleamed with the memory.

"I have a gun—an unusual design, for riot-control—that may need some adjustments. Are you set up for that?" He indicated the shop. "You are just getting started."

"In a month, perhaps I will be able to work on your gun. I will send you word when we're ready. God willing, my wife and our daughters will be here by that time." He fumbled with his pocket watch, peering at it to make out the time. "Are you a family man, Sheriff?"

"No, Mister Smithers, I am not," said Russell, sensing that Smithers knew the answer before he asked.

"Sad, very sad," Smithers said, then returned his watch to his pocket. "Well, it is a pleasure to meet you, Sheriff. I hope we will have the opportunity to serve you quite soon." He indicated the shelves. "Is there anything I can show you while you're here?"

"I will need to purchase ammunition before long. My deputy will bring you a list, if that is satisfactory?" He started toward the door. "I hope you and your family like Charity, Mister Smithers."

"Oh, I'm sure we will. It's such a glorious opportunity, don't you know." He nodded several times as Russell went out the door, then stood by the window, watching where he went.

While Sheriff Russell sorted through his latest letters from other lawmen, Luis Guerra stood at his side, attempting to read over his shoulder. "You think this is going to work, Sheriff?" he asked after a while.

"It's better than waiting for another murder. And it will give us more information to pass along if the killer has left Charity." He sat back and stared at the letters separated into three stacks. "These have no murders on record, not of the type I've described. They're to the north of here, mostly. These are the ones that might be what we're looking for—no real pattern to them—and the last look like the same killer: young women with fair hair, killed with a knife, sexually molested, mutilations in most instances. One from Taos; the murder there is almost three years old. The family does not want any investigation. According to the marshal, they're too ashamed. They want the whole thing forgotten."

"Fools," said Luis comprehensively.

"Yes, but one can see why they might feel that way." He tapped the pile of possibilities. "I'm taking these home with me tonight. I want to go over them. And if I find anything that looks possible, we'll talk about it tomorrow."

"You still planning on doing a street patrol tonight." Guerra waited for the answer, knowing he would have to accommodate the sheriff's decision.

"Around nine, and another at midnight. You can do the nine and I'll take the later one; I'll be up in any case." He glanced at his deputy. "Something's bothering you."

"I..." He slapped his hands together impatiently. "I don't think it's enough. I want to do more. I want to find this killer and see that he is punished."

"I want to see him brought to justice," said Russell mildly, adding to the quizzical look in Guerra's raisin-brown eyes, "It's not quite the same thing, Luis."

"You do not want him punished?" Guerra demanded, his amazement intense.

"Yes, but that is not what I am paid to do. I want to bring that man to the law, and it is for the law to punish him." He could not smile at so heinous a crime, but there was a quirk in his manner. "If I were not an officer of the law, then I would want to punish him."

"Aha," said Guerra, satisfied that the sheriff was not shirking his moral obligations. "Then we understand each other."

"Oh, yes." Then Russell looked at Guerra. "But Luis, you are my deputy, and much as you might want to be the instrument of vengeance, you can't be; you are sworn to uphold the law, not take it into your own hands. Or to stand aside in order to let others take it into theirs." He cocked his head in the direction of the cells. "What right do we have to put people in there if we do not uphold them law?"

"You are as bad as Padre Antonio," said Guerra, his face becoming sullen. "Very well. I will try to do as you suggest. I swear I will not forget my oath."

"I know you will not," said Russell, getting up from his desk and gathering up the letters. "I'm going to have supper at the hotel, and then I will be at my house. If you need me, send for me."

"That I will, Sheriff," said Guerra, who loved being left in charge of the jail. "If I need you."

As Russell left the jail, he heard the sounds of hammering—this noise was a constant now in Charity as new buildings were raised at a ferocious rate. In the almost ten months Russell had been in Charity he had seen the town change dramatically, growing both to the west and the north where the slope of the mountain afforded the easiest purchase on its flank. More than twelve houses had been started since the thaw—his own included—and another three were being readied. If the alterations were striking to him, what must they be like, he wondered, to those who had lived here longer, for five, or ten years? Not that there were many who had been here ten years, other than the Padre and Sister Mercedes.

Liam Cauliffe was at the hotel, seated in the dining room with his wife. While he was not smiling, for smiles did not come easily to this dour Scot, his face was filled with quiet satisfaction. He nodded to Russell as he came through the door. "Are you going to join us tonight, Jason?"

"If you will allow," said Russell, about to sit where he often took his meals.

"No; come over here with us. I've wanted to talk with you for several days, but there never seems to be a chance." He indicated the chair opposite his. "I thought that giving up the circuit would allow me more time to myself, but that's not the way of it." He rasped his fingernail along his chin. "I'm having a bath and a shave tonight."

"One of the advantages of owning a hotel," said Russell, looking around. "The only other place with rooms is the tavern, and they don't offer baths."

"Don't make light of it, Jason; bathing can be a terrible vanity." He looked as if he might launch into an impromptu sermon, then changed his mind. "I spent some time with Missus Fletcher today."

Since Frederick Fletcher and his wife were still in Denver or Boulder, Russell assumed that Cauliffe meant the mayor's wife. "And what did she have to say?"

"She's worried," said Cauliffe.

"Not unusual with her," said Russell carefully.

"She is a very...correct woman." Cauliffe signaled to Sun. "We will have soup, if you please."

"Both of you?" Sun inquired politely, and in much better English than he often displayed to the patrons.

"If you will, please." Cauliffe dismissed him. "She is concerned that this dispute between her daughter-in-law and Reverend Wachter will end in litigation, and she is distressed to think that anyone of her family might have a hand in acting against a man of God." He paused, giving Russell tacit permission to comment.

"And what do you think?" Russell asked. "Not about the mayor's wife, about Dona Elvira's complaint against Reverend Wachter? Does it trouble you that there may be litigation?"

"Well," Cauliffe allowed, "I do not find myself in agreement with Reverend Wachter. When he says that a husband is obliged to beat his wife regularly to correct her faults, I cannot completely concur. It may be necessary, if she is very wayward and contrary, but otherwise, I think it is something a man must judge for himself. And when he declares that it is the obligation of all parents to select the spouses of their children, because the parents will always be wiser than their children, I cannot wholly support him. Certainly it is best if a child is guided by its parents, but there are instances when wisdom is with the child, not the parents."

"What he believes is not in question—except that he believes he has the right to claim the land where his community is being built." Russell lifted an open hand. "Is he entitled legally to be there. That is the heart of the issue, and it has nothing to do with his calling. If he isn't, then, reverend or not, he is in the wrong, the more so because he has not made any attempt to acquiesce to the requests presented to him in regard to the Arreba y Corre Rancho."

"But it is going to lead to hard feelings, Jason," said Cauliffe heavily. "It is going to cause more hardship."

"I'm sorry to say that I fear you're right," said Russell, looking up as Sun brought soup. He wished now that he were hungrier.

"I cannot condone Reverend Wachter's behavior that brought about Missus Fletcher's...sad loss. At the same time, think it was capricious and ill-advised for her to venture to Reverend Wachter's community without appropriate escort. If anyone was to speak to Reverend Wachter, it was her husband who ought to have done so."

Russell heard him out. "And you, Missus Cauliffe?" he asked
the very silent Dorabelle, who was staring at a half-empty plate of
soup that had been before her so long it was cold, not steaming
like the preacher's and Russell's. "You have said nothing."

"Because I do not want to argue with my husband," she said
quietly, looking at him with an expression between sorrow and
defiance. "And if I speak, it may come to that."

"My dear—" began Cauliffe, without any idea what to say
next.

"Why don't you agree?" asked Russell.

She lifted her chin. "It would not be right for—"

Liam Cauliffe touched her hand briefly. "Speak your mind,
woman; you're not a giddy child. I'll try to listen to you without
protest."

She gave him a quick smile. "If you permit," she said, then
turned directly on Russell. "I was a widow for many years, and I
fended for myself. There was no one else to do it. So I think Missus
Fletcher was right to do what she did—if it were my land, I
would go anywhere, risk anything to keep it. If someone came
into this hotel and tried to damage it, he would have to over-
power me first. Missus Fletcher was not being foolish or impetu-
ous or any of the other things I have heard her called. She
miscarried! She risked that to save her land, and all that you say
is that she was not prudent about what she did. Who else would
stop the theft of her land? No one else was taking care of the
matter—everyone is afraid because the man is a minister of God.
She did the thing she had to do, and now all that you can do is
say she was not right in her conduct."

The dining room of the hotel was silent as Dorabelle Cauliffe
finished. One or two of the early diners blinked and made more
noise with their cutlery than usual; Russell looked at Mrs. Cauliffe
thoughtfully. "Suppose she had shot Reverend Wachter? What
then?"

She glared at him, as if suspecting he was mocking her, but
there was only curiosity in his pale blue eyes. "She did not shoot
him."

"But she might have," said Russell. "Would you still defend
her if she had done that?"

"I don't know," she admitted after she had considered it.

At last Liam Cauliffe spoke up. "I don't know what to say, my dear. I had no notion you harbored such intense feelings for Missus Fletcher's plight."

She said nothing, suddenly very interested in her cold soup.

"I wouldn't be surprised if Bess Mattington agrees with you," said Russell. "She hasn't spoken to me, but she did say that if anyone tried to move in on her ranch, she'd chase them off with shotguns and bear traps."

"And the town would stand by her," said Dorabelle Cauliffe, "provided it was not a minister coming onto her place. It helps that she's a Protestant, too." She turned to her husband, "Mister Cauliffe, I don't cast doubts on your calling, but you yourself have told me that there are many scoundrels wrapped up in the New Testament. How can you know that Reverend Wachter isn't one?"

"I have spoken to the man," said Cauliffe, but his frown grew deeper. "Nothing he has said has made me think that he might not be true to his calling."

"An opportunist would do the same thing," Russell said.

Cauliffe looked at him. "I need no Devil's Advocate, Jason." He took a spoon of soup in order to have something to do while he thought. "I do not approve of disrupting the worship of others, even those whose faith and worship is different than my own. But it offends me to the very gates of heaven to see the Word of God abused." He regarded Russell carefully. "I will do what I can to help maintain an even disposition in the town. I will try to explain what you have said—that this is not a matter of religion but of law—and I hope that some few of the congregation will be listening."

"Thank you, Liam," said Russell.

"I feel," the minister went on, "that I have an obligation to you; if I had not recommended you to the Town Council, you would not have come here."

"Oh, possibly not here, but somewhere like it," said Russell. He tried his soup at last. "This is very good."

Grateful that their distressing conversation was over, Dorabelle Cauliffe nodded eagerly to Russell. "Yes, Sun is a treasure, isn't he?"

Chapter Twelve

Luis Guerra pulled his horse up in front of Russell's house, raising dust and shouting, "Come quick, Sheriff!"

Russell emerged from the second barn, going up at right angles to the first. Sawdust clung to him and his shirt was dark with sweat. "What is it?" He pulled his large handkerchief across his brow, then stuffed it into his pocket. "What's wrong?" For he knew it was something wrong; nothing else would bring Guerra to him in such haste.

"A fight. In the tents!" He yelled so loudly that his horse pivoted nervously. "Over cards."

"Damnation," said Russell softly, then nodded. "All right. The roan's saddled. I'll get my baton and be with you." He had already started toward his porch when Guerra called after him.

"Bring a pistol, too. Maybe that volley-gun of yours. It's turning into a riot, Sheriff."

Russell took a deep breath. "Very well," he said, thinking that what he had feared was now happening—guns were replacing knives for fighting. "I'll bring it."

He checked the volley-gun, satisfied it was fully loaded, then buckled on his baton holster. His eyes ached and the air weighed on him. He decided it had to be the heat that was causing the trouble. There had been fights the night before, nothing serious, but irksome; five men were spending the day in his jail because of them. And now there was something worse brewing. He pulled his door closed and jumped off the porch, signaling to Guerra as he jogged toward the door. Once in the barn he went straight to the roan's stall. He tightened the girths on the roan's saddle, then slipped on the bridle, fastened the throat latch and led the horse outside. As he swung into the saddle, he called out to Guerra, "A fight over cards?"

"In the tents. You know what it's like," said Guerra, referring to the cluster of tents that had sprung up on the southwest side of town, near the dairy. Only a few shacks had been there before, and in the last month, the tents had sprung up around them like mushrooms. "It started in the big tent, the round one?"

"Yes," said Russell, picturing it in his mind. "I know which one you mean."

"In there." They had reached the Denver Road and turned west into town. "I didn't think I could manage it myself."

"You did the right thing. I hope it doesn't get too bad." He had warned the Town Council about the tents not more than a week ago. "How many were fighting?"

"A dozen, maybe more," said Guerra. "I only have my pistol, so there wasn't much—"

"I'm not faulting you, Luis. You were right to bring me. And now, I want you to keep with me until we attend to this." He swung off on Mission Street, past Sagrada Caridad and the jail, then across Charity Street. Guerra kept behind him, urging his pinto to keep up with Russell's roan.

Two blocks away from the fight and Russell could hear it. He drew his roan from a trot to a walk, and halted him at the outskirts of the tent settlement. Tieing the horse to the porch post in front of the barber shop, he slung his volley-gun over his shoulder and started toward the center of the tents.

"What do you want me to do, Sheriff?" Guerra shouted.

"Follow me. Mounted. If anyone tries to bolt, you catch them." He saw a man come out of one of the alleys, his face covered in blood. "Let him go, Luis."

"He might—" Guerra began.

"He isn't going to do anything," said Russell, moving more quickly as the sounds of conflict—shouting, breakage, an occasional shot—grew louder. "Don't shoot unless it's necessary. We don't want to get into a pitched battle."

"No time to reload," said Guerra in an attempt at humor.

"Something like that," Russell agreed, his attention now on the men he saw milling outside the large, round tent. He brought the volley-gun down where he could use it, and shouldered his way through the shouting spectators into the middle of the brawl.

All of the tables in the tent were overturned, and at least half the chairs were broken, and one of the poles was bent and could clearly give way. More than thirty men were embroiled in the fray, while a number of others hung at the edges of the fighting, nursing injuries. The noise was furious.

Russell stood in the side door of the tent, took aim at the bent pole, and fired one of the volley-gun barrels, smiling a little as the other half of the tent collapsed, dropping canvas onto the battle, bringing bellows and shrieks of dismay, and sudden confusion as the men sought to escape the enveloping tent. Outside, most of the men started to flee, their encouragement of the fight turning to consternation. Howls of indignation joined the chaos.

"Now then." Russell fired a second time, this shot directed well over the top of the sagging tent. "Gentlemen!" he shouted, and waited while an uneasy calm settled over the combatants. "Gentlemen," he said in a lower voice, "I cannot allow this, whatever the cause is." He stepped back so that he was clear of the long flaps of the tent. "Each one of you has broken the peace, and each one of you is guilty." He made a point of aiming his volley-gun at the other tent pole. "I expect all of you to surrender, either to me or to my deputy, and to do so without any further disruption."

Someone cursed Russell, his mother, his brothers, and all possible offspring.

"You, sir," said Russell in his calmest tone, "will apologize. If there is another outburst of any kind, I will bring down the rest of the tent. Is that understood?" He waited, his gun at the ready.

Someone threw a rock; it landed harmlessly a few inches from Russell's boot.

"Deputy Guerra," said Russell, "arrest the man who threw the rock." He stepped to the side, but kept his aim on the pole. "If anyone else is considering mischief, stop it."

This time a pistol was fired, and the man next to Russell sitting on the ground with a bruise forming on his jaw fell to the side, screaming obscenities and clapping his hand to his bleeding ear.

"Arrest that man as well," Russell instructed, not moving from his place. "At once, Deputy Guerra." He heard rather than saw Guerra push his horse through the crowd in pursuit of the man who had fired the pistol.

"That is the last, I trust," said Russell. "Now then," he went on, speaking to the men inside the tent. "I want you to come out, one at a time, hands up, no weapons. My deputy and I will gather them up and see that they are returned to you in a day or so, when we have recorded your roles in this."

A few of the men inside the tent shouted protests, and one of them rushed at the sheriff.

Russell fired the third barrel, bringing down the tent.

This time the protests were louder but muffled by the tent. Now the canvas spread out at Russell's feet, lumps and mounds under the cloth showing the location of men and ruined furniture.

"Deputy Guerra, I want this crowd disbursed. I hope that someone will fetch Doctor Clayton. See to it at once."

"Yes, sir," called out Guerra from a little distance. "I have the man with the pistol, too."

"Excellent," said Russell, using the barrels of his volley-gun to lift the edge of the canvas. "Now, I will repeat my instructions, gentlemen. Perhaps you will follow them this time?" He saw two men crawl out from under the far side of the tent and bolt down the nearest alley; he watched them go with the sense that it would be folly to pursue them with so many others to arrest and charge. "I want you to come out, one at a time, without weapons. Is that clear?"

The man beside Russell had curled into a ball, whimpering.

"If you are injured, Doctor Clayton will attend to you when I am done." He held up the edge of the door-flap. "All right, one at a time."

The first man, a slight, bearded fellow of uncertain age, crawled out, holding up hands with bruised and torn knuckles. "It was just in fun, Sheriff," he said sullenly.

"Was it?" Russell asked as he took his notebook from his pocket. "Your name, please."

"Bernard Schultz," he said. "Barney." ·

"You're new to Charity," said Russell, who did not recognize the man or the name.

"Arrived ten days ago." He coughed and spat. "Hell of a town you got here, Sheriff."

Russell nodded. "What weapons do you have?"

"Two knives and a Bell pistol. I left 'em in there, like you said." He looked around. "What now?"

"For the moment," said Russell with a sigh, "you can wait here for Doctor Clayton, or you can return to your...residence."

"I got a room at the tavern." He lowered his hands and stared at the damage. "I can tend this; I got some horse balm."

"The fine for brawling in public is five dollars."

Schultz stared at him. "Five dollars!"

"Pay it now or leave town by noon tomorrow," said Russell in his most even tone.

"Five dollars!" Schultz repeated, more outraged than before. He kicked at the dust, then started away from the sheriff, muttering at the high cost of amusement in Charity.

The next fellow out was barely out of childhood; he had a bloody nose and a blackened eye, and his expression was sheepish as Russell said his name. "You won't tell my uncle about this, will you, Sheriff?"

"I'm afraid I have to," said Russell. "What Mister Sampson does is up to him." He put the boy's name in his notebook. "Don't let me catch you back here again, Patrick."

"No, sir," he said, eyes on the ground. "Will I have to pay five dollars?"

"Yes," said Russell.

"Can I work it off instead? My uncle won't let me have five dollars, especially if he knows how I came to owe it." He stared at Russell. "Please, Sheriff."

"Go over to the jail, Patrick." Russell did not want to be drawn into the boy's predicament. "I'll meet you there."

He lowered his head again. "All right."

The third man was Silas Fitzroy, who glared at Russell. "I don't have five dollars, and it isn't likely that I'll get any by tomorrow." He held his arm across his chest, protecting his ribs. "I don't plan on leaving yet, either."

"Five dollars by tomorrow, or a job and the promise of five dollars by the end of the week. Is that clear?"

"I got to have the doc look me over." Fitzroy refused to answer Russell's challenge. "I think something got broke."

"Then stand over there and wait for Doctor Clayton," said Russell with a sigh, and turned his attention to the next man.

Barton Purvis was attempting to get the attention of the people jammed into the hall of the Charity Protestant Church for the meeting of the Town Council. He rapped the table where he and George Fletcher sat; he gestured to Mayor Fletcher to show that he did not know what else he could do.

"I saw the last of your victims yesterday—Fitzroy," Henry Clayton said to Russell as he came up to him through the crowd. "I ought to thank you for providing me so much business."

Russell was not able to smile. "That could have turned quite nasty."

"So it could have," said Clayton. "And you right in the middle of it with just one deputy to help you out." He shook his head. "What the devil are we going to do with you, Jason? You aren't going to be satisfied until you face the whole town."

"I may be doing that tonight," said Russell carefully.

"Don't be absurd," said Clayton. "After what you've done for Elvira Fletcher, Mayor Fletcher would not permit that to happen. He has taken his family's interest to heart."

Hosea Olfrant, a little out of breath, came panting through the crowd and took his place at the front table with George Fletcher and Barton Purvis. He nodded to everyone and apologized to the mayor.

"I've suggested to Mister Fitzroy that he talk to Missus Bell; she could use a hand while Miss Rossiter is ailing." He saw the surprise in Russell's face. "Well, he has a fine to pay, and you've given him until tomorrow to pay it. With cracked ribs he isn't up to house building, so this might be an answer."

Russell shook his head. "What did he say?"

"Not very much. I told him where he could find their farm; I have faith in Missus Bell, Jason. She is a sensible woman, and she has been trying to run their farm and attend to Miss Rossiter at the same time. Fitzroy can feed the stock and make sure they have water. He won't earn much, but he won't starve, and you'll get that five dollar fine. Not on time, but you will get it." He looked down at his feet. "I spoke to Cora Vreeland. I was worried about her, with that riot so near the Howe dairy."

"And is she well?" asked Russell politely.

"I don't know why I bother; it serves no purpose."

"It lets you know she is well," Russell said gently. "You see that man there, near Mister Sampson? He's building the barn on the west end of town. He says he's going to bring in hogs."

"I suppose we ought to welcome them all," said Clayton, accepting the change of subject gratefully. "Word is that Smilin' Jack is putting up a building across from the park."

"Is that whose it is?" Russell asked, and then fell silent as Barton Purvis finally managed to bring the meeting to order.

"First order of business," said Hosea Olfrant after the proper introductions and announcements were made, "is the question of a school. Missus Mattington has given Charity the sum of three hundred dollars to build a school, and she says she will give three hundred more if we will build a school and hire a schoolmaster within the next year." The generosity of the offer brought a murmur of surprise. "But the cost will then fall to this town and the people in it. Since Reverend Cauliffe has said he would be willing to teach for a while, we might prefer not to take on such a large burden as a school and a schoolmaster quite yet." He coughed delicately. "The on-going cost has to be considered."

"Six hundred dollars is a lot of money, Purvis," someone in the gathering shouted out; his comment was endorsed with nods and whistles.

"But the six hundred dollars are only the beginning," said Purvis. "That is why we need to vote on the matter, because you are the ones who will have to provide the next money, once the six hundred is gone."

Samuel Gall stood up, his hat clutched to his chest. "Well, it won't come to that much each, will it? The children need a teacher, and that's a fact. Most of us aren't so good at letters, and we don't have the time to teach for ourselves." He looked around. "We'll have to spend it one day. Why not have it now, when Missus Mattington is being so open-handed?"

"There are many factors here," growled Purvis, looking at Mayor Fletcher. "The continuing cost is much too—"

"You're a man with one girl," someone else in the room protested. "You don't have to worry about her making her way in the world, but those of us with boys, we got reason to want a school."

"Listen to them," Clayton said softly to Russell. "They can't see that it's money well-spent." He shook his head. "It'll keep the youngsters off the streets and away from bad company. Never mind how well they learn their letters, at least they won't be throwing dice or—"

"I have this to say," Mayor Fletcher announced as he got to his feet. "We are a growing community. There are many new faces in Charity, and there will be more as time goes on. If we want to continue to grow and prosper, we must keep pace with our growth, and I have come to think that it would be wise to have a school. It would establish us as a town with foresight and a place where a man might bring his family and live well." His words were clearly intended to evoke applause; there was a spattering of it.

"Mayor's right," said Wilson Travers, who owned the tavern on the south side of town. He was the most disreputable of all the men of business in the town, and his endorsement brought speculative murmurs. "I want to say this." He got to his feet, smiling angrily at the three men seated at the table. "We don't often agree, Banker Fletcher and I. But this once, I say he's right, and that any man with a lick of what's right in him will vote for the school and the schoolmaster. And I'll add a hundred dollars to what Missus Mattington has offered, to show I mean it." He sat down amid a flurry of excitement.

"I say we vote right now," declared Daniel Calvin, not waiting to be recognized by Purvis. "We all know our minds, don't we?"

The agreement was emphatic.

"Well then," said Purvis, coloring at having his hand forced, "we will vote. All in favor of building a school and hiring a schoolmaster within the year allotted by Missus Mattington and Mister... Travers, raise your hands."

Both Purvis and Olfrant counted the hands, and each of them scribbled down their counts before comparing them. "Sixty-two in favor, Mayor Fletcher," Olfrant said.

Though sixty-two was a clear majority, Purvis went through the motions as the stickler he was. "All those against building a school and hiring a schoolmaster within the year, raise your hands." He and Olfrant agreed that twenty-seven men had voted against the school.

"Well, we are to have a school, then," said Mayor Fletcher, signing the page where the votes were recorded. "I am certain that this is a wise decision."

"The second order of business concerns the tents near Spring and Water streets, by the road to the Howe dairy," said Purvis.

"Here it is," whispered Clayton to Russell.

"Mister Howe has said he does not want the tents permitted so near his barns. He has had two calves taken in the last month. He cannot prove his allegations, but he is convinced that they were stolen by men living in the tents. There have been unfortunate outbreaks of violence there. The matter to be discussed is whether or not the tent settlement may be allowed to continue." He looked over the gathering. "I know that many of you have hired men to work on your buildings, and some of those living in tents are putting up homes of their own, living in tents only until their houses are ready for them."

"This is a town for families, not drifters and single men," said Jock Bruder. "Anyone living in the tents ought to be those who are going to settle here, live here." He folded his arms and went on, "Not everyone can stay in Missus Cauliffe's hotel; it's costly and she hasn't room enough. And not all can stay at Travers' tavern. But it ought to be required that a man staying in the tents have land and be building on it. Otherwise they can go somewhere else."

"Wait," said Matthew Challiser, whose family lived in the tents while they worked to put up a house. "I am one who is going to stay here. Me and mine are building a house. But I tell you, if it weren't for the men, the drifters living in the tents, there wouldn't be enough labor about to do the work before the end of summer. The tents are necessary."

Another one of the men living in the tents got to his feet. "I'm Goren Meikelmanns, and I have my family with me. We are building a farm. Most of you know where it is—just the start of Cowley Pass Road. I've got three children, all too young to be much help. I have to hire others to work with me. Now, I'm willing to do it, but if I have to put my family into the hotel or the tavern, it'll be too costly and I won't be able to afford to remain here. The tents are necessary."

Samuel Gall was on his feet again. "It's bad enough that Lorinda Dooley keeps her house in Charity, but it's getting so that there's no place for decent folk here. You say that you need laborers to get you into your houses before the snows come, and I say well enough. There's men enough in Charity, men living here, to give you the help you need. When I came here, we all did for each other, putting up barns and houses. Ten men working together can get a house up in a few days, at least up enough so that you could live in it. Nothing fancy, nothing grand, but enough so that the door could be bolted and there was a roof to keep the rain out."

Elias Riverton, who was over fifty and stooped from his long work in a New Jersey paper mill, rose politely. "My wife and I want to bring our grandchildren to live with us. Our house is almost done. Our daughter died, and her husband, and there's only us to take care of their children. I don't want them coming here if the town is rowdy and filled with men who have no families, no ties, and only their amusements to keep them in order. I don't think this town should welcome drifters. They're dangerous men, most of them. Some of them are criminals." He gave a little bow and sat down.

Henry Clayton got to his feet. "I have a few words to say, Mayor Fletcher. I'm a single man, and I came to Charity to have a home of my own. I'm not the only one. We all know men who want to make Charity the home they have not had before. But I am a physician as well, and I tell you that the tents are not good sense. They promote fights and other problems, and the men who live there often do not take much care in how they live. I have seen more illness and injury from those men than I have seen anywhere other than on the deck of a ship at sea."

"But would it be otherwise if the tents were not there?" asked Hosea Olfrant. "Aren't we merely going through what every town experiences as it expands?"

"Some of it is unavoidable, I'm sure," said Clayton impatiently. "But some of it comes from the circumstances of how these people are living."

"I do not like your tone, sir," said Matthew Challiser. "I am not 'these people,' as you call it."

Clayton made a placating gesture. "No, not in that sense, surely. But there are many who have come only because they can pass with little notice. And while they are here, we must be prepared for more disruption." He decided to address the matter more directly. "That fight in the gambling tent, the one that Sheriff Russell ended so well, is an example of what I mean. There were many injuries, most of them superficial, but a few more serious. Two men have cracked ribs, and one man has an injury to his eye that I fear I cannot remedy. The fight happened during the day, when, if we are to believe what is being said here, all of the able-bodied men are working, earning money putting up buildings. But that was not the case. I discovered that two of the men were ill, one with consumption. I am afraid that had I not tended to his bruises I would not have found his illness until others had contracted it. As it is, I have instructed him in ways to keep from spreading the disease. But don't you see that the tents increase the likelihood that there will be more disease and more injuries. To say nothing of how often there are brawls there." He stared at George Fletcher and then sat down.

"Uh," began Barton Purvis, not knowing what more to say. "Does anyone else want to—"

Nathaniel Howe stood. "I want those tents moved, and that's all there is to it."

Hosea Olfrant looked nervous. "There are reasons to permit them to remain," he said, glancing up from the notes he was attempting to keep. "We do not want to keep people away from Charity, especially now when it is possible for us to grow."

"Begging your pardon," said Liam Cauliffe, raising his voice in order to be heard over the sudden buzz of talk that filled the room. "I have my calling, and as a preacher, I know that those men who come here to prey on the people of Charity are not eager to build or to work the land; they come to steal and to usurp the work of others. You have seen it happen in other places; it can also happen here if we permit it." He took a step forward. "I do not think we should turn away from those who are willing to work, who lead lives that are filled with honest industry. But those who are here for nothing more than plucking pigeons, then those we must deny."

This time there was a greater reaction, and a man toward the back of the room snorted loudly. It took Purvis more than a minute to restore order. He signaled to Louis Kinsman. "What do you say, Mister Kinsman? You came here just over a year ago."

"And have buried my wife in the cemetery on the hill," said Louis Kinsman. "I have my house, and I thank God for it. There is nothing keeping me here now but my desire to remain, and that is strong. Those who are here, who have come to this place to make it their own I welcome. Those who wish to fleece whomever they can and pass on, I wish Godspeed, and would like to hurry them on their way." He flushed, his own eloquence surprising him.

"Amen to that," said Purvis. "But that does not answer the question of the tents. Are we to permit them to continue."

"There will be trouble as long as they remain," said Nathaniel Howe, not bothering to get to his feet. "Places like that are traps for sinners, and they have all the hook in hell to hold those they capture."

"We have to live somewhere while our houses are being built," protested Mr. Riverton. "What do you want us to do?"

"Put up your tent next to your house, of course," said Howe. "I did that when I came, when there wasn't anything here but the mission and a couple of shacks." He looked toward the front of the room again. "We didn't have a bank then, either, did we, Fletcher?" Since Howe's disdain of banks was well known, this attack made little impression on anyone.

"But you...your circumstances were not the same," said Mister Houghton. "It's different now."

"It's easier now," was the rejoinder from Nathaniel Howe.

"They could keep at this forever," Clayton muttered to Russell.

"And they may. I hope they move to another topic." He sighed and got up. "Mister Mayor," he said, his voice loud enough to carry through the room. "I have some comments to make."

"Sheriff Russell," said George Fletcher.

"There is no immediate solution to this problem, but some decision must be made—an arbitrary one if necessary—because if it is not, next year will see the same problem but compounded tenfold. I would recommend that there be specific areas of land set aside for those who are building in that area where they will be able to pitch a tent and have the company of other newcomers who will soon be their neighbors. For those who are not going to remain, or who are here only for the purpose of getting money or working for a few months, I would suggest that there be other arrangements made, so that we will not have a place like the tents, where families are forced to live with vice all around them."

"You are the expert on that, living with vice," said the familiar, insinuating voice of Robert Spaulding. "I notice your drive leaves the road across from the drive to Lorinda Dooley's house. Old habits die hard, sheriff."

There was a sudden, angry outburst of conversation that almost drowned Spaulding's laughter.

"All right," said Russell quietly, "that is enough." He strode toward the front of the room, his face set. "Mayor Fletcher, I am sorry to intrude, but under the circumstances I would like your indulgence."

"Of course, Sheriff," said George Fletcher, who was still well disposed toward Russell.

Taking a deep breath and steeling himself for what he had to do, Russell faced the townsmen gathered in the room. "Recently there have been rumors about me which have troubled many of you. It has been suggested that while I was employed by the Governor General of Australia I broke the law. Insofar as I lived with a woman who had been transported there, yes, that accusation is true." He let the shocked whispers die away before he went on. "I asked for permission to marry her, not once, but several times. But she was a convict, and my request was always denied."

"Tell them why she was a convict," Spaulding jeered. "Tell them that, Jason Everard Nicholas Russell. Or are you too proud, given who your father was?"

Russell regarded Spaulding. "You're late with that news, I'm afraid. And being a bastard in this part of the world is not the same as being a bastard in England." He looked away from his tormentor, and went on resolutely. "Let me tell you a little about the woman I lived with and would have married if I could: her mother sold her to a brothel when she was nine. There were many brothel-keepers who paid well for children. Have you any conception of what her life was?" He saw the answer in their faces. "No, of course you don't. When the brothel was raided, she was tried and sentenced to transportation—and at seventeen she was put on a ship to Australia. She told me once that she was glad that she was not put in prison, where she would have to whore to get enough to eat."

"An easy answer for an easy woman," said one of the men.

"You think so?" Russell asked. "When she landed, she was met by that man, by Spaulding and his cronies. They were officers of the Governor General, but they had a little enterprise of their own; they had set up a brothel. This woman was sent there, to do what she hated. For three years she lived in fear. When she rebelled she was beaten, and when the men used her harshly she was blamed. Finally she ran away, and I was sent to find her. She tried to kill herself when I caught up with her, because she could not endure going back to Spaulding and his partners."

"So you say," Spaulding mocked.

"My word on it," Russell responded seriously. "It took me three days to get the truth out of her. She trusted me finally because she knew I had been a Runner; I had arrested her uncle when I was in Bow Street. I promised her that she would be safe if she brought charges against Spaulding and the others. She did, and there was an investigation. Spaulding, Downs, Nettleton, and Alden were accused and convicted. Or has he failed to mention that? He and the other three were sent to serve their sentence on an island off Burma. The sentence was for eight years." He looked over the faces, seeing questions there, and doubt. "I lived with that brave, fragile woman until she died. That was three years ago." He swung around to look at Mayor Fletcher. "There are records of this, if you want to review them. I can request they be sent."

"You can have them concocted, you mean," Spaulding countered, this time without a trace of geniality.

George Fletcher was genuinely shocked; it took him some little time to gather his thoughts to form an answer. "I think, Sheriff Russell, that it might be best if...if we obtain the documents, or copies of them." He looked at the other two Town Council members. "Gentlemen?"

"This must be settled," said Barton Purvis with greater resolve than Russell had ever heard him show. "We cannot have such allegations remain disputed in the man we have hired to keep the peace."

Hosea Olfrant spoke up, "Well, he has kept the peace. We can't deny that he has done his work." This was met by a variety of shouts and mutters from the men in the hall. "He brought Mayhew's gang to justice, and he managed that fracas at the tents without loss of life or great damage to property. It should count for something. I don't hold with consorting with harlots, but that was another time and another place."

"True, very true," said George Fletcher at his ponderous best, taking the lead once again. "Well, Sheriff, we all thank you for your...candor. When the documents for your story arrive, I will be pleased to present them to the Town Council and the town meeting." He looked down at the table as if the wood grain might contain a secret message for him. "I will be sure to find out the whole of this question. In the meantime," he went on, his words directed to the gathering at large but intended for Robert Spaulding, "there is to be no spreading of rumors and no repeating of what the Sheriff has said here. Now," he said in another, more harried voice as he looked from Russell to Olfrant to Purvis, "what are we going to do about those tents?"

Chapter Thirteen

When she left Charity, Elvira Fletcher had been trim but well-fleshed. Now she was gaunt, her skin stretched over her face so tightly that every expression seemed painful. She stood in her father-in-law's office, her stance so straight that she appeared carved. Then she extended her hand to Sheriff Russell and said, "I asked you here so that I could thank you; you have already done a great deal for me, and it is not necessary that you do more."

Russell inclined his head. "Missus Fletcher, I would be remiss in my duty if I did not accompany you to your hacienda, just as I would be remiss if I fail to serve Reverend Wachter with the papers you have brought."

"As you wish," she said with a slight smile that was almost cruel. "I have men who work for me and they can attend to these tasks, if you would rather not."

"I am an officer of the law, Missus Fletcher," said Russell, trying to guess what was actually on her mind. "I am sworn to carry out the mandates of the court." He turned as Frederick Fletcher came into the office, and was struck again at the change that had come over the mayor's son: gone was the wastrel, the gambler, the would-be rake, and instead there was a thoughtful man with a hardness about his mouth. "Good morning, Mister Frederick," said Russell, holding out his hand.

Frederick took it in a quick, hard grip. "My father tells me you are willing to pursue our interests for us."

Russell was not certain he liked Frederick's choice of words, but he did not question them. "I am sworn to act for the court; you have writs to be served." He walked to George Fletcher's desk and said, "Unless you have objections to me serving these writs, I will attend to them today."

"Very good," said Mayor Fletcher. "It would be as well to settle this matter as soon as possible."

"Yes, it would," said Frederick, his eyes like flint. "I want those trespassers off our land at once. You can inform them that we have been more than generous in obtaining them deeds to land of their own. It is certain that they have no right to be where they are." He nodded to his wife. "You do not have to come with us if you would rather not, my dear."

"I very much want to come with you," said Elvira Fletcher, her voice sharp. "I have tolerated this abuse much too long, and now I want to see my rights vindicated." She turned her hot gaze on Russell. "If there is any delay, you are to evict those criminals by force. I want them gone."

The passion of her words made George Fletcher shake his head. "No, my dear girl. We have come this far through the power of the law; let us continue in the same way. I fancy you do not want this dispute to continue."

"No, I do not want it to continue," said Elvira Fletcher, pouncing on her words. "I want it settled. I want no further argument. You are right, father-in-law."

If George Fletcher was relieved to hear this, Russell was not, for he heard the implacable note in her voice and saw the militant light in her eyes. He went to her, coming as close as was proper. "Missus Fletcher, I think it might be wisest if you were to remain here. The last time you confronted Reverend Wachter there were…terrible consequences for you. Let me urge you to permit me to act for you."

"No," she said. "No one will act for me, Sheriff." She looked at her husband. "Not even Mister Fletcher will act for me. I will tend to this myself, for the honor of my family."

Russell abandoned the idea of persuading her, and could not dismiss the doubts she had waked in him. "All right. I have the papers and my horse is ready. If you wish to ride with me"—he faltered, uncertain now if she still rode—"then meet me in ten minutes at the jail."

"Thank you," said Elvira Fletcher with cold propriety, and stood aside so that Russell could leave the mayor's office.

"I hope you are not planning anything unwise," George Fletcher said to his son, all the while looking at his daughter-in-law.

"I am planning nothing at all, Father," Frederick answered. "I leave that to Reverend Wachter."

"And you, my dear?" the mayor asked Elvira with a good deal less authority.

"I will do whatever I must," she answered with a wide, hurtful smile.

Paco was waiting at the head of the tree-lined avenue that led to the hacienda. He held his wide-brimmed hat in his hand and he bowed in the saddle to Elvira Fletcher. *"Señora, tengo mucho allegrarse de verla a usted."*

*"Gracias, Paco, me gusta regresarme aquí. Mi esposo y...*my husband and the sheriff have come with me, as you see."

"Si, señora," said Paco, giving no notice of her shift to English. "The accounts are at the hacienda. You can see them." He turned his ram-headed chestnut toward the hacienda. "Follow me, *por favor.*"

"Frederick," said Elvira Fletcher. indicating that her husband should ride beside her. "And you, Mister Russell," she added, letting him know he was expected to ride behind them.

On the quarter-mile to the hacienda, Paco proceeded to fill his patrona what had happened in her absence. He spoke in rapid Spanish, paying no attention to the men who accompanied Elvira Fletcher. Only as they came to the hacienda did he return once more to English. "We have prepared a meal for you. In the dining room. *La señora* will show you where it is. Marta and Clara will attend you." With that he got off his horse and bowed to Elvira Fletcher. *"Señora, mia patrona, bienvenida."*

"Quanto hay amabile," said Elvira Fletcher, waiting for Paco to hold her horse as she dismounted.

Frederick got down without assistance and handed the reins to Paco. "You've done very well here. We are grateful."

"De nada," said Paco, starting to lead the three horses toward the stable.

As Russell dismounted, he called after Paco, "Where do you want me to put Horatio?" He had named most of his horses now; today he was on the blood bay.

"Follow me, señor," said Paco without turning as he continued toward the stable.

Russell shrugged and did as he was told, determined not to be offended. "Where shall I put him?" he asked as they entered the long, wide walk between the stalls.

"The second from the end, señor," said Paco. "We will bring water and hay for him."

Leading Horatio into the designated stall, Russell noticed with approval that it was clean and there was fresh bedding. "Better than what you have at home, boy," he said to the horse as he removed his saddle. "We'll be away from here in two hours or so. Get your rest." He took his saddle and bridle and carried them out of the stall, securing the door after him. "Is there a place where I can put these?" He heard no answer and Paco was nowhere in sight. Puzzled, Russell looked around, then saw a tack stand not far away. The stall beside the stand was empty and had no bedding; Russell supposed he could use the stand. He called for Paco again, and when there was no reply, he put the saddle on the stand, draped the bridle across it on top of the girth, then went back to the hacienda, wondering if he ought to find the side-door instead of the front. Elvira's father had admitted him through the front door, he recalled, and he would enter there again.

"Where did you get to, Sheriff?" asked Frederick as Russell was led to the dining room by one of the servants.

"The stable," said Russell.

Frederick laughed. "Horse-breeders. You're never content to leave your animals in the hands of others, are you?"

Russell decided to make no comment on that. "I had better speak to the housekeeper before I eat. I want to be sure it's understood about these papers, so that they can be produced at any time they are required."

"Oh, that can wait," said Frederick, a little of his old manner showing in the easy dismissal.

"I would prefer to tend to it now, Mister Fletcher," said Russell. "Will you or your wife tell me where to find the housekeeper?"

"I suppose that would be Inez. She was Missus Fletcher's maid, her—what do you call it?—duenna?—yes, that's it. Her duenna. She has been left in charge here, so you might want to tell her. But there's also a…kind of butler. He's the one who actually runs the place. Inez only oversees the house, but Ruy manages the place." He gestured toward the large table that was laid for the three of them. "They've got quite a spread planned."

"So I see." It had been years since Russell had sat down to so formal a meal, and he hesitated now, wondering if he would remember the entire procedure. He nodded toward Elvira Fletcher where she stood by the window that opened onto a little courtyard with a tiny fountain. "If it would not inconvenience you, Missus Fletcher?"

"If you would prefer to do it this way, go ahead, Sheriff. I will have Marta bring sherry while we wait."

The day was very warm, and sherry seemed an odd way to begin a meal in such weather, but he only said, "Fine. I will not take long. If you would rather begin without me—?"

"It is unthinkable," said Elvira Fletcher in a tone that could not be questioned.

Marta escorted Russell to the far wing of the hacienda, and into a spartan white-washed room that looked more like a monk's cell than an office. *"Momentito,"* she said before she left Russell alone.

Belatedly Russell wondered if Ruy spoke English, for his few, stammering words of Spanish would not help him here. He was relieved to see that in the single bookcase one shelf had titles in English—if nothing else, Russell decided, they could write notes.

A few minutes later a man in late middle-age came into the room and said, "I am Ruy Barcofirme. You are Sheriff Russell. It pleases me to meet you." He shook hands and stepped back. "You have instructions for me."

"Yes. And I am more pleased than I can say that you speak such excellent English." He took the wide leather satchel from his shoulder.

"Don Maximillian insisted," said Ruy. "He did not want anyone to take advantage of him." He went to his place behind the desk and sat down; it was the only chair in the room.

"Very wise," said Russell as he thumbed through the papers in his satchel. "I have a court order here, brought by your patrona, which states that the land of the rancho belongs to her." He held it out as he spoke.

"Of course it does," said Ruy indignantly. "There is no question about that."

"Well, this is something you can use to be certain that her ownership is never questioned. It has the seal of the court on it, you see? If anyone comes on this land and tries to lay claim to it, you need only show this to have the authority to force the others to go." He saw approval in Ruy's guarded expression. "I have other copies of this order, and I will present it to the people who have started their community on this property. I will make certain that they understand they cannot remain here.

"How many men do you want to take with you?" Ruy asked at once, delight in his voice. "We have a dozen who could ride on short notice."

Russell shook his head. "No. That will not be necessary. I have the documents and I will present them, and stipulate that they have a reasonable period—sixty days at most—to move to the land your patrona has so thoughtfully provided." He paused, then went on, "I want you to make it clear to your men, Ruy, that they are not to harry those settlers. We can do much good with the writs I have, and the law will support everything we do if there is no harassment. If you or anyone here causes trouble for those settlers, then the law will not be able to protect you as well. I would appreciate it if you would explain that to the men who work the rancho."

Ruy was sitting stiffly as he listened, as if Russell were offering him the most serious affront. "I have my duty."

"And I have mine," said Russell. "I must uphold the law. If you break it, I will have to hold you accountable."

"If we do..." Whatever the rest of his thought was, he did not utter it. "I will do as you ask, Sheriff. I will tell Dona Elvira's men that they are not to drive the trespassers off. I will promise them that you will do it for us. In sixty days." The last was an ultimatum. "If they are not gone, I cannot answer for what these men might do."

"I understand you," said Russell. "And it had better not come to that, for everyone's sake." He indicated the paper. "Keep this with the records; there are copies on file, but you will want to have this where you can reach it."

"As you say," said Ruy, opening the top drawer of his desk. "I will keep it here, locked in." He looked narrowly at Russell. "Don Maximillian told me of you; he wished us to meet. You understand, while he lived, I was often away to conduct his business. Now, who knows? Who can tell?"

"You are not certain about Missus Fletcher?" Russell asked, and corrected the name to "Dona Elvira? I would have thought she'd proven her mettle by now."

"But she is a woman, Señor Russell, and she is wife to her husband. What becomes of her, and of this land, depends upon him, does it not? And the paper you have given me."

"The order stipulates that this land is the property of your patrona." That was not entirely correct, for the document said the land was owned by Mr. and Mrs. Frederick Fletcher of Charity, the Colorado region of the Texas Territories, but Russell suspected Ruy would not approve of that description, or would look upon it as an ill omen. "The words cannot be altered, and if any person tries to change the words, they will be committing a crime."

"I would not change the words," said Ruy indignantly.

"Of course not. I thought that there might be those who would want to steal the document. I want you to know that it would make no difference. This is a matter of record." He slipped his satchel back over his shoulder. "I will hold you to your word, Ruy; I expect to have no interference with the settlers."

"For sixty days, we are agreed," said Ruy, a faint threat in his polite words. "After that, it is another matter."

"It will be tended to," said Russell, hoping that he would be able to convince the Reverend Wachter that he would have to move to the new location or face armed men.

"You have said so," said Ruy. "I thank you for this, Sheriff, for this paper." He rose from his chair. "Now I have duties to attend to. When Don Maximillian was alive, he ran the rancho, but these days, I have that task."

"You were good to give me your time and attention," said Russell, recognizing the manner that would mark a superior butler in England. He went to the door of the austere office. "I will rely on you to keep me informed, as you may rely on me."

"*Muy bien*," said Ruy, and bowed Russell out of the door.

As Russell sat down to the lavish meal, he found himself doubting he would receive so cordial a welcome again if the settlers were not off the rancho in the allotted time.

"Here's the five dollars," said Silas Fitzroy as he all but threw the coins onto Russell's desk.

"Very good. I will waive the penalty for late payment," said Russell, taking care not to challenge the man again. "I will prepare a receipt for you, if you wish."

"Signed and sealed," said Fitzroy, adding, "How many of the others paid up?"

"Eight men have left town without paying. There are two more who still owe their fines. One of them is ill and cannot work, and his fine has been deferred."

"Because he's ill?" Fitzroy asked, angrily amused.

"Because he might make others ill as well," said Russell, refusing to argue with the young man. He wrote out a receipt and handed it to Silas Fitzroy. "There you are. And"—he took out his register—"you can see that I am entering the date of your payment and the amount you have paid."

"And there will be no other payments required to clear my record here?" Fitzroy inquired belligerently.

"No," Russell answered, closing his register and putting it back in his desk. "I gather that Missus Bell has paid you."

Fitzroy squinted at him. "Yes. She paid me. She said they'll keep me on for a while. Have you got any objections?"

"Not I. In fact, I'm pleased that she and Miss Rossiter have help just now, with Miss Rossiter doing so poorly." Russell watched Fitzroy as he went on. "They have worked very hard, the both of them; it is a pity to see them in such straits now."

"Foolish, women trying to get by that way. Farming without a man, that's right foolish." He gave a single laugh. "What can you expect, women like that?"

"They have done well until recently," said Russell at his most neutral. "It would be distressing to learn that they had more to endure."

"That supposed to be a warning, Sheriff?" Fitzroy demanded. "Well, they have nothing to fear from me, two middle-aged women like that, a widow and a spinster, who would rather spend time together than making a place for a man." He looked around Russell's office. "They got the place in hand, though. It isn't real hard work. I have some spare time. I could lend a hand here at the jail."

"That's not necessary," said Russell.

"Why?" Fitzroy asked. "Because you already have that Mexican to work for you? You think he's enough by himself?"

"Not entirely," said Russell. "I will keep your offer in mind, Mister Fitzroy. But I would feel more satisfaction knowing that the Cousins have help and assistance than I would with a bit more aid here. You do more for Charity working for the Cousins, Mister Fitzroy, than you would do stacking wood for the jail."

"Who wants to do anything for Charity?" He chuckled at his own feeble joke. "I want to be part of keeping the law. That's what matters. Lawmen get respect. People look up to you, and do what you tell them. I could do things for you. You won't let me yet, but one day—"

"Mister Fitzroy, even if I were inclined to employ you—which, to be frank, I am not—there is no budget for another assistant for me. Luis Guerra works for Missus Mattington and she continues to pay half his salary. Unless you have a similar sponsor, the Town Council would never tolerate the cost. And I would not recommend they spend the money now, not when getting a school is so important." He went toward the window, looking out into the morning, knowing that by afternoon it would be too hot to do more than stroll around the town. "It would be best if you would return to the Cousins now. You'll want to get your chores done before the heat of the day. They'll need you before noon if I remember their schedule." He went to the door.

"I'll find a way to convince you, Sheriff. I can be a better deputy than that Mexican. I know how to handle myself in a tight situation, which is more than that boy does. Give me a chance and I'll show you. I got two guns of my own and fifty rounds of ammunition for each of them. You wouldn't have to buy anything for me."

"We have discussed this before, Mister Fitzroy, and my answer remains firm." He stood, holding the door open. "Please give my regards to the Cousins."

"It's not a tea party, Sheriff. Regards!" He shook his head in disgust and went away.

Russell watched Fitzroy as he went to mount his raw-boned gelding, wishing still that he could determine what it was about the man that made him so uncomfortable. He kept coming back to the eyes, to the way that Fitzroy would not look directly at anyone except in anger. He was still pondering this when Luis Guerra came into the jail through the rear door.

"Buenas días," he called out, and went on, "Smilin' Jack is at the hotel; he's brought five wagons this time, three for one man. The name is Skye. Smilin' Jack says he's rich as Midas and fine as sugar."

"And this splendid rich man is coming here?" Russell asked, the corners of his eyes crinkling with amusement. "Why on earth?"

"Well, you came here, Sheriff, and you're not poor." Guerra beamed at him. "Now we will have another fine man."

"I was asked here, and not because my father provided for me, but because I have experience in the law." Some of his good humor faded. "Who is he?"

"Smilin' Jack said his name—"

"—is Skye, yes I heard that." Russell started to roll up his sleeves, his eyes distant. "And does he have a wife named Flora, do you know?"

Guerra was taking off his spurs, but he stopped. "What?"

"Nothing," Russell said, regretting his speculation. "Nothing important." He came back toward the desk. "When does this paragon arrive, do you know?"

"According to Smilin' Jack, Skye will be here by next Wednesday. Maybe Thursday, if the weather gets much hotter." He hung his spurs on a peg and put his hat over them. "Smilin' Jack wants to talk to you, by the way. About horses."

"This evening," said Russell, taking his baton holster and buckling it on. "How are the tents?"

"They stink, but so does the tannery and the dairy in this heat," said Guerra. "I've made sure the gambling tent is closed. They don't like it, but so long as the Town Council says you have the authority, they'll abide by it, I suppose." He went to the desk, remarking, "If we could make coffee without lighting a fire in the stove..."

"Yes," Russell agreed. "But as it is..."

Guerra took his seat. "Doctor Clayton wants to talk to you, too. I told him you'd be making your rounds soon."

"Thanks; I'll make a point of seeing him." He did not like to be obvious in the watch he kept on Clayton, but every time Smilin' Jack arrived in Charity, Russell dreaded that Clayton would receive another packet of opium.

"That fellow Cole Ritchards is down at the tavern," Guerra added. "Not speaking to anyone, of course, and getting pretty drunk, but Travers says he can handle him. You should see Ritchards. He's all scarred up. Got into a fight with a bear a couple months back."

This news startled Russell, who kept an occasional eye on the misanthropic woodsman. He realized that he had not seen Ritchards for almost three months. "Is he all right?"

"He looks pretty bad. But he brought in a bear pelt, so I reckon he's fine." He waved as Russell went out the door.

Russell crossed Charity Street, holding his hand to his face because of the dust. From Spring Street to Park Street there was nothing more to see than a dozen boys inventing a game with rocks and a length of twine. He went up Park Street to Doctor Clayton's house and office only to see a note tacked to the door indicating that Clayton would be back later. Russell shrugged and continued on west toward where the tents clustered.

"Four of the mares have settled and I'll know about the other seven in a week or so," William Red Pony said to Russell as they sat on the porch eating supper. "There's more to do here than just the two of us can handle, Jason."

"I know," Russell admitted. "We'll have to hire someone, I suppose."

"Three men, even four, could be kept working here. You got a good-sized herd there, and you're breeding them careful. It won't be long before you got more." He made a gesture to show how inevitable this was.

"No dispute there," said Russell. "And then there will be the foals to train, and two-year-olds to train, and—" He looked over at William Red Pony. "You're right. We do need someone. I wish I had arranged something with Othery."

"Why him?" William asked.

"Because I'd like someone with experience with these horses. I might be able to hire someone from Missus Fletcher, but—"

"Is it true she and Mister Frederick are moving back to her hacienda, to run her rancho?" William interrupted, which was a rare occurrence for him.

"That's what they say," Russell confirmed. "Frederick's taken this possession being nine-tenths of the law dictum to heart and intends to show that he and his wife are maintaining that property and living on it, in case Wachter tries anything in court to show that the rancho was not a home." He looked at the last of the thick lamb chops on his plate, and the small heap of boiled onions. "We'll need a cook, too, won't we?"

William Red Pony shook his head. "You need a wife," he said, and continued eating.

Russell was shocked at this bluntness. "What did you say?" he managed to ask.

"I said you need a wife. You need a woman. You're a man who likes the company of women." He directed his gaze across the yard to the newer barn. "Don't mind my mentioning it, Sheriff."

"I...no, of course," Russell said, at a loss to know what to say. He continued with his meal, completely unaware of what he ate. Finally, as he took the last of his biscuit and soaked up the remaining meat juices, he said, "Given what's being said about me, who would have me, even if I were to ask."

"Women have more sense than you think, at least the good ones do," said William Red Pony. "They're like horses that way. They know who the good riders are, and the rest don't matter."

Russell stared at William Red Pony in the fading light. "How can you say this?"

"I see things. Keep them to myself most times. But I figured I owed you a word or two." He smiled a little. "Don't listen to me if you don't want. None of my business." He put his plate down. "Thing is, when I was at the mission—I stayed there after they schooled me because my people didn't much want me back—I remember there was this teacher. You should have seen her, Sheriff, a little bit of a Quaker lady out of the east, always wearing grey. Her name was Sarah. Sarah Foxe. It's a good name, white or Indian. We didn't talk much; no one allowed it and we were both too scared, because we both knew it wouldn't be just talk. She said so, when it didn't matter. If she hadn't been at the mission I would have been gone from there four years before I left. As it was, I couldn't leave her. There was no sense to it, there was just Sarah Foxe and that was enough. She was more real than the rain, and I couldn't—I've had two wives since then, but they weren't Sarah." He paused, surprised at how much he had said.

Russell knew that he had no right to intrude on this confidence but he could not stop himself from asking, "When did she tell you? When didn't it matter?"

"When she was dying, of course," said William Red Pony. "She got her foot into a nest of young snakes, when they've got all that poison. I did everything I knew. So did the mission doctor. It didn't make any difference, not any of it." His voice grew very soft. "So she stayed with me 'til the end. It didn't matter then." He looked out at the mountains where the last glow of sunset lay. "No one ever loved me like that. Sometimes I think I can still feel her skin on my hands."

Chapter Fourteen

Two big lanterns burned in the gambling tent, once again raised and welcoming. Although it was nearly ten, the canvas still held most of the day's heat and inside the men sweltered. A makeshift bar was manned by two rough men carrying big skinning knives, and there was a large, bearded man near the door. Most of the men who worked building houses during the day and who had no families could be found here at night; its only competition was on the far side of the town—Lorinda Dooley's house.

At one of the three round tables a game of poker was in progress; dice were being tossed at the second and at the third the game—played by older men—was piquet.

Tim Flannery, the older of the two bartenders, had been passing the last hour singing bits of songs he recalled from his long-ago childhood in County Wexford. He had left that, the poverty and the piety far behind; only the songs remained. His voice was scratchy from over-use but still had a few good notes left in it, and one or two men listened to him with interest.

> "And they found the English lord all alone
>   Deserted and crazed and afraid;
> In his madness he could never atone
>   For his—"

A scuffle cut short the denouement of the ballad. Andrew, the bearded guard at the door, began to move away from his post, his hands half-raised. "I tell you, you can't come in here."

"I can go wherever I must," came the answer, and the woman's voice penetrated to every part of the tent. "Stand aside."

Tim Flannery looked at Jamie Smith, who worked the other end of the bar. "What the devil?" he asked.

"I can't see," answered Jamie.

The tent was suddenly filled with the murmur of conversation and the shuffling of chairs.

"You can't come in here," Andrew persisted. "Go away, Sister, before you cause some trouble."

"Sister, is it?" demanded Tim, who despised the Church and every part of it. "What sister comes here?" He ducked under the bar, between the barrels of low-grade whiskey that held it up. He pushed his way toward Andrew, a satisfying wrath boiling through him.

Sister Angelica stood in front of Andrew, her hands closed on her rosary, her face filled with purpose. She directed her stare at the big man. "You cannot keep God and His messengers out, not even out of this den of sinners. It is my task to bring the Word of God where it is most lacking."

"You can't do that here, Sister," said Andrew as politely as he knew how. "Leave, won't you."

Tim reach Andrew and saw the nun with grim delight. "So, Andrew, what have we here?"

"The Sister wants to come in," Andrew said helplessly.

"Does she now?" Tim asked, too heartily. "And what would the Sister be wanting here? A drink, is it, Sister? Not enough of the grape at Communion?" He shoved Andrew aside brusquely and confronted the nun. "You must be the one who made such a stir at the whore's place. And now you're coming here." He indicated the men in the tent. "This isn't the place for you, Sister. Less than the whore's place. There's no women here."

"God is everywhere, and His servants should not fear to go where He is." She glared at him, taking her stance more firmly. "I ask you to stand aside."

"You can ask whatever you want, Sister, but you won't get it, not from me, not here." Tim grinned at her, his eyes glittering. "I'm warning you—come in here and no one will answer for what happens to you."

Andrew moved back as far as the press of the men would permit. He glanced miserably from Tim to Sister Angelica, and wished he could get away. "Tim," he said, the name a protest, though he could not say what it was he protested.

"Let me tell you, Sister, that you're taking your life in your hands in this place. We don't want trouble. We've been warned, don't you see?" He put his big hands on her shoulders and would not let her wrench away. "So we'll try not to let the worst happen. But it might."

"Release me," said Sister Angelica, her dignity failing her as she strove to break away from Tim Flannery's iron hold. "Let me go, sir."

"Why? You came here, Sister. You were not asked here but you came. And now it's for you to bear the consequences." He gave her a sneer that was meant to be a smile.

"You cannot do this," she said, her voice getting higher.

"Do what?" he taunted her. "Throw you out into the street? Strip that habit off you? Who's going to stop me?"

A few of the men voiced their encouragement, one of them damning the Pope; there were others who objected, but not so loudly, for fear of the wrath of the rest.

"I demand you release me at once." Sister Angelica had turned pale and as she struggled against Tim, she began for the first time to feel dread.

"Leave her alone, Tim," called Jamie Smith from his place behind the bar. "You don't want the sheriff closing us up for good."

"What can he do?" Tim called out. "He can't stop us."

"They'll close us down," Jamie warned, more loudly, and this time the hoots and shouts were more for leaving the nun alone; no one wanted trouble with the sheriff again.

"I say we keep her here and let her know what's what," said Tim at his boldest. "Poor creature probably hasn't been touched in her life, thinks that God is as good as a man." His laughter was echoed by a few others. "Who is she going to tell?" he challenged, looking directly at Sister Angelica.

"That priest," said one of the poker players, but with an avidity that took any prudence from his words.

"Hell, the priest can't tell anyone; he'd hear it in Confession and they can't talk about what they hear there," he said, his voice getting louder. "And she won't tell him unless she must—she'd be thrown out, wouldn't you, darlin'? Got to be chaste; God likes to keep His women to Himself, isn't that right?" With one hand he pulled at her wimple.

"You *stop* that!" Sister Angelica screamed, and began to kick at Tim's legs.

"You bitch!" Tim bellowed, and struck out at her, pulling her wimple off and tearing her veil.

One of the piquet players lurched up from the table so suddenly that it was overset, which started a scramble for the money that had fallen to the dirt floor. At the poker table, two of the men rose and prudently put distance between them and what promised to be a worthy fight.

"I'll put two dollars on Tim," said the oldest of the piquet players to the man on his right.

"Done," said the other, offering his hand to seal the bet.

Sister Angelica had broken away from Tim, but stood in shock as she realized her head was uncovered, revealing close-cut mouse-colored hair. Her gorget hung at her neck like a scarf. Belatedly she turned to run.

Tim threw himself at her, catching her around the waist with his arm and bearing her to the ground. As they fell they struck a chair, which started to overturn but struck a tent pole instead.

The men in the gambling tent were suddenly in chaos. Four men were able to get out of the tent before the actual melee began; they hurried away from the tent. Only one of them struck out in the direction of Mission Street and the sheriff's office.

Now Sister Angelica was screaming, her rage more hot-burning and pure than her faith had ever been. She raked at Tim's face with her nails and tried to gouge his eyes with her thumbs; her blood pounded.

Behind the bar, Jamie got out the long, solid bat he kept for such emergencies, and prepared to use it on anyone who got near him. He had it up at the ready when the tall man who had been throwing dice came hurtling toward him, knocking him off-balance and swinging him around so that his bat crashed into the nearest lantern, setting it swinging precariously.

Another three men made their escape, including Andrew, who held his massive hands to his face and whimpered as he bolted.

Jamie could not stay on his feet. He staggered against the bar, felt it shift behind him, and then one of the barrels tipped over, spilling as it fell. Jamie landed in a spreading pool of whiskey, his shirt soaking through at once.

In spite of Tim's size and strength, Sister Angelica had almost broken away from him. Her habit was torn now and she had lost a shoe, but she had had the satisfaction of feeling Tim's collar bone crack under her heel, and that was worth the loss. She started to crawl toward the edge of the tent, praying that she could get under the flap before she was caught again. She was so intent on her goal that she did not see one of the men caught in the fight trip as he was shoved backward, flailing his arms as he fell, landing hard on the nun.

The pain was enormous. Sister Angelica gave a small, anguished, sound and fainted as the man who had felled her tried to right himself by grabbing the nearest tent pole.

Canvas billowed, almost as if it were striving to take flight. Then the tent pole collapsed and both lanterns dropped onto the rioters. The flames flickered, and one of the two went out, guttered on its own oil.

But the other big lamp cracked, and flames ran out with the oil, seeking other fuel. Almost at once the whiskey was alight, along with part of Jamie Smith's clothes. He shrieked in fear and pain, lurching to his feet as he attempted to escape. He blundered into the sagging canvas, then floundered away from it, leaving a wake of flame behind him.

The fire was taking hold, sinking its ravening fangs into the tent and tables and chairs. The men succumbed to fear as it grew and those who could strove to escape, leaving those who were not so swift or so determined to fend for themselves.

Three more men managed to crawl out from under the fallen side of the tent just as the canvas was starting to char. In his haste the last of these three pulled the flap near the adjoining tent, empty because the men who had shared it were inside the gambling tent.

For a little time Sister Angelica slipped back to near consciousness, roused by her own coughing. Pain and smoke made breathing impossible, and she drifted once again into delirium and stupor.

Tim Flannery had almost made it to the door in spite of his useless arm and the agony of his broken collarbone. He heard the voices of men around him, and somewhere he thought there was a bell ringing. He shook his head to clear it, and stumbled into the supine figure of one of the dice players. He went down, striking his shoulder on the same side as his broken collarbone. Without a sound he crumpled.

The fire had gobbled almost half the gambling tent and had started on the next two closest tents. Shouts and shrieks and yelling accompanied its progress as men and families fled the tents and shacks.

Russell was in his shirtsleeves and there was hay in his hair as he rushed across Charity Street, dodging those running the other way. He carried his baton and his volley-gun, and his light blue eyes were like ice. "You!" he shouted as he recognized one of the men. "Come with me."

"There's a fire," the man howled.

"And we must stop it," Russell shouted back. "I want you to go to every house and get buckets. And men to man them. Come to the park, to the spring. We'll start a bucket brigade there. And one at the other end of the tents, from the spring on Water Street." There was a third spring nearby but it was little more than a wet place on the ground and useless now. "Luis! Get the mayor out here. Now!" He did not look over his shoulder to see if his deputy had obeyed his orders.

Through the crowd came a familiar figure. Henry Clayton carried two buckets and his satchel. "We'll get the fire under control first, and then I'll tend to the injured. The Sisters can look after them until then. Lord Almighty, look at the smoke! How bad is it?"

"I can't see enough to know," said Russell bluntly. "But there's enough dry grass around here to make it very dangerous. The wind's not very high, but a few sparks..." He pointed to an alley. "We'll go that way. I want to see where it is." He set off with Henry Clayton following. He heard the growing noise and it sickened him, for he knew how dangerous this panic was, and how quickly it could get out of hand.

One of the men running from the fire crashed into Sheriff Russell and found himself in a strong, unrelenting grip. "Let me go!" he shouted.

"What happened?" Russell demanded.

"The Sister came. The tent fell. It caught fire from the lanterns." He shook his head wildly. "There's four or five tents burning now. It's going to get worse."

Russell lessened his grasp. "All right. I want you to help Doctor Clayton. Right now. I want you to do just as he says. He will tell you where to start the buckets. I want you by the well, filling buckets. Go to the park with Doctor Clayton." He signaled to Henry Clayton. "Take this man with you and get the buckets going," he shouted.

"That I will!" Clayton responded.

As he made his way nearer the panic and the blaze, Russell thought over what he had just heard. The man had said that the sister came. He could not believe that it was anyone other than Sister Angelica, and he cursed her for meddling. He could feel the heat from the fire now, and hear the roar of it over the shrieks and cries of the people. Soot clouded the air and the stink of burning was everywhere.

A mother shepherding four crying children ran by, calling to her man and to God to help them.

In less dire circumstances Russell might have gone to assist her, but with the fire so near, he could not be detracted from his task. He pulled his baton from its holster and used it to push his way through the crowd.

Tent Street was little more than a wide walkway and now it was jammed with people attempting to drag a few precious belongings from the path of the fire. One man struggled with an enormous trunk bound with leather straps and held closed with two enormous padlocks. When another man all but fell over the trunk, the first man struck out at him with a long-bladed dirk.

Russell stepped between the two men. "Move that back to Western Street," he told the man with the trunk. "You," he said to the other, "go to the park and start filling buckets." He took hold of a corner of the trunk and began to drag it backward.

"Thief!" shouted its owner.

Russell stopped and grabbed the man by the front of his vest. "Look at the badge," he ordered. "I am Sheriff Russell. You are needed for a bucket brigade." He resumed dragging the trunk and looked to the second man. "I told you to go to the park. Doctor Clayton will be in charge." He wanted to shove the man but saw how close the fellow was to bolting.

In another five minutes Russell had dragooned four more men into helping, and he had been surprised when two women came up to him and offered to help with the injured. He told them where to find Doctor Clayton and went back to organizing the bucket brigade. He needed sixteen men at a minimum to keep the buckets moving. If only the wind did not shift back toward the main part of town, he thought, the losses would not be so great that it would strike a death-blow to Charity.

George Fletcher, looking ghastly in the light of the fire, appeared at Russell's shoulder. "What do you want me to do, Sheriff?" he asked, adding, "Mister Purvis and Mister Olfrant are with me."

"Good," said Russell, indicating the men struggling with the buckets. "We need more men on this line. Now."

"Excellent," said Mayor Fletcher, and without further ado shed his coat and took his place in the line, nodded to the other two members of the Town Council to do likewise.

The fire was spreading to the south; four small shacks were gone as well as more than two dozen tents. Only the barns of the Howe dairy lay beyond, though there were houses building west of the fire. Russell shouted for more men, and extended the bucket brigade so that twenty-two men fought the blaze from two places.

"Sheriff," said Sam Ramsey, hurrying up to the line of men. "Preacher Cauliffe sent me."

Russell continued to work but he gave the boy his attention. "What is it, Sam?" He hoped it was not more unwelcome news.

"Preacher Cauliffe has started a line like this from the west spring," he said. "He's got nine men on the line. He wanted you to know."

Russell did his best to smile. "Thanks, Sam," he said, hearing how hoarse he had become with smoke and shouting. "Tell him to watch the south as well as the west."

"You bet," said Sam, pleased at his sudden elevation to such importance.

Two men back, Martin Corley choked and fell, only to be replaced by the elder Twyford brother. The buckets continued to move, bringing water to quench the flames.

A little later Samuel Gall came down to the fireline, his eyebrows singed and his arms red from heat. "I thought you'd like to know that we've got the north end of the fire stopped. Four tents completely gone that we can count. We're working our way south."

"Fine," said Russell, though now it hurt to speak at all.

"Anyone know how it started?" Gall asked.

"Lantern knocked over," said Russell, his voice so rough that it was hardly audible.

Gall shook his head. "My brother got his hands burned pretty bad. Where's Doc Clayton?"

"At the park, I think. He's in charge of getting the buckets filled." The last ended on a rasp.

"I'll find him," said Samuel Gall as he started back along the line of men who kept the buckets moving.

Russell was about to call after him, to ask him to bring some word from Clayton, but had not voice enough for it. Then he saw that the man at the very head of the line, three away from him, was weaving on his feet. Russell moved quickly to the man's side—to his amazement it was Frederick Fletcher, all but unrecognizable under the scorching and soot—and took his place, signaling for others to carry Frederick back to the park. He moved automatically now, taking each bucket as it was swung to him, throwing the water on the fire, then stepping back to hand the bucket on to the man on his left and take the full one from the man on his right. He was remotely aware of a sting on his shoulder and the taste of burning on his cracked lips; he hardly noticed that he moved forward from time to time, that the fire was diminishing. He never knew when his own strength gave out and Hiram Mattington replaced him at the head of the line.

"You'll be fine," said Clayton as Russell coughed at the brandy trickling down his throat. "Sit still and don't try to get up until I get a chance to look at your shoulders." Clayton himself was clearly exhausted, his face pale and drawn, his eyes sunk in shadowed sockets that owed only a little of their darkness to smoke.

"How long?" Russell wheezed.

"Too long, by the look of you," snapped Clayton. "Oh, you mean how long have you been out? Ten minutes, more or less.

The heat and smoke did it. I've got others to tend to," he said as he moved on.

Russell leaned back, trying to concentrate, but unable to hold any thought for long. He stared up at the night sky, looking away from the fire so that he saw only stars and the faint, massive shape of the crest of the mountains. Now that he was lying down, his shoulders were fiercely sore and after one painful attempt he did not try to explore the damage. Somehow or other he had been burned, he knew it, but had no idea how it had happened. He closed his eyes, wishing he could find a little peace.

"Sheriff Russell," said a voice he recognized, that brought him fully awake.

"Missus Lilhius," said Russell, wishing now that he could speak without growling. He wanted to ask what she was doing in town, but he could not frame the phrases properly.

"Everyone for miles around has come," she said, kneeling down beside him. "Missus Mattington sent hands to all the ranches and farms."

"Trust Bess," Russell murmured, liking the indomitable Hepsibah Mattington more than ever.

The next news was more difficult for Mrs. Lilhius to impart. "Reverend Wachter's community would not answer the summons."

"Probably just as well," whispered Russell.

"Possibly," Missus Lilhius agreed. "Reverend Wachter said that the fire is a judgment on Charity."

Russell nodded. "Is there anything more?" His throat hurt when he tried to speak, but he could not make himself be silent.

"Doctor Clayton asked me to look at you. He said your shoulders are badly hurt. You were burned."

"I think so," Russell said, embarrassed that she should see him this way.

"I was told you were at the front of the line." She was peeling back his vest and his shirt, frowning at what she saw. "What on earth—?"

"I don't know," he said, and remembered the man he had replaced. "Where is Mister Frederick?"

"He's dispensing brandy and coffee. Doctor Clayton does not want him back on the line until he stops coughing." She began to unbutton his shirt, then peeled it and his vest from his upper body, her eyes avoiding him. "Are you in much pain?"

How could he answer that, he wondered. "It's better than it was," he lied.

"Doctor Clayton will want to put a salve on the burns," she said in that direct, steadfast way he liked so well.

"William Red Pony can do that for me," said Russell. "He's tended my horses and he's tended me. I trust him to know what's best." He sensed her reluctance to accept this. "He is a good man, and he is skilled with herbs. The life I've led, I've come to put more faith in that than what physicians do with their powders and nostrums." Saying that had deprived him of what little voice he had left.

"Well, I will let you explain that to Doctor Clayton," she said, adding, "and I wash my hands of the results."

Russell smiled and tried to think of something he could do to keep her at his side a little longer. Without intending to, he touched her arm. "Missus Lilhius," he croaked.

"You shouldn't try to talk, Sheriff Russell." Her weary smile was so welcome that he tried to answer it with one of his own; his aching skin stretched and creased.

"I've got others to attend to, but I'll be back to you shortly. If I can find William Red Pony, I'll send him to you if he's not on the fireline." She rose, paying no heed to the earth clinging to her skirts. "Try to rest, Sheriff."

He nodded twice, and watched her as she made her way to the next person, lying several feet away. The pain in his shoulders seemed more bearable now, and his eyes no longer felt as if they had been burned with pokers. He rolled onto his front so that his shoulders would not touch the dirt, and he hoped that no one would brush against him, for it would shame him to scream.

"Sheriff?" This time it was Hosea Olfrant who hunkered down beside him.

"I can't talk," Russell grated.

"The fire's almost out. Another hour and we ought to have it stopped." He hesitated. "I hear you're the one who got the buckets going."

Russell could think of nothing to say.

"Well, it goes to show what matters in a sheriff, doesn't it? That woman in Australia was a long time ago, and you tried to do the right thing. What happened there doesn't mean much about what happens here. People will forget about the other, you'll see. It's just too bad that Spaulding had to find you, or no one would have known. Give them time, Russell. They'll remember how you dealt with Mayhew and the fire and the other won't be important." He might have patted Russell on the shoulder but stopped himself in time.

When he was gone, Russell let out a long, angry sigh.

By dawn most of the men were through with buckets, and a second group, those with shovels and picks and stretchers were making their way through the still-smoking wreckage. Russell, his shoulders and hands bandaged, stood where one of the shacks had been and kicked at the ashes.

"Ten casualties so far," said Silas Fitzroy who had arrived two hours before. "They've got them over in the park where the Preacher and the Padre can look after them." His eyes were bright with excitement. "Can't tell what some of them were—men or women. Must have been quite a blaze."

"Yes," said Russell, his voice still little more than a rusty imitation of itself.

"Wish I could have got here earlier, but we didn't get word until three in the morning. That fellow Hunt came to the Cousins' place. I came as quick as I could. Missus Bell, she came too."

"I saw her," said Russell, looking down at the length of charred wood that had been a rafter, perhaps.

"Missus Mattington must've roused the countryside." He continued to turn over ashes and debris with his shovel. "They say Aaron Gall found a bunch of coins a while ago, just lying in the ashes."

"You'll hear more such stories before this day's much older." Russell was tired to the marrow of his bones. He wanted nothing more than to go back to his house and sleep the clock around. But there were unfinished chores to do here, and his horses to tend to once he left this area. He walked away from the ruins of the shack and went down the narrow track that had led between the rows of tents. Now there were mounds where the tents had been, blackened, misshapen, like enormous, discarded, diseased flowers.

"What do you think, Sheriff?" Fitzroy asked as he came after him. "You looking for something?"

"I don't know," said Russell, wanting to be free of the eager young man. He moved a little quicker.

"Can I keep any coins I find, Sheriff?"

There was something taunting in the way Fitzroy asked, and it irritated Russell. "Anything you find, you bring to me, like every-one else," said Russell, although he had made no such stipulation until that instant.

"Of course," Fitzroy assured him, his manner more insolent than ever.

Russell had had enough; he rounded on the young man. "Listen to me, Fitzroy: if I hear one complaint—*one*—from anyone in this town about anything being taken from the fire area, I will hold you accountable. Is that clear?" He was not able to raise his voice much above a whisper, but his intent needed nothing more than the cold look in his eyes.

Fitzroy took an involuntary step backward. "Yeah," he muttered. "You bet. Sheriff."

Chapter Fifteen

She lay on the table in Henry Clayton's office, her face waxen, her eyes closed now that Clayton had tended to her. He stared at Russell who stood in the door. "We found her in the calving shed, at the Howes' dairy. It had to be the smoke that got her." He stretched his hand out to Cora Vreeland's body and brushed a wisp of hair back from her face. "Two cows dead, a couple in poor condition, five dead calves, and Missus Vreeland gone with them."

Russell nodded and stepped through the door, closing it behind him. "I'm sorry, Henry."

"So am I," said Clayton softly. "Oh, sorry for myself as much as for her." He arranged her hands, touching her tenderly, as if she were still alive to feel his fingers. "I would never have imposed on her, but I took heart because she was there, and the day might come when it..." He was unable to continue. Wiping the wetness from his eyes he turned around to look at Russell. "You've had that Indian work at you, haven't you?"

"William took care of my burns this morning, as soon as I got home." He went to the window that overlooked the street. "How many were killed last night?"

"Counting Cora? Eighteen. There are three more who were badly hurt and might develop infections. If they do, I doubt I can save them. Infections in burns, you know, have no laudable pus, only pernicious." He could not stop looking at Cora Vreeland, but he managed to speak evenly.

"And injuries?" Russell asked.

"Those that were serious enough for me to see? Fifty-seven if we count you." He touched the side of her face with the backs of his fingers. "She had lost so much, and now this."

"Henry."

Clayton was weeping now, tears filling his eyes though he did not sob. "If I'd known, I would have taken her place."

Russell wanted to look away but did not. "What would that have done, Henry? She would still be lost to you."

"But I would not have to know it," he said, so softly that Russell almost failed to hear him. Suddenly he turned away from the body and wiped his hands over his face. "I've been doing this since I found her. I've told myself that I will not lose control and then there are tears on my face again, and I do not know how I came to shed them." He went behind his desk and sat down. "How are you doing."

"Well enough," said Russell cautiously.

"Have you been able to sleep?"

"Some," said Russell, remembering the blank hours that left him heavy-minded and unrested by late afternoon. "It will be better in a few days I'm certain."

"I want you to let me change that dressing tomorrow. You may have more confidence in that Indian than you do in me, but I want to satisfy myself that you will be here by the time the summer is over." He leaned back and stared at the ceiling.

"And you?" Russell prodded. "Have you got any rest?"

"No. How can I rest?" He changed the subject deliberately. "Frederick surprised me. He was an example to all of the town."

"Yes he was," said Russell.

"You don't seem—" Clayton began.

"No, I am not surprised. Mister Frederick is not the wastrel he was when I arrived here, and you can thank his wife for that. Dona Elvira wrought a change in him as no one else could have. She may have been a rebellious adventure when he eloped with her, but she is his world now." He gave a tactful cough. "Are you going to make arrangements for Missus Vreeland?"

"I've already spoken to Liam, if that's what you mean. I'll arrange for a proper stone for her, and money to keep her...her grave." He shivered as if the hot evening had become abruptly cold.

"And the others?" Russell asked, trying not to press his friend and at the same time wanting an answer. "What decisions have been reached?"

"Padre Antonio and Preacher Cauliffe have taken care of that. Some of the victims were too burned. No one can tell anything about them. Padre Antonio will say prayers for them and Preacher Cauliffe will see to the burying of them. That way, no matter what their faith, the right thing will be done. They found Sister Angelica in the ashes. Did anyone tell you that?"

"Luis Guerra brought me word a short while ago. She was probably at her good work again. If she was looking for martyrdom, she found it, I suppose." Russell shook his head slowly. "Poor, infuriating woman."

"It's too bad. The air still has that burning stench in it." He looked over at Cora Vreeland. "I know she is dead. But I want to be wrong. I watch her, as they used to watch the dead long ago, to see if she will move again. She won't; but I hope she will." He tried to make a gesture of apology, then doubled over, crying wretchedly.

"I want it understood," said the newcomer to the Town Council, his lowland Scots accent blurring his words, "that I don't do this for favor. I have other means to obtain favors when I want them."

"And I wonder what they might be," Cauliffe whispered to Russell.

"We'll find out in time." Russell watched the man skeptically, recognizing his type from his Runner days, more than twenty years ago.

George Fletcher cocked his head. "You are certain that this is what you wish to do? Your offer is so generous, I fear you may come to regret it. You have only been in Charity a week, Mister Skye, and it is—"

Charles Skye held up his hand. "Your Worship...or what is right?"

"Your Honor," murmured Hosea Olfrant.

"Your Honor," Charles Skye said mellifluously, "I am quite sure that I can afford the offer I have made. It is my belief that Charity will thrive more quickly if those who were deprived of the homes they were building were able to resume their work at once, and with minimal costs for their misfortune. I am in a position to be of assistance; that is all there is to it."

"I doubt that," Cauliffe murmured.

Russell shrugged and gave his attention to the portly man in the good clothes who stood before the Town Council. What was there about him that made Russell distrust him? He admitted to having made his fortune in trade and said he wanted nothing more now than to make his life on the frontier. Why? Who was he running away from? for try as he would, Russell could not convince himself that Charles Skye—if that was his name, which he doubted—was not running away.

"As I have stated in my proposal, I want to place five thousand dollars at the town's disposal for aid to those whose homes and belongings were destroyed by the fire, to the end that the funds go to building houses for those people. I do not believe that it would be proper for the town to charge interest on such loans, or at least not to charge interest for a reasonable period, such as a year." He put his hands at the small of his back and rocked on his heels. "Charity has made me welcome at a time when it could be said that the town might well turn newcomers away. It would please me to do this."

"And a generous offer it is," said Barton Purvis, anxiously looking at George Fletcher to be sure he had got it right.

"No more than any other in my position would do." Skye bowed a little. "I know what it is to scratch to get by, and I am willing to share my good fortune. What is the difficulty in that?" He beamed at George Fletcher. "Do not refuse my offer, Your Wor...Honor. I am sincere, I assure you."

In desperation, Fletcher asked one question that had not yet been posed. "How does Missus Skye feel about your donation? Surely your wife has some opinion about what you have done. Does Missus Skye consider this wise?"

"She was the one who first suggested it," said Skye with a satisfied grin. Now that he had the attention of the Town Council, he went on in his most expansive style. "She looked upon the devastation on the west side of the town and she said to me, 'My dear Mister Skye, what is to be done? How can you see such

misfortune and do nothing, when you have so much at your disposal?' and I thanked her for her gracious heart. She's a very
good woman, is Missus Skye, and I am not ashamed to praise her
to you."

"Very neat," said Cauliffe softly.

"Truly." Russell took Cauliffe by the arm and drew him aside
where they would not disturb the private meeting of the Town
Council. "What bothers you about the man, Liam? Something
rankles with you. You are usually more charitable than this."

"I know," Cauliffe said thoughtfully. "And God help me, there
is no outward sign that makes me question the motives of the
man. He is doing the very thing I ought to be the first to approve,
and doing it a manner that any Christian ought to wish to emu-
late, yet something stops the words in my throat." He looked at
Russell. "Do you believe what he has said?"

"You mean that he came to his fortune late? Yes, I believe
that. It shows in his behavior. What I do not believe is his account
of how that happened. It may be true that he was made the heir of
his mother's estranged brother in token for the disgraceful way in
which his mother's family reacted to her marriage, but...it has a
smell to it, doesn't it?" Russell was secretly glad that he was not
the only one who doubted the tale of the prosperous newcomer.
He rubbed his chin. "I suppose the town cannot afford to be too
fussy about the teeth of this horse."

"It troubles me, the offer and everything about it. Mister Skye
troubles me," said Cauliffe. "But I can give no good reason for it."

"Do you think you might recognize him?" Russell suggested
without much hope.

"No, I've asked myself that question already. But I know his
sort, and so do you. That's why we're having this conversation."
He took a step away from Russell then came back. "I've asked
Missus Cauliffe if she can shed any light on the man, but aside
from her remark that she would require every cent of his stay at
her hotel paid in advance, she can point to no specific thing. She
tells me that he does not smile with his eyes, but that's not a reason to mistrust a man."

"She's right about his eyes," said Russell, musing as he watched
Skye continue his appeal to the Town Council. "I suppose that

Fletcher will take his offer. He can't refuse now that most of the town has heard about it, can he? They'd hang him by the lamppost for sure."

"That's part of it, I think," said Cauliffe. "Everyone heard about it, no one quite knows how. I am unchristian enough to think that we need look no further than Mister Skye for the author of this information." He took a hard, short breath. "If I err, I pray that God will forgive me."

"Amen to that," said Russell ironically, adding, "Shall we go back into the hall and find out if Skye has convinced Fletcher of the merits of his offer?"

On the steps leading to the church door Reverend Wachter stood surrounded by his tallest followers, every one of them holding something that could be used as a weapon. "You will leave this place at once!" he thundered as Russell brought his horse to a halt at the foot of the steps.

"Reverend," said Russell as patiently as he could, "you're making this more difficult than it need be. I have to present this writ to you, and to be sure you understand what it says."

"There is no reason to do that. It is not for men to tell me how I shall live, and where. I am answerable only to God." He threw back his head and began to sing a German hymn.

"Oh, stop it, Reverend, do," said Russell as he got off his blood bay and opened the larger saddle bag. While Reverend Wachter continued to sing, Russell went on steadily, finding nothing amusing or intriguing in Wachter's game, "You have been notified that you are trespassing, and you have chosen to ignore that notification. The court has upheld the petition of the owner of the land to evict you. You have been notified that you have been given—given—other land where you can establish your community and you have chosen to reject that gift, although it was not required of the donor, and is not a necessary condition of your eviction." He looked at the faces of the men surrounding Wachter and noticed with shock that Abigail Lilhius' boy Jonah was among them. "Now I have to present you with legal notification that if you do not move from this place you will be subject to arrest and prosecution for what you have done." He saw Reverend Wachter take a step toward him. "If you do anything or cause anything to be done to stop me delivering this document, I will take you into custody right now, sir."

"I have my men with me," Reverend Wachter interrupted his singing to say. "They are steadfast in their purpose."

"I doubt any of them want to spend time in prison for assault. You could already face such a charge, since your conduct had such grievous consequences for Missus Fletcher. Another such episode can only be to your disadvantage." He took the writ from his saddlebag and handed it to Reverend Wachter. "Read it, Reverend, and frame some kind of answer. I strongly advise you to study this writ. If you do not respond, it will be construed as consent. That is the nature of the law, Reverend. He who remains silent gives consent." He nodded to the minister. "You have ten days to file your response or your relocation will go forward and you will have no legal recourse to stop it." He was about to get back on his blood bay when he added, "I wish you would permit the relocation to take place. I'm tired of the dispute you and Frederick Fletcher are pursuing, and my sympathies are with the Fletchers, not with you. They have been much more responsible than you and your followers have been. Why not consider the Fletchers' very reasonable terms? Think about it tonight. Pray, if it will help you reach a prudent decision." He put his foot into the stirrup and swung up. As he gathered up the reins, he nodded to Reverend Wachter. "You have no basis to maintain your claim here, Reverend. Whatever you want to do in this place, you would be better doing it at this other location."

Reverend Wachter tore the paper in half. "You may deliver the pieces to that Papist hoyden, if it suits you," he declared to the obvious gratification of his followers.

"As you will," said Russell, and turned his horse away from the church and the men standing there. He knew better than to hurry his mount, for any pace faster than a walk would be considered flight. Under his shirt his half-healed burns itched and ached as he struggled with the current impasse, and the sun was hot enough to make him irritable. It troubled Russell to know how obdurate Wachter could be, and he tried out various ways he might use to explain this to Elvira Fletcher in a manner that would not make the predicament worse than it was. He was still puzzling over the problem when he reached the main road; he was about to turn toward Charity when, on impulse, he took another side road, one that led to Abigail Lilhius' farm.

"Sheriff Russell," she called out with real pleasure as he came out of the trees and approached the house, "How good to see you. I was almost ready to shout so that I would feel a little less bored."

Russell drew up his blood bay. "Bored? How can that be? You have excellent society in your own company." He came up the steps to the porch. "You've certainly got your hands full with all that wool to card."

"Yes, and that's part of the boredom. I had as much to do yesterday, and I will have another lot to do tomorrow and the next day." She gestured to the large basket by her chair.

"And you have managed it all on your own, I think," he said as he removed his hat; he did not know how open his face was, or what Abigail Lilhius read there.

"Yes; Jonah has been—"

"Pardon me," he interrupted, to save her any possible embarrassment, "I know he is with Reverend Wachter. I have just now come from there, and your boy was in his community."

She nodded, looking upset. "I do not see much of him now. He is often away from the house."

"I'm sorry, Missus Lilhius," he said. "I wish I could do something that would be of use to you. Your boy will not listen to me, even if you gave me leave to speak with him. I am one with the Antichrist in the eyes of Wachter and his followers, or so it seems." He leaned his head back and looked up toward the sky. "I've been told that with those clouds on the horizon we might have a storm tonight or tomorrow. Make sure you put your stock in."

She regarded him, her eyes startled. "Are you certain?"

"No," he said, his face easing into a smile. "But those people who have lived here the longest are getting ready for a storm. William Red Pony told me that he thought it best to make sure the horses were under cover. I trust William's judgment."

"I'll consider myself warned, and if there is—" She broke off, aware that he was looking at her again, with that kindness and longing she had seen in his eyes the first day they met. "Mister Russell?"

"Let me sit a little while, and then I'll be glad to help you, since your son has forgot what he should do." He rubbed the back of his neck, taking care not to touch the healing burns.

"He has not been himself since Mister Lilhius died, though it is more than a year since. I think sometimes that he imagines himself an orphan thrown on the parish." She did her best to smile but failed.

"He's a young fool, if he assumes that." It was all he could do not to reach out to touch her arm in comfort. "If there is anything I can do—other than help you with the stock—I wish you will tell me."

She did not trust herself to speak, but nodded her acceptance. There was heightened color in her face as she went back to carding wool. "Hot work for so hot a day," she observed a little later, feeling safe to speak to him.

"Yes. My mother used to knit, but I did not see her prepare wool for knitting." His voice was quiet with his memories. "She was an excellent woman, my mother. The school she had was always run well, and she made sure she was not dependent on my father once he had heirs."

For a short while she worked in silence, and then she asked, "Does it bother you? I mean...I have been told that...most men..."

"I was fortunate: my father was fond of me and truly loved my mother. He provided for me far better than many another has done for his children." He looked at her. "When I was a boy, it was hard to be his bastard son, but not because he made it so. I have had a good education and opportunities that would not have come my way if my father had not been the honorable man he was." He paused, discovering it was both very easy and extremely difficult to speak to Abigail Lilhius. "He named me Jason, for he said I would have to go far to attain my goals. He made sure neither my mother nor I had to live in want. His bequest to me was most generous, for he did not have to remember me in his will at all. His solicitors have made it very plain that his generosity was far in excess of their recommendations."

"Did you know him at all, your father?" She watched his face as he answered, her carding set aside.

"Oh, yes. I did not see him often, but he was kindly when he visited, and he took me once to his hunting box in the West Riding. I remember walking with him." His eyes were distant now, back in the fine green hills. "He told me that it was a pity he could not recognize me properly, but that the times were not good for that."

"They say in Charity that he is a titled gentlemen," she said, fascinated in spite of herself.

"The Earl of Mindenhall," said Russell. "My half-brother has the title now." He almost sighed, his breath deep and slow. "His son writes to me from time to time. So far his father has not forbade the communication."

"Do you think he will?" She was facing him now, her eyes on his. "Why would he do that?"

"He has the boy's position to think of, and his own," said Russell. "It might not be advisable to permit my nephew to make too much of a hero out of me; I gather that is the worry." He laughed. "When I was told of how he perceives me, I did not believe it. I still do not entirely."

She stood up, and the subtle link between them was broken. "Well, Sheriff Russell, I hope for your sake that your half-brother does not keep his son from corresponding with you. I think it would be cruel and despotic of him to do that, not only for his son but for you."

"You're very kind, Missus Lilhius," he said, rising with

"And so are you," she said, "for stopping to help me. It is very good of you."

With an odd smile he fell into step beside her as she went

"Damn you for a meddling whoreseon!" Henry Clayton raved as Russell pulled the last drawer out of his desk.

"Call me any name you like," said Russell calmly, his manner so correct and controlled that it was apparent he was angry. "But I will find that bloody opium before it puts paid to you, Henry."

Clayton shook his head. "I have not had recourse to my pipe at all, until the—

"—Until Cora Vreeland died and you saw her buried," Russell said harshly. "And now you are determined to follow her there with all dispatch." He tossed the drawer aside and knelt down to examine the desk itself. "You have a compartment for it some-where. Smilin' Jack said he brought you two parcels of it since the beginning of summer: where are they?"

"Leave me alone!" Clayton had slumped into the corner, and now sat with his knees drawn up to his chest. "For the love of God, Jason, just leave me alone."

Russell continued to look through the desk. rapping at it, pressing the undersides of drawers and the inner panels of the sides. "I can't do that, Henry. It is more than a question of friend-ship, it is the safety of this town. You are the only physician for more than thirty miles, and I cannot permit you to destroy your-self. Too many people need you."

"Send them to your William. You say he knows herbs and the rest of it." He scratched at the three-day stubble on his chin.

"William is all very well for some things, but you and I, and William, for that matter, know that we need a physician here." He left the desk and started to work on the large wooden chair. "Ah!" As he turned the chair over he saw the small chest strapped to the underside.

"A physician!" His laughter was humorless. "I have no right to call myself that, nor do you." He leaned his forehead against his knees. "Go away," he said in a muffled voice.

Russell had the little chest unstrapped and was opening it. "I will not."

"For pity's sake, Jason, go away." He looked at the sheriff, his eyes so hollow that they seemed to come from the recesses of his skull. "I can't continue this way."

"On that, at least, we are agreed," said Russell as he put the chest on the desk. "Is this all of it?"

Clayton nodded. "I want enough for a pipe. Please."

"No," said Russell politely. "I have asked Sun to make you a good supper and bring it to you. He has orders to watch you eat it. Missus Cauliffe is expecting you at the hotel. I have paid for a room there for you for three nights; they are going to have a hot bath for—"

"Hot! In this weather?" Clayton shook his head weakly.

"Hot. You stink of opium and sweat and all the rest of it, Henry. The sooner you stop, the sooner you will cease to miss it." He crossed the room and pulled Clayton to his feet. "I know you mourn her, Henry, but this is not a worthy tribute to her memory. Consider that."

Clayton refused to look at Russell. "Consider her? I can do nothing else. I would sleep with my hands clapped over my eyes if that would keep my visions of her away." He broke away and stumbled toward the coatrack. "I have to put on…"

"Fine," said Russell, watching as Clayton took care to pull on his coat. "Is there anything else?"

"I would like some tea. There's water in the pot, I think. I haven't laid the fire." He raked his fingers through his lank hair. "Why, of all the people in this wretched town, did I have to fail her? Why could it not have been anyone else?"

Russell watched his friend with concern. "You did not put her in danger, Henry. She did not go to that shed because you sent her there."

He shook his head. "It doesn't matter. She's dead." He put his hands together. "I can't seem to think anything else is important but that." He was not strong enough to right his chair, and so stood while Russell did it for him. "It was marvelous, you know, not having her lost for a while, and not caring that she was gone." He sat down and placed his folded hands on the desk in front of him. "That gunsmith—Smithers? is that his name?—he came here yesterday, I think it was, and I told him to go away. Maybe you would go to his place, and find out what he wants."

"All right. As soon as Sun comes with your food." He glanced out the window. "They're coming along with the new buildings."

"Is William going to rebuild?" Clayton asked without any genuine interest.

"No. He has decided to live at my holding." He picked up the little chest. "You have overcome this before. You can do it again."

Clayton shrugged. "I wanted to before. Now, what reason do I have? The dreams are better than living, Jason, no matter what you want to believe. Perhaps not today, or tomorrow, but sometime I will not have to waken." He gave a travesty of a smile. "This time you prevailed, but one day the opium will best you. "

There was such calm certainty in Henry Clayton's demeanor that Russell was chilled. "Think what you are telling me," he said urgently. "You're wrong. It isn't a contest between your opium and me, it is between the opium and you, Henry."

The terrible smile broadened. "That battle, Jason, was lost long, long ago."

Chapter Sixteen

Judge McConnell was new to the circuit; at thirty-four he was a fine-looking man with a short beard of bright ruddy-gold and hair the color of rust. He came accompanied by two marshals, saying when he presented himself at the jail, that he had read the report Sheriff Russell had submitted and concurred that the gravity of the situation required he be prepared for resistance from Reverend Wachter's community.

"I fear that nothing has been settled, Your Honor," said Russell when John McConnell finished his observations. "Nothing I have been able to say has convinced Reverend Wachter that the law will prevail."

"Reverend Wachter's calling does not set him above the law," said Judge McConnell, motioning to the two marshals to leave them alone. "I know they are useful, but they are both army men," he said when the men were gone. "They see every opponent as one of the enemy, and they are more inclined to shoot than to enforce the peace. There have been times I have been grateful for their inclination, but this will probably not be one such. I have been reviewing a little of your record, such as it is, and I see that you are not and were not a solider."

"No," said Russell.

"I did not mean any offense by my remark," said McConnell when Russell did not go on.

"None taken," said Russell. He hesitated. "I was unaware that there was any record of me. Where is it kept?"

"Such as it is, it is on file with the provost at Fort Leavenworth. There are a few reports, and records from the circuit judges who have been here before. Not a great deal. But your dealings with the Mayhew gang are recorded, and one or two other incidents, as well as the letter of recommendation from Reverend Cauliffe. He speaks very favorably of your conduct in Australia." He waited, giving Russell every chance to make his own comments. When none were offered, he went on. "So in a sense I have the advantage of you."

"Possibly," said Russell. "Do you have records on criminals in those files?"

"Certainly, those who have done something noticeable, or have been brought to trial." He raised his brows. "Is there someone you're curious about?"

"Two of them, actually," said Russell.

"Including the murderer you have been making inquiries about?" Judge McConnell inquired. "I have heard about the letters you've been sending all over the Territories. An unusual approach to the problem."

"It worked in Bow Street," said Russell pleasantly.

"This is not Bow Street and the frontier is not England," McConnell pointed out unnecessarily.

"They are more alike than you might suppose," Russell said, and scribbled two names in his notebook, along with descriptions. He handed this over to Judge McConnell. "Both men may have used aliases at various times, but the description could help if they have. If you would be good enough to send me any information you have on them?"

McConnell read the names. "Charles Andrew Skye and Robert Spaulding. All right. When I have finished my travels I will tend to this for you." He leaned back. "Do you anticipate trouble in evicting Reverend Wachter?"

Russell gave a single derisive snort. "Trouble? I'm anticipating war."

"I found another two horses mauled," said William Red Pony the next morning. "It looks like bear again. Cats don't tackle horses in groups, not usually."

"Could the horses be saved?" Russell asked as he drank his coffee and tried to fasten his collar-button properly.

"No; you would not have wanted them saved. I shot them both, and dragged the carcasses away, so that they would not bring more hunters near the herd." He glanced around the kitchen. "Is it all right with you if I go after the bear? I'll take two horses; I shouldn't be gone more than three days. If I am, then you'd better send someone to look for me."

"There's stock that needs us both," said Russell making a gesture in the general direction of the twin barns.

"One of the Ramsey children will do the work for a day or two, if you give them half a dollar. They're fit and they know how to work." He folded his arms. "There's no point feeding the horses if all they're going to do is fatten bears."

Russell gestured his indecision. "Do as you think is best, William. If I didn't have this hellacious trial, I'd be tempted to come with you. As it is, the Fletchers are ready to ask for Reverend Wachter's hide stretched on the door."

"That is the price of ownership," said William, and then added, "We learned it from the Spaniards, and it has not been a pleasant lesson. If it becomes unpleasant enough, we may forget it entirely." He reached for a mug and poured out some coffee. "It will be very hot today. I hope that they open all the windows in the church or people will faint from it."

Russell nodded twice. "While you're out there, see if you can find Cole Ritchards. I should have gone after him before now, but there has been so—"

"Charity is getting larger and you have more duties here," said William for him. "All right. I will carry your regards to him, but I doubt he'll return them."

"Probably not," said Russell, picturing the misanthropic fellow in his mind.

William chuckled as he poured himself more coffee and was content to remain silent while Russell put aside his coffee and set about tieing a proper knot in his neck cloth. When he was finished, he got up and went to put on his best coat. "Wool on a day like this, Sheriff?" William called after him.

"It's not as heavy as some," said Russell from the small closet by the stairs. "It was made in India, and the weather there is worse than it is here." He pulled the coat on. "Probably out of fashion by now, but who will notice?"

"Missus Fletcher will notice, both of them," said William. "Are you taking your pistols?"

"Of course not. I will not bring a pistol into a court of law." He stepped back into the kitchen. "I'll carry my baton, but nothing more."

William looked him over with narrowed eyes. "What is that?"

"The coat? It's called a frock-coat, but this one is shorter than most." He smoothed the lapel. "I felt like a dandy when I first wore it, but that was years ago."

"Will the judge wear robes?" William asked. "I've seen a judge in robes once, at the mission. He came to settle a dispute about hunting. My family was very impressed with his robes."

"I don't know. I suppose he will. In England he surely would, and a wig as well." He paused. "Do you want to see?"

"No," said William Red Pony. "I would rather go after the bear that's killing the horses. You have a contract with Smilin' Jack to honor, and you won't be able to if this bear keeps attacking your stock."

"True enough," said Russell, going to pick up his hat—this was not his usual one, but a proper beaver with a suitably low crown—and buckle on his baton holster. "I will look for you in three days, or come after you myself."

"Fine," said William, and raised his hand as Russell left the house.

The whole town of Charity seemed determined to attend court that day. The hall of the church was packed, and the air so hot and close that it was like being enveloped in steam. Some of the people had spilled over into the church itself, and Reverend Cauliffe was doing his best to move them out of that portion of the building.

Russell left his horse at the jail and walked up Charity Street, past the hotel and the bank to the Protestant church. He made his way through the crowd to the front of the room and a chair near the table where the Fletcher family sat.

"Sheriff Russell," one of the marshals said as he tapped Russell on the shoulder.

"Yes?" Russell asked as he turned.

"Judge McConnell would like to see you, if you will follow me." He was polite enough, but it was apparent that he would not accept a refusal.

"All right," said Russell, and followed the marshal to the small room where Reverend Cauliffe put on his vestments for services. In his way, the Judge was doing the same thing. "Good morning," said Russell as the marshal escorted him through the door.

"Mister Russell," said McConnell. "I have been told that feeling is running high. I am going to do something that is not quite correct, but I hope you will assist me, if not in the name of law, in the name of justice." He pressed his hair back into place now that his robe was on.

"How do you mean?" asked Russell, instantly suspicious.

"I understand that there are those who do not support the Spanish land grants in this part of the world, and they are eager to see them overturned. So they are taking Reverend Wachter's part, not against the Fletchers, but against the claim of the land grant itself. The land grant is not the question, since whether or not the woman is entitled to it, her husband most certainly is under the laws of the land. But since Reverend Wachter intends to discredit the Fletcher claim, I hope you can find me someone who could discredit Reverend Wachter." He fussed with the knot of his tie. "Well?"

Russell frowned, then nodded. "I know one person who might be able to do it, but..." He faltered. "She keeps a house on the east side of town. Many people in Charity do not like her being there."

"I see. She is a loose woman." He folded his hands and looked down at them. "I doubt she would help."

"There is one thing," said Russell, wondering as he spoke if he would be able to convince Lorinda Dooley to appear in court at all, let alone speak out against Reverend Wachter. "When the minister visited her house, he beat her and stole her money. He apparently thought he had the moral right to do it." He watched the judge. "She is the only one I know with an actionable complaint."

"And she runs a bawdy house." He pursed his lips. "He beat her and stole from her."

"I have my notes on her complaint, and the reasons for not pursuing her claim." He shrugged. "I saw the bruises, and I can testify to their severity. There are girls at her house who can identify Reverend Wachter as the one who beat Lorinda Dooley."

"Let me think about it. I will tell you my decision when we recess for dinner." He started toward the door. "I have also heard that Missus Fletcher, the Spanish Missus Fletcher, is a woman of majestic temperament."

"There is some truth in that," said Russell.

"You should have been a diplomat, Sheriff," said Judge McConnell. "You're wasted keeping the peace."

Russell smiled a little. "Keeping the peace is diplomacy of a sort, Your Honor." He did not add that his father had been one of the most respected diplomats of his day.

"Point taken." He hesitated again. "Will you speak to this woman for me, and persuade her to come forward?"

"I'll try," Russell said.

"Then go tend to it now, Sheriff." He went out of the little room quickly, and one of the marshals called the court to order.

Russell waited a little while, then sighed. He had not intended to spend the morning at Lorinda Dooley's house, but he supposed he would have to. He went to the side door and let himself out into the bright heat. As he walked down the hill, he hoped that his horse was still saddled so that he could be about his task more quickly. He knew he would be called to testify and he wanted to be composed when that happened; if he spent all his time trying to break down Lorinda Dooley's reservations, he would be ill-prepared for his own part in the trial.

Reverend Wachter was represented by one of his own followers, a man of middle years who had presented his credentials to Judge McConnell before the proceedings began. He had also given the judge a brief in which he challenged not the Spanish land grant, but Dona Elvira's right to inherit it. The argument was that since she was not in fact a true heir, the land was no longer part of the land grant unless some United States citizen could lay legitimate claim to it. He stated that the law and custom required that the land pass to male heirs, which ruled out Don Maximillian's daughter.

"I want to draw the court's attention to the records of the land grant," said Mr. Turner. "Since it was given to the family, no heir has been female. When there were no sons, the land passed either to the husbands of daughters or to cousins. Since Don Maximillian died before his daughter married, and was opposed to the match, so would doubtless have withheld his—"

"Your Honor," interrupted Mister Bradford, who had come from St. Louis to represent the Fletchers, "no one can say what Don Maximillian might or might not have done. Since he was dead at the time of his daughter's marriage, his approval or lack of it cannot be a factor."

"Objection upheld," said Judge McConnell.

"But, Your Honor," Turner protested, "it is a matter of record that Don Maximillian opposed the match. He sent his daughter away when she attempted to elope with Mister Fletcher the first time."

Bradford was on his feet. "The state of Don Maximillian's mind cannot be argued. He might not have felt the same way."

"Don Maximillian was Spanish and a Catholic!" Turner shouted. "The Fletchers are Protestants!"

"Padre Antonio blessed the marriage," said Elvira Fletcher sharply. It was the first time she had spoken since the trial had begun, but her silence had clearly been an effort.

"Gentlemen," Judge McConnell said, "any discussion of the intentions of Don Maximillian Arreba y Corre cannot be relevant to these proceedings, as the man himself cannot be called, and he left no documents to indicate his intentions beyond what was in his will, which I have already reviewed and have found inconclusive. If the will were less subject to interpretation there would be no need for us to be here."

"Your Honor, his intentions are crucial to our case," said Mr. Turner, glancing at Reverend Wachter as he spoke.

"I am sorry to disappoint you, Mister Turner, but I will not allow you to speculate on the man's position when the man himself cannot be called. Just as you may not claim that Don Maximillian did not support the match or his daughter's inheritance, so Mister Bradford may not claim that he did. Is that clear?"

Both advocates nodded, and Jared Bradford whispered to Frederick Fletcher, "That might be a problem."

"It seems more of one for Wachter than for us," he said softly. "They cannot assert he was—"

"No, you must approach it from another direction; we cannot now claim that Don Maximillian was prepared to break with tradition and leave his estate entirely to his daughter. It may be important to have that possibility."

Frederick frowned, then reached over and put his hand on his wife's. "We'll prevail," he said, but for the first time he had doubts. "The land is yours by right."

Mr. Turner continued with his presentation and the hall grew so hot that the rear door was opened in a futile attempt to get more air into the building. By noontime there were people standing outside the hall in the shadow of the building where they could hear the proceedings through the open windows and not have to endure the stifling heat indoors. Neither side of the dispute was any closer to a resolution.

"If only they had not challenged the inheritance, this would not have come up. The eviction would have gone as required." Jared Bradford wiped his brow and prepared to offer up notarized copies of all the documents filed and served on the Fletchers' behalf, adding that the attempt to break the will of Don Maximillian was a ploy of desperation, not of conviction. He pointed out that Dona Elvira's inheritance was deemed permissible by her priest and by her surviving relatives, since no one had been sent to claim the property for the family. He added that the attempt to call Dona Elvira's right to inherit into question was nothing more than a tactic intended to obscure the very real matter of trespass.

At one Judge McConnell called a recess, ordering the trial to reconvene at two. Then he went into the side room and pulled off his robe, taking a deep breath and running his finger around the inside of his sweat-soaked collar. Quickly he hung his robe on a peg, then called for his marshals and headed off for Dorabelle Cauliffe's hotel and his dinner.

He was polishing off a venison chop when Jason Russell came into the room. "Your Honor," he said formally as he approached the table where the judge and his two marshals sat.

"Russell. Good to see you. Sit down. Have them bring you some dinner." He motioned to the empty chair at the table. "Tell me how you fared."

Russell drew up the chair, but waved Martin Corley away when he brought a plate. "Coffee, just coffee, if you would?" Then he looked at the judge. "I've spoken with the witness, and she has agreed—very unwillingly—to let me question her on the stand. She will answer questions from you, but she refuses to let the advocates for either side speak with her. If they try, she says she will not speak at all."

"Very irregular," said the judge, shaking his head. "But this whole proceeding is damned irregular." He buttered a slice of bread, frowning. "All right. Tell her I will accept her testimony in the capacity of *amicus curiae*. I don't know if it will be accepted if the case is ever reviewed, but—" He drank more of his coffee. "Congress will have to make a decision about the Spanish land grants before much time goes by. And they will have to uphold them."

"Why do you say that?" asked Russell, startled to hear the judge express that opinion.

"Because half the major land holdings in the east were granted by royal charter of one kind or another, and so far only occasional contests of eminent domain have be upheld against them. Don't think the men in Congress are unaware of that; many of them are the heirs of such grants. If the Spanish land grants are not upheld, then the French and English charters can be questioned as well." He had the last of his coffee, saying, "Why must we go back to that insufferable hall? It's worse than a hot stove in a bakery."

One of the marshals laughed, the other continued to eat without any indication that he had heard.

"When do you want me to bring Lorinda Dooley to court, Your Honor?" Russell asked, taking his cup of coffee from the tray as Martin Corley came to the table again.

"Three o'clock should be about right," said McConnell. "Most of the statements should be finished by then, and the basic dispute will be defined. It should never have come to this. If Reverend Wachter were not a man of the cloth, it would not have." He sighed. "Missus Cauliffe has a fine kitchen here. You don't expect to find cooking of this sort in an...out-of-the-way place like Charity."

"She has a very good cook," said Russell, and drank his coffee quickly. "I'll bring Miss Dooley to court, and I will question her, and then I will escort her to her house. That is the arrangement we made."

"Quite acceptable under the circumstances. Tell her I will only ask her about specific points in her testimony in order to establish clarity, if that will reassure her." Judge McConnell pulled his watch from his vest pocket. "Thirty-five minutes yet. Is that enough time for you, Sheriff?"

"It will do," said Russell as he drank down his coffee and rose to leave. "Thirty-five minutes."

There were disapproving stares and the susurrus of whispers when Sheriff Russell brought Lorinda Dooley into the hall of the Protestant church, and many of the townspeople turned to stare at the woman most regarded as a necessary evil.

"Are you certain this will work," Frederick Fletcher asked as Russell came up to the front of the room. "I do not like having to depend on this woman."

"She isn't your witness," said Russell calmly. "She is appearing as a friend of the court, at the request of Judge McConnell." He said this loudly enough that most of the people gathered in the crowded hall could hear him.

Jared Bradford touched Frederick's shoulder and whispered to him, "It's very clever; don't interfere."

Judge McConnell indicated the chair where Lorinda Dooley was to sit, and then addressed the assembly. "I have asked Sheriff Russell to act for the court; he will question the witness about certain aspects of—"

He got no further. Roland Turner was on his feet, one hand raised in outrage. "I must protest!"

"On what grounds?" Judge McConnell asked with a smile that promised only disapproval. "The witness is appearing at the request of the court."

"She is…she is—" Turner sputtered.

"She has information that bears on this case." He looked straight at Reverend Wachter. "Have your advocate sit down, sir, at once, or I will order the marshals to escort him out of the room. To continue—"

"Bide your time," said Reverend Wachter to Turner, his voice raised enough to carry over the judge's words. "We will have our opportunity to redress any lies she tells."

"Since she is to be sworn," said Judge McConnell, "she will be under pain of perjury if she lies." He then turned his attention to Lorinda Dooley.

For the occasion she had put a bonnet over the glorious tangle of her hair and worn her most demure dress. She wore no paint on her face; the heat of the room and the unforgiving curiosity of the people in it gave color to her features that hid the fever spots in her cheeks. "I…I will not lie," she said, her voice growing stronger with each word, her chin defiantly up.

The judge nodded to one of the marshals. "Stevenson. Bring the Bible," he said, and swore Lorinda Dooley to tell the whole truth and only the truth. "Now," he went on when Stevenson took the Bible and went back to the side of the hall, "do you understand that you are to answer all Sheriff Russell's questions to the best of your own knowledge, and then to answer any I may put to you?"

"That's what I agreed to do," she said as if accepting a challenge to a duel.

"And that you do not have to answer any questions from either of the parties in this case? No one but the sheriff and I will require responses from you. Has that been made clear to you?" The judge was serving notice on the two attorneys in the case, and did not wait for her acceptance before he motioned to Russell to begin.

Russell had brought his notebook with him, and he made a point of opening it. "Miss Dooley, do you recall a day last April when you came to my office?"

"Yes," she said, sitting a little straighter. "It was sunny. You had a fire in the stove."

"That's right," said Russell, trying to encourage Lorinda Dooley so that she would not be so tense, for her tension made it seem she was lying. "You came to make a complaint."

"Yes," she repeated. She took hold of the trailing ribbon of her bonnet.

"About a man who had come to your house." He was prompting her, hoping she would not fail him.

"A Scripture-quoting man," she said, no longer looking at Russell, but staring at Reverend Wachter. "A tall man, big, with a beard and talking with an accent."

"What did this man do?" Russell asked.

"What does anyone do at Lorinda Dooley's?" called a voice in the crowd, and there was a spattering of malicious laughter.

"That will be enough of that," said Judge McConnell.

With a toss of her head, Lorinda answered the sheriff. "He had come to pleasure himself, same as all the rest. He drank whiskey, and then he wanted a woman."

"Will you tell us what happened then?" Russell inquired.

A few whistled and catcalls drowned her answer.

"Stevenson, Eldrich, if there are any more such interruptions, clear the hall." Judge McConnell raked his gaze over the crowd. "I will not have a valuable witness mocked. Miss Dooley, will you repeat what you just said?"

"I said he asked for me." Her reply seemed very loud in the constrained silence. "He would not have another. He wanted the woman who owned the house, and I am that."

Russell gave her a quick, encouraging look. "Did you agree?"

"Well, I didn't like it. It's never a good thing when a man who's there for the first time wants the head of the house. It always leads to trouble. But he was big and he could cause trouble, and there was no one there that night who could be depended on to throw the fellow out if he got too eager, so I said yes. Up to then, it had been a pretty good night."

"And what happened then?" Russell moved so that Lorinda Dooley could look at Reverend Wachter as she answered.

"He insisted that we use my room. I don't like that. But the others were full and the man was very set in his wants. I took him to my room for the business. He went at it without art. While he was about it, he kept hitting me, cursing me and quoting from the Bible. I tried to make him stop, but it just made him madder. He hurt me. Doctor Clayton saw what he did, and he said that it was bad. I felt sick after the man was through." She turned to look at the judge. "I might not make my living the way nice folk do, but it's what I know, and it pays to keep my daughter in school. I don't want her living like me."

Russell cleared his throat. "Did this man do anything else to you?"

"Yes," said Lorinda, and this time she was bolder. "Yes he did. While I was trying to get up, still so sore that I couldn't see straight, he went and took my money. I had my money in the chest on my dresser, and he opened it and took it." Her eyes were bright with fury and tears. "I want my money back. It took years and years to earn it, and I want it back."

Judge McConnell interrupted her outburst. "Please confine your remarks to the events, Miss Dooley."

She did not speak for several seconds, then she wiped her face and said, "All right. I said he robbed me. He took my money. He said I wasn't entitled to it because I got it through sinning." Her hands shook in her lap. "If I could have got up, he wouldn't have walked away."

Russell nodded. "We're almost through, Miss Dooley. Just a few more questions and then you can leave."

"Do I get my money back?" she asked, and her shoulders sagged. "It's all I've got."

"Miss Dooley, the man who beat you and robbed you—is he in this court today?"

She nodded once and lifted her hand, pointing. "That's him. Right at that table. The reverend with the beard. That's the man."

There was an outburst in the room that rose in intensity; the shouts of the marshals could not end it. Finally Judge McConnell got to his feet and held up his hands for silence. Slowly the noise diminished.

"This is calumny!" burst out Reverend Wachter, already on his feet. "This...harlot! has no right to speak against me."

Russell turned on his heel and faced Wachter. "Tell me, Miss Dooley, is there any identifying characteristic about this man you can offer as proof of identification?"

"I can," she said in a kind of triumph. "His dog-tooth is missing. And he has a long scar here"—she drew her finger along her upper arm—"that looks like a fish hook on the top, right here—"

With a wordless cry of rage Reverend Wachter lunged across the table only to find his attack stopped by Russell, who shoved the head of his baton against the minister's chest. "She cannot!" Wachter shouted. "She *cannot!*"

"Reverend Wachter," said the sheriff in a level tone as he lowered his baton a few inches, "I think it best if you return to your place. Now. I will not hesitate to use this if you attempt to reach Miss Dooley again." He paid no heed to the shocked exclamations in the hall of the church; his attention was on Wachter. "Sit down."

"She is lying," Wachter insisted. "It is all lies."

"He's the one who lies," Lorinda Dooley said loudly, once again pointing at Wachter. "He beat me and he robbed me. I had saved that money for years and he *took* it!"

Questions and expostulations became louder as everyone in the hall vied for the attention of everyone else, the better to show how confused they were, how dismayed at what had been revealed, how this revelation astounded them.

"Everyone be quiet!" ordered Judge McConnell. "Reverend Wachter, sit down and remain silent until I speak to you. Miss Dooley, confine yourself to answering questions, either from me or from Sheriff Russell. I want proper conduct in this court. Is that understood." He waited, then nodded to the sheriff. "Is there anything else, or have you completed your interrogation?"

"I have no more questions at this time, Your Honor," said Russell, stepping back.

"I have a few questions to address to Miss Dooley," said the judge. "Are you acquainted with Elvira Fletcher?"

"Her?" Lorinda shook her head. "No. I've seen her before; everyone in Charity knows her. She wouldn't speak to the likes of me; it's not done. I used to see Mister Frederick from time to time, but not for, oh, months and months now."

"I see." Judge McConnell waited a moment. "Have you had other men at your establishment who would fit the description you have given of Reverend Wachter? Is there any chance you have confused one man with another?"

"No. Even the worst whore would remember that one," she said darkly. "You don't forget a man who beats you and takes your life savings."

Something else occurred to the judge, and he said, "One more thing, if you will." He waited while she nodded. "If you had a legitimate claim against this man for abusing you and stealing from you, as you say you did, why didn't you pursue it? The sheriff has told me he was prepared to act on your charges, but that you withdrew them. Why is that?"

"Are you joking me?" Lorinda asked incredulously. "The man's a reverend. Who would believe someone like me making charges against a preacher? They'd probably take everything, just because I said something. I know how it is, and I know who is favored. No, I decided I'd had trouble enough on his account. I didn't want any more."

Russell took a step forward. "Miss Dooley, will you tell me why you decided to speak out today?"

She laughed, gently and self-derisively. "Because it's easier saying no to an avalanche than to you, Jason Two-Middle Names Russell. You said I had to, and you made me think I had to. So here I am."

There was a sound in the hall that was not quite an echo of her laughter.

"And would you want to file charges now?" Russell asked.

"If I still can," she said after she had thought about it for a short while. "Yes."

Judge McConnell looked at Stevenson. "Marshal, take that man into custody. He is to be held here overnight, and not be allowed to return to his followers. I will hear the case tomorrow, after Doctor Clayton has examined him and determined that he has the scar and the missing tooth Miss Dooley describes. In the meantime, I see no reason to stay the order of eviction. See that Reverend Wachter's followers are off the Fletchers' land in the next five days." He tapped the table where he sat with the flat of his hand. "This court is adjourned."

As Stevenson approached Reverend Wachter, the minister stood once more and raised his hands to heaven. "'O Lord, Thou knowest: remember me and visit me, and revenge me of my persecutors; take me not away in Thy long suffering: know that for Thy sake I have suffered rebuke.'" He joined his hands before him. "It is written: 'They return, but not to the most High: they are like a deceitful bow: their princes shall fall by the sword for the rage of their tongue: this shall be their derision in the land of Egypt.' My people are not misled by this—"

As Elvira Fletcher started to leave the hall, she paused long enough to spit on Reverend Wachter's feet.

Chapter Seventeen

Summer began its lazy slide into autumn; the nights grew cooler now, and the wind was brisk enough to make people glad to wear jackets after dark. Charles Skye started building his grand house at the end of a new street that was quickly named Overlook. The rest of the Smithers family arrived and moved into the incomplete house on Water Street. Reverend Wachter was taken to Pueblo and his community was moved to the land the Fletchers had purchased for them. William Red Pony killed two bear and lost three fingers on his right hand in the process, which he said was a fair trade. Padre Antonio performed four marriages and seven requiems, declaring that life in Charity was improving.

Cole Ritchards came into town in early September, his mule-drawn wagon filled with lumber and kindling. He set up a tent in the park and started selling the wood and taking orders for more. His scars were no longer raspberry-colored, but their white pucker gave his face a terrible look, and a few people avoided him because of his disfigurement.

"Good afternoon," said Russell as he came by the tent. "How is business for you?"

"Oh, it's brisk enough—too brisk in a way; there's too many people coming into this place." He glowered up from his stool. "I been thinking I'd head further west, maybe up into the Oregon Territory. No so many people there."

"True enough," said Russell, his eyes crinkling as he smiled.

"When I come here, there wasn't sixty people in Charity. Look at it now." He gestured with his maimed hand. "In a few more years it'll be big enough to have the Army notice it. I can't stand the notion, can you?"

Russell gestured his helplessness. "What can I say, Mister Ritchards?"

"Ah, you're one as would like to have the town grow, I know that. They brought you here because it was growing. Well, I don't fault you for that. They're wanting more lumber than fur now." His grudging approval was marked by a sudden change of mood. "Something I should have told you before, when I found it."

"What is that?" Russell asked, recognizing the somber tone in Ritchard's voice. "Tell me."

He scowled, as much from sorting out his thoughts as from his misanthropy. "About two, three weeks back I was over by the Cousins' place. I hadn't been there in a while. I had skins and some cut lumber with me." He hawked and spat. "I don't know how to tell this part. Sorry, Sheriff."

Since apology of any kind was rare with Ritchards and he had offered the approximation of two, Russell knew something was worrying the man. "Tell me, Ritchards."

He shook his head slowly. "I never seen anything like it, and you can swear that at the Pearly Gates. I found what was left of a girl, just slung away. She'd been there a while, maybe ten, twelve days from the look of it."

Russell went cold. "A girl. How old?"

"Oh, close enough to being a woman, I suppose. There was a little bit of clothes left, the kind you see the young ladies wear. She'd had a bonnet on. Some of it was left, and a little of her hair. I took a bit of it, and a medal from a chain around her neck. I thought you should have it, in case anyone's looking for her." He stared down at the ground as if he were searching for hidden gold. "She was young. I could tell it. And someone got her with a knife."

Russell swallowed against the knot in his throat. "Did you notice anything else about her."

"Well, not too much. The animals had got to her, you know. But her face was cut up, and so were other parts. She was awful high when I found her. Wouldn't have found her if she hadn't been stinking. I reckoned someone wanted her lost; whoever killed her, most likely. Lord of the Prophets! and you wonder why I want to get out of this place."

"I have to know more, Mister Ritchards. I don't mean to distress you, but I need to find out more." He saw two men approaching, one with a hammer, and he said, "Tell me later. Come by the jail so I can have a report."

"If it's necessary," said Ritchards grudgingly. "Poor thing, lying out there. It gave me a turn, Sheriff, I don't mind owning it." He then looked toward the men. "I got sanded lumber here, and I can bring more if you order it. I got hides, too, if you trading them."

"Lumber," said one of the men. "Good lumber, cut true."

"I have the best." Cole Ritchards straightened up, a hard light in his eyes. "I'll talk to you later, Sheriff." And then he turned away from Russell.

The bundle on the stretcher dragged behind Guerra's horse was pitifully small. The pinto sidled and tossed his head in protest at the nearness of the decomposing body, but Guerra held him and continued to swear in Spanish under his breath.

"You found her, I see," said Russell as he came out of his house. "Where Ritchards told you?"

"Yes," said Guerra, dismounting and leading his horse to the hitching rail. "I see they got the last of the windows in," he added, pointing to the upper story.

"I'm glad of it," said Russell. "It was getting too cold at night." He came down and looked at the stretcher. "Poor child."

"I found a shoe that might be hers. With what Ritchards gave you maybe we can find out who she was." Guerra took off his hat. "I don't know, Sheriff. I can see getting mad at a woman, but this—"

"Yes," said Russell quietly. "Well, I'll hitch up the wagon and take her to Doctor Clayton to look at. He won't like it, but I've warned him it might be coming." He hooked his thumb on the belt of his holster. "Have Jonah feed your horse and brush him down. It's the least I can do. There's food in the kitchen. Help yourself."

Guerra frowned. "Jonah?"

"Missus Lilhius' boy. He spent most of the summer at Wachter's community, but now that they're gone, he's still here. His mother asked if I'd employ him four days a week." He cocked his head toward the barn. "He's learning."

"Is he good with horses?" Guerra inquired as he unstrapped the tow-poles from his saddle.

"Well, he's not bad with them," said Russell circumspectly. "He seems willing to work, that's a start."

"That's good," said Guerra, and was able to lead his pinto away from the ominous stretcher.

"Tell William to hitch up the wagon for me. I want to get my notebooks." Russell started back into his house.

"Sure thing, Sheriff," Guerra assured him as he continued on to the larger barn.

By the time William brought the spring wagon out, one of the big coaching bays harnessed to it, Russell was ready to go. He got onto the driving box and called out to William, "Don't wait supper for me. I'll get something at the hotel if Clayton decides to keep me around while he examines the body." He did not want to have to watch that procedure, but if he remained with Henry Clayton, he would be able to have notes which might be needed later.

There were a number of carts and wagons going up Charity Street, including two long-bedded drayage wagons filled with supplies for the hotel. Russell held his spring wagon at the corner of Denver Road, wanting to cross without incident. He finally drew up in front of the office side of Doctor Clayton's house and tied the bay to the porch post. He went up the steps two at a time, anxious to get the remains inside, away from public curiosity.

"Henry!" he called as he pounded on the door.

There was no answer, and no note to say where he had gone.

"Damnation," Russell whispered. He started down the stairs, trying to think where he might go to find the physician when he caught sight of something through the curtained window.

Russell stopped and peered, leaning over the railing as far as he dared in an attempt to make out what seemed to be a supine figure on the floor. Then he was hurtling back up the stairs, his baton out and his shoulder braced as he slammed into the locked door, trying to break it open.

Henry Clayton still held his pipe in his cold fingers; his eyes were half-open, rolled back so that only the whites showed. The air was heavy with the sweetly rotten odor of opium and death.

Russell knelt beside the body. "Henry," he said softly. Then, very gently, he took the pipe from Clayton's stiffened hand. In the next moment he threw the pernicious thing at the wall with all his strength, and clamped his teeth against the howl of wrath and grief that burned in him.

He stood for several minutes while his breathing became more regular and the pounding in his head and neck subsided. Then he went back to Clayton's body. "Damn you, Henry," he said conversationally. "I told you not to do this." He bent down and tried to lay the body out, but it was stiff, unyielding. "Oh, God, Henry, what are we going to do now?" Reluctantly he went to the door and looked down onto the street, looking for a face familiar enough to entrust with a necessary mission. Finally he saw young Sam Ramsey sauntering down Spring Street, and he raised his hand, calling out to the boy.

"What is it, Sheriff?" He shaded his eyes as he looked up. "Something sure stinks."

"Yes," said Russell. "Sam, I need Preacher Cauliffe, right now. Will you go find him for me? There's half a dollar in it for you if you'll bring him here in fifteen minutes or less."

The boy's face brightened. "Right you are, Sheriff. I know where he is—at the schoolhouse." He took off in the opposite direction at a scampery run, the promise of money making him fleet.

Russell went back into Clayton's office and began his search for the opium supply he had not found before. He was checking the wall for hidden doors or similar hiding places when he heard someone coming up the stairs. He turned and found Liam Cauliffe staring in at Henry Clayton's corpse.

"God forgive him," said Cauliffe as he closed the door behind him. "Opium?"

"What else?" Russell asked, more bitterly than he knew.

Cauliffe folded his hands and bowed over them, praying silently for the departed soul of the physician. "Does anyone else—?"

"I don't think so. The door was locked when I came." He gestured toward the window. "I saw him through the window."

"We'll have to inform the mayor and the Town Council. How are we to manage without a physician? There's a physician in San Isidro, but none closer that I know of." Cauliffe caught his lower lip between his teeth. "How could he have done this? He knew the chances he was taking, and..." He could find no words to express the futility that threatened to overcome him.

"He wanted to die, Liam." Russell said it with blunt kindness. "He had lost his will to resist. It was...it was easier to die." He walked over to Cauliffe. "Remember in Australia, that skinny thief from Portsmouth? There was no reason for him to die, either, but he did. He was fit one day and dead three days later, all because he no longer cared." He stood over Clayton. "Henry was the same. I didn't want to see it, but I know it's true."

Cauliffe started toward Clayton's desk. "Did you find the opium? Have you looked for it?"

"Not yet; I've searched the desk and the examination table." He half-leaned and half-sat on the edge of the desk. "In the mean time, there's the corpse of a girl outside that may be another victim of the killer who murdered the Grover child and the—"

"I was sure he had gone," said Cauliffe in renewed shock. "Are you certain?"

"No. That's why I brought the body here, so that Henry could examine it and tell me if she had been killed in the same way. But now—" He moved away from the desk; he was becoming restless, not wanting to be still. His head ached and there was a cold knot under his holster buckle. "I have to know."

"We can send word to San Isidro," suggested Cauliffe without conviction.

"I'd rather get a message to Judge McConnell and ask him to find someone for us. He travels enough, and he is a sensible man." Russell gave a sudden, hard sigh. "I'd better notify the mayor and...the rest. Can I leave you here to tend to him, whatever needs to be done?"

"Yes, of course," said Cauliffe. He hesitated. "I do not know what any of us could have done to prevent it."

"No," said Russell, "neither do I." He went to the body again and stood looking down at it. "Henry, Henry, what were you thinking of? What was the point?" The questions hung in the room, persistent because they could never be answered.

* * *

An hour before Henry Clayton's funeral was to begin, Smilin' Jack strode into the jail with a sheaf of letters for Russell. "I picked some up in Denver and some in Pueblo. Seems no one rightly knows where this town of yours is," he said, adding with a nod toward the mourning-band on Russell's sleeve. "I heard about Doc Clayton. Too bad, him going like that."

"Yes." Russell was half-listening as he sorted through the mail. A letter bearing Judge McConnell's name was set aside to be opened at once, while the others were stacked. The last one caught Russell's attention, for it carried the Mindenhall arms and was banded in black.

"More bad news," suggested Smilin' Jack, looking over Russell's shoulder. "Fancy paper. And no stamp."

"Earls have franking privileges," said Russell absently as he held up the envelope. It had left England in April; it had made good time crossing the ocean and the vastness of the United States. Russell tapped the envelope speculatively as if the sound of it might give some indication of its contents.

"Open it, why don't you?" Smilin' Jack said.

"Yes," Russell said, still bemused. He broke the seal that closed the letter and spread it on the desk in front of him. "Lord Almighty," he murmured as he read.

"Well?" Smilin' Jack asked.

"Uh..." Russell folded the letter carefully. "My half-brother was killed on April 20th. He fell while taking a jump on an untried horse and broke his neck. His son is Earl now, or will be when he comes of age. This is written by my aunt, asking me..." His expression changed, becoming remote. "She asks me to come back to England, to serve as guardian for my nephew."

"God's holy truth!" exclaimed Smilin' Jack.

"It seems that I've been left a portion of my half-brother's estate, beyond the horses and bequests my father left me." He said it as if the words had no meaning. "Poor Reginald."

"Reginald? Your brother?" Smilin' Jack was confused.

Russell shook his head, his eyes fixed on something far, far away. "No. My nephew." He rubbed his face suddenly. "I've been left twelve thousand pounds."

Although Smilin' Jack was not certain how much money that was, it sounded like a tremendous sum, and he whistled in appreciation. "So you're a rich man."

"Twelve thousand pounds," he repeated. "What on earth possessed him to do it?" He put the letter into his vest pocket. "I can't answer this now. There's too much…"

"You're not leaving, are you?" Smilin' Jack asked, alarmed as he realized what the letter from England might mean.

"Yes," said Russell absently as he went to get his jacket. "It's Henry Clayton's burying. I have to be there."

"Oh," said Smilin' Jack, relieved. He picked up Judge McConnell's letter and handed it to the sheriff. "Here. You might want to look at this one, too, while you're at it."

"Oh. Thank you." Russell started to put the envelope in his pocket with the one from England, but then, on impulse, he tore it open and glanced over the four pages. Gradually his features changed, and he was able to smile once. "Well, well, well," he said as he refolded the sheets.

"What is it?" Smilin' Jack demanded.

"The answer to a few questions," said Russell, looking pleased. "I've been waiting for this."

"Are you going to tell me what it's about?" Smilin' Jack said impatiently. "Damn your eyes, I brought you the letters; the least you can do is tell me what they say."

"It's not correct," said Russell carefully. "I have to speak to…to one or two men. Once that is done, you have my word I will tell you what has transpired." He patted the pocket where he put the letters. "Come by the hotel this evening, and have a drink on my purse. I'll tell you what the news is then, when I can do it properly."

"You're a stickler, Sheriff." He started to follow Russell out the door, then said, "What about the horses? You agreed to have twelve for me before winter. Are you going to do that?"

"Certainly," said Russell without hesitation. "William and I have selected them already, and in a little while I'll start to work them in teams, so they'll be ready for you." He reached in his pocket for keys. "I don't like having to lock doors, but with so many new people coming to this town, I don't know who might decide to come into the jail, or what they might do."

"Doesn't that trouble you?" Smilin' Jack asked while Russell turned the key.

"No. It saddens me a little, but when I was a boy we always locked our door, and so I see nothing unusual in doing it." He pocketed the key and started up the street. "Are you coming?"

"No," said Smilin' Jack. "I'm not fitting for a funeral. I'll get a room at the hotel and meet you there later. I need a little sleep before we talk business." He clapped his hand to his chest. "Time was I could have gone for two days without sleep and danced with every lady in the room as well. But those days are gone."

"For us both, my friend," said Russell as he strode away from Smilin' Jack. He was almost to Bank Street when he saw an old-fashioned gig come rattling along the road, the driver pale as muslin. Russell stopped, watching the gig bowl along, trying to decide if Miss Rossiter needed any help handling the team. He raised his hand in greeting as he reached the corner.

"Sheriff!" she cried as she caught sight of him. "Oh, thank God, thank God." She tugged on the rein and the horse swung aside, then set his legs and came to a sharp halt. Miss Rossiter leaned down from the driving box, panting as much as if she had been running. "Mister Russell, please, please, you must come. I don't think he knows I've gone yet. Please."

Russell had never seen this placid, sensible woman so distraught. He took off his hat and came to her side. "Miss Rossiter, what has upset you?"

She grasped his arm. "It's that Mister Fitzroy. He's got Missus Bell in the barn. He's bolted it closed. I heard Cloris scream." She started to cry. "It was worse than anything, how she screamed. You've got to come."

"When did this happen?" asked Russell, alert.

"Just a short while ago. Missus Bell was going to load the milk cans onto the gig, to drive them into town. She called Mister Fitzroy to help her. Then he closed them into the barn and put the bolts on. Sheriff Russell, you have to help her. I couldn't bear it if anything happened to her. I couldn't."

"Of course," said Russell. "Yes. But I'll need your help." He indicated the gig. "I want you to drive me as far as Daniel Calvin's stable. My horse is there, ready to ride. As soon as I'm away, I want you to go to the church, the Protestant church—"

"Of course," Miss Rossiter interjected.

"—and speak to Preacher Cauliffe. Tell him what you've told me and ask him to bring four good men with him, sensible men. I'm depending on you to do this, Miss Rossiter. Do you think you can?" He had reached for the driving rein of the gig and was pulling the horse a few steps closer. "I'll help you up. Hurry. We have no time to lose."

"You can't imagine how her scream sounded, Sheriff," said Miss Rossiter, her voice fainter now and her color poor, the hollows of her eyes almost slate blue.

"Don't dwell on it, Miss Rossiter." How was this poor woman to manage with Doctor Clayton dead, Russell asked himself as he scrutinized Miss Rossiter's face. "There is too much to do. As soon as you have reported to Preacher Cauliffe," he went on as he helped Miss Rossiter onto the driving box, "I want you to go to the hotel and have Missus Cauliffe give you a cordial and a room where you can rest. Tell her it's my request, will you?"

As Miss Rossiter struggled with the reins, Russell climbed up beside her and took them from her. "I'll...I'll do as you ask," she said, but so timorously that Russell wondered if he ought to leave word with Calvin as well.

"Good for you," he said as he turned the gig down the street. I'm sorry, he thought as he drove, I'm sorry I can't be there to see you laid to rest, Henry. I have the living, a woman who was your patient, to attend to. Don't be angry with me.

"Sheriff, is something the matter?" Miss Rossiter asked as they passed the edge of the park.

"No," he told her, doing his best to offer her a smile. "No, I am only thinking of what I will have to do next."

Chapter Eighteen

Russell dismounted a quarter of a mile from the Cousins' farm. He left his grey tied to a tree and made his way on foot toward the empty house and the barn. He went warily, listening for every sound, his baton up and ready. Aside from his baton he carried two knives, choosing them for their silence; a pistol would be useless, he thought, unless Mrs. Bell was already dead. That notion, once he had admitted it as a possibility, blocked out all other considerations, and he found himself assuming that Fitzroy had killed her.

The door to the house was standing open, and the smell of something overcooked on the stove told Russell that the barn was still the place he had to go. He glanced toward the pens on the north side of the barns where the stock was kept: both pigs and sheep were waiting, the sheep starting to blunder about nervously. Russell knew he would have to avoid that place. There was nothing to the east of the barn but the feed shed, but he was certain the animals would set up a ruckus if they saw a person go there, for they would expect food. He looked into the small field beyond the shed, and counted nine cows grazing there. Good, he thought. No cattle in the barn. That left the west side—which was the wide drive between the house and barn—or the south.

"The south it is," he whispered to himself, and made his way back toward his horse so that he could cross the road out of sight. It was growing dark as clouds rolled in off the prairie and piled up against the mountains, and that was helpful to his search. So long as the storm held off a while, the lowering light would be to his advantage.

There came a scream, long, high and ragged, more like an animal than a woman.

Russell steadied himself as he heard it, and cursed. Unbidden a terrible memory from India came to him; the sight of living women burning on the funeral pyre of their dead husbands. He forced that from his mind, knowing that he could not afford to let his mind wander, not for an instant. He braced himself to hear more screams.

There was cover to the south most of the way to the barn, first trees and then scrub. He would have to be careful about making noise as he went, for the brush was dry and twigs snapped easily. While he was fairly certain that Fitzroy would not pay much attention to one or two broken twigs, he would certainly be distracted by a number of them.

Unless...Russell smiled to himself...unless he ran right to the side of the barn. Then Fitzroy would be sure to ignore it, for no man would be so loud. He would probably attribute it to deer trying to get into the feed shed. With that for consolation, Russell surged forward, trotting through the woods and brush, heedless of the sound of his passage. Once he reached the open yard at the side of the barn, he stopped, and hunkered down in the last of the brush, waiting to see if there was any response from the barn.

After three minutes there was another scream.

Russell moved carefully, going toward the barn's flank, keeping low so that he could not be seen out the windows from the inside. He huddled against the wall and listened, hating what he heard from the inside.

He would have to go in through the front or the back. Using the high, narrow windows was out of the question. He had to decide which would protect Mrs. Bell the most, for she was the one in the greatest danger. He rocked back on his heels and thought. Finally he started to make his way, carefully and slowly, toward the rear door that opened onto the feed shed. While he knew he might rouse the animals, he hoped that Fitzroy would be put off-guard if a disruption came from that end of the building. He could hear whimpering now, and an occasional obscenity from Fitzroy. The first raindrops spattered into the dust and tapped on the wood. He sensed it would not be much longer before the young man would have to kill his victim. Hatred like vitriol burned within him, and he had to wait as he mastered himself once again.

He was almost in position when he heard his horse whinny, and the sound of an approaching wagon.

With sudden desperation, he rushed the door, his baton in his left hand, his throwing knife raised. He hoped that Fitzroy was more disoriented than he himself was.

Cloris Bell lay in the center of the barn, her clothes gone, her body streaked with blood. Fitzroy, his trousers hanging around his knees, stood over her, a skinning knife in one hand and a baling hook in the other. His eyes, when he turned toward Russell, were as glassy as those of a man with a high fever.

Russell stopped long enough to throw his knife, and had the satisfaction of seeing it bite into Fitzroy's side at the waist.

Fitzroy screeched and dropped the baling hook. He reached for the knife and roared at the added pain his touch brought.

"Get back, Mister Fitzroy," said Russell, breathing hard but keeping his voice even and low. He came a step nearer. "Get away from Missus Bell."

In erupting fury Fitzroy flung himself toward Russell, howling as the knife in his side brought him to his knees.

Outside the wagon had stopped and a woman was calling loudly for Miss Rossiter and Mrs. Bell. It was now raining in earnest, and the sound of it rattled over the barn.

Fitzroy remained on his knees, roaring in pain with every breath he took. His face was ashen and his eyes had gone feral.

Someone began to pound on the main door of the barn, calling again for Miss Rossiter and Mrs. Bell; Russell knew that voice, and hearing it shook him. "Missus Lilhius!" he called to her. "This is Sheriff Russell. The door is bolted."

"Sheriff!" she shouted, and the sound of her voice seemed to reach Mrs. Bell, for she moaned and her eyelids flickered. "Let me in."

Russell watched Fitzroy closely as he looked for a length of rope. He was determined to secure Fitzroy's hands before he did anything else. As long as that knife was in place, Fitzroy would not move much, he was certain of it. And as soon as it was removed, he was in danger of bleeding to death. The sheriff continued to look for rope.

"Sheriff!" Abigail Lilhius called to him. "Please."

Russell had found the rope he needed, but stopped to answer. "Missus Lilhius, it is very…very bad in here."

"God save us!" she cried. "Let me in!" She renewed her pounding on the door, and the noise seemed to rouse Mrs. Bell a little more.

Russell went to the door, pausing before he lifted the bolt. "Missus Lilhius, I warn you: you do not want to see these things."

She hesitated an instant. "Is Miss Rossiter or Missus Bell inside?"

"Missus Bell. She has been badly…injured." Russell did not know what more to say to the determined woman on the other side of the door. As much as he wanted to bring aid to Mrs. Bell, he wanted to spare Mrs. Lilhius the knowledge of what had happened here.

"Then she needs my help," said Mrs. Lilhius. "And I will tend to her. Open this door!"

Russell pulled the door open reluctantly, but stood blocking her way. "I know you are not easily shocked, but this…is quite dreadful."

She shoved him aside and started forward. As soon as she saw Cloris Bell she stopped and gave a choking cough. "Missus Bell," she forced herself to say. "What…oh, gracious, you are so…" She did not finish but went to her neighbor's side and knelt. "It's Missus Lilhius," she said, pulling a large linen handkerchief from her apron pocket, but doing nothing more with it. "Can you hear me, Missus Bell?"

To Russell's surprise, Mrs. Bell gave a little mutter and one hand flopped at her side. She tried briefly to get her elbow under her, then stopped.

Fitzroy was still bellowing with each breath, throwing his head back when he tried to pull the knife free. His face shone with sweat.

Russell stepped behind him, his baton at the ready, and said slowly and distinctly, "Mister Fitzroy, I want you to put your hands behind your back. Immediately." He took hold of the man's wrists and skillfully secured them with the rope he had found. "I am placing you under arrest for the attempted murder of Missus Bell, and suspicion of two other murders."

Silas Fitzroy brayed in pain as Russell finished tying his hands.

"You have to get to your feet, Mister Fitzroy." Russell did his best to lift the young man, trying not to hear the gobbling shrieks he gave as the knife shifted in him. "Missus Lilhius," he said without taking his hand from the ropes that bound Fitzroy, "how is Missus Bell?"

"In great distress, Sheriff Russell," came the answer. "I am afraid that she might...and there is little I can do for..." She could not continue.

Though her mouth was cut and swollen, Cloris Bell burst out, "I'll kill him."

"The law will do it," said Russell, painfully relieved to hear her speak. It was impossible to imagine her surviving long, but at least for a while, she was alive.

"Don't try to—" Abigail Lilhius said, attempting to hold Mrs. Bell without adding to her hurt.

"Kill him!" she repeated.

"Please, don't strain yourself," Mrs. Lilhius pleaded.

Fitzroy bayed up at the ceiling. "Take it out take it out take it out!"

"If I do, you will bleed to death," said Russell bluntly. "As it is, you may live long enough to be hanged. When we are back in town, where we can bandage you properly, we'll take it out. For now, you must bear it." He found himself wanting to shake Henry Clayton for dying, especially when he was so much needed. How could Charity get on without a physician? He looked at Fitzroy. "You won't have to walk to the wagon. You won't have to get on a horse. Be glad of that, Fitzroy."

"Take it out!" he screamed.

"That would be murder, Mister Fitzroy," said Russell at his most patient, then looked back at Mrs. Lilhius and Mrs. Bell. "How is she?"

Mrs. Lilhius shook her head. "She's not doing well. All that blood." She clamped her teeth together so they would not chatter.

"Do what you can, Missus Lilhius," said Russell. "Will you permit me to borrow your wagon? I'd need you to come with me, for Missus Bell if nothing else. I'll tie my horse behind the wagon and drive if you will—"

"Certainly, Sheriff." She looked around. "I should find something to cover Missus Bell, but I don't want to put anything over those open wounds. The pain is terrible now, and if I cover her, it will be worse."

He nodded. "Yes. But with the rain she must be covered."

"And for modesty." She looked around again. "There will be something in the house, I am sure of it." She eased Cloris Bell into a sitting position and braced her back with the farrier's bench. "Missus Bell, I am going for a blanket. I will be back very shortly. Do not fear. The sheriff is here to guard you."

Mrs. Bell opened her eyes again; Russell noticed that the left one had been cut, for the white was red and it did not move with the other. "Where is he?"

"I'm here, Missus Bell," said Russell coming a few steps nearer.

"Where is he?" she repeated more distinctly.

Mrs. Lilhius hurried out of the barn, running through the cloudburst to the house. Russell glanced after her, then knelt down beside Mrs. Bell. "I have him. He is tied up and he is wounded. I promise you he will pay. He'll be hanged at the next circuit court."

"I want him dead," she said with such strong emotion that Russell was surprised by it.

"I promise you," he said, "he will pay for what he has done to you and the others."

"*Now*," she insisted, levering herself more upright. "Now."

Fitzroy urinated and blasphemed as he did.

Russell saw that Fitzroy's trousers were wet, and he sighed. They would have to remove them, and be damned to shame. He started toward the man, only to have him try to edge away. "Now, Mister Fitzroy, if you do anything more, you will hurt yourself very badly. Stand still. If you try to run you will fall and the knife…"

Fitzroy cursed him roundly. He continued to move with mincing steps, his trousers hobbling him as surely as the rope held his hands behind his back.

Russell was working to the other side of the man so that he could bring him down without driving the knife deeper when he saw that Mrs. Bell had moved. His eyes flicked toward her, then back to Fitzroy in time to see him stagger forward, doubled over. Blood fountained from his mouth and nose, and the sound he made would surely haunt Russell for years to come.

Mrs. Bell collapsed, her hand still on the baling hook she had grabbed and sunk into the soft flesh of Fitzroy's belly.

Outside Mrs. Lilhius was hurrying toward the barn with a quilt folded in her hands. She bent over it to keep it from getting wet.

"Missus Lilhius," called Russell, hearing his voice crack, "Stay where you are. Please."

She hesitated, then came nearer. "What is the matter?" she cried.

"Missus..." He did not know what to say next: Mrs. Bell has killed Fitzroy? It was true, but there had to be another way to explain it. "Missus Bell has hurt herself."

"Oh, no." She started toward the open door again.

"No," Russell insisted. "No, stay where you are. I must do... something about Fitzroy. Then you can come in." He knelt down and took Fitzroy's boots in his hands, then dragged him into the nearest stall, grateful that the stock was not inside. It was bad enough with human beings to contend with—had there been hysterical animals as well, Russell knew he would not be able to accomplish anything.

"What are you doing?" Mrs. Lilhius asked as she came as far as the door.

"Mister Fitzroy seems to have collapsed. He may have fallen on the knife." He came back toward Mrs. Bell and knelt to find out if she was still breathing. He could barely hear the working of her lungs and her pulse was ragged. "She's fainted. I will help you wrap her securely, and then I will carry her to the wagon."

"Nonsense," said Mrs. Lilhius with as much practicality as she could summon. "You will go bring the wagon and I will tend to Missus Bell. She will be ready to travel by the time you have the wagon here."

Russell could only agree with her good sense. "If it will not trouble you too much."

She had knelt beside Mrs. Bell, but she looked up at Russell with something enormous and stricken in her eyes. "Mister Russell, I have buried my husband and three of my children. Surely I can attend to Missus Bell."

Russell went for the wagon.

George Fletcher looked up from the reports Russell had prepared for him. "A most appalling business, all of it," he said ponderously. "That such a man could have killed those women and gone undetected for so long, well." The last was accompanied by a gesture of helplessness. "It is a great pity about Missus Bell."

"Yes, but it might have been a greater pity had she lived, for she would surely have been an invalid. I am sorry that she suffered so much those last three days." He stared down at the carpet. "But Fitzroy is gone, that's something."

"A damnable creature." Fletcher cleared his throat and used the spittoon. "What of Miss Rossiter? I understand this has shocked her very much, and she was doing poorly already."

"Yes," said Russell slowly. "She has been through such tragedy." He stared out the bank window to the people going by in the street. "Preacher Cauliffe has asked her if she would assist him to run the school until a proper schoolmaster is found; not as a teacher, you understand, but to tend to the records and to keep track of the students. She has accepted if the Town Council will approve a reasonable salary for her. If she sells the farm, she should be quite secure."

"And is she going to sell the farm?" Fletcher inquired, pursing his lips now that they were in the more familiar territory of finance.

"She has an offer of eleven hundred dollars, for everything; stock, land, buildings and most of the furniture. It is a good offer, but not overly generous, considering the size of the place and their stock." He still thought of Maude Rossiter as one of the Cousins, though Mrs. Bell was dead. "She has accepted it tentatively, assuming that the buyers are satisfied with their bargain."

"Well, it could be worse for her, and that's a fact; and I suppose so long as she is not ailing, it would be right to give Preacher Cauliffe some help," said Fletcher, then tapped the next pages. "What do you wish me to do about this material about Mister

Spaulding? Surely he should be held and sent to Fort Smith to answer these charges."

"Assuming he can be found," Russell said. "I know him of old, and he has a talent for vanishing." He caught his elbows in his hands. "Do you want me to pursue him, or merely detain him if he should come to Charity again?"

"There is so much to do here," said Fletcher, clearly weighing his options.

"Yes, and Luis is a good man, but we are both needed here." He took a turn about the room. "I have personal reasons for wanting to find the man and see him brought to justice. But I also have an obligation here. While I am sheriff of Charity, I am obliged to give the town my first consideration." He hesitated, then went on. "And I am willing to have the past die, if Spaulding is not here to resurrect it."

"Indeed," said Fletcher, going plum-colored. "About the things he said of you: I assure you I never believed the half of them. It was not...useful to have such rumors circulating about you, but considering what you vouchsafed us, and what we now know of Spaulding, I cannot think that there will be any further unpleasantness from his mendacity."

Russell was almost willing to smile. "I am grateful, Your Honor."

"Well, well, it's nothing to go on about. All in all, I would say that you have executed your duties most admirably."

"Thank you," Russell told him, wondering what was coming next, for Mayor Fletcher was plainly trying to address some concern and was not succeeding.

Finally Fletcher cleared his throat and looked squarely at Russell. "I have heard that your...half-brother died. Let me offer my condolences."

"You're very kind. But truth to tell, I did not know him, and while I am sorry he was killed, his loss is not hard to bear." Russell did not dare to sit down during this interview, but briefly wished that Fletcher had offered him coffee.

"Ah. Yes." He folded his meaty hands on the center of the desk. "I was informed that you had been asked to assume the task of raising your nephew."

"That's true," said Russell.

"I see," said Fletcher after a short silence. "Well, I cannot say that I blame you."

Now Russell smiled. "I'm afraid you misunderstand me, Mister Fletcher. I have told the solicitors and my aunt that I do not wish to return to England." He read astonishment in Mayor Fletcher's face. "I gave it serious consideration, and in the end, I realized that this is where I have decided to live. If I returned to England, it would be for an interim period, to help my nephew until he is of age. But I would once again be a bastard and I would be welcome only so long as my nephew had need of my presence. After he reached his majority, I would be expected to leave again."

"You exaggerate," said Fletcher.

"No," Russell said bluntly. "I have been over most of the world looking for a place where I wanted to live. This is where I have settled, with my house and my horses. I have a contract with Smilin' Jack, I have my work as sheriff, and when that is done, I will have a respectable breeding farm."

Fletcher said nothing for a long moment. He stared at his linked hands and ground his teeth. "I suppose," he said at last, "you will want us to vote you a better salary when your year of probation is over."

At this Russell chuckled. "I know my worth, Mister Fletcher, and I know what this town can afford to pay. With the growth of the last year, it might be wise to give me a little more because of the increased work, although I would prefer a second deputy instead, at least one who is available some of the time. Mister Guerra is very good at his work, but with so many newcomers in the town, and all the new faces, we need at least one more pair of hands to deal with the work." He saw the mulish set of Fletcher's shoulders, and did his best to be more persuasive. "If I had someone whose task it was to look after the jail. Nothing very dangerous, you understand, but quite necessary. It would make it possible for both Mister Guerra and I to work more effectively."

"Another salary," grumbled Fletcher.

"Yes, but there are seven new streets and thirty-six new houses, if you count my own, since I arrived here eleven months ago. We have well over a hundred new residents here, and more are coming." He rubbed his chin. "And if your daughter-in-law releases her rancho lands on the south-west side of town, there will be more land for farms to bring settlers here."

"Elvira Fletcher has been very generous of late," said her father-in-law, frowning as he calculated. "And I agree that it is not unlikely that we will have more growth in the next few years. The frontier is becoming more crowded every day."

"So it is," agreed Russell.

Fletcher took a long breath. "Well, I will think it over and discuss it with the other Council members. We have a Town Meeting in three weeks, and we should have reached a decision by then." He pulled another report from the pile. "As to this—"

Russell dared to interrupt. "I have one other favor to ask, Mister Fletcher."

It was not usual for anyone to make such requests of George Fletcher, and for that reason alone he stopped. "Yes?" he demanded in irritation. "What is it?"

"I would prefer that my election as sheriff be left to the Town Meeting, not simply a vote of the Town Council." He saw how startled Fletcher was, and attempted to explain. "The year we agreed would serve as my trial, my probation, it was well enough that I answered only to the Town Council, for the administration of the town is in your hands. But if I am to be sheriff for a term in office, I should be elected as you members of the Town Council are. If the town itself does not want me to be sheriff, then I cannot discharge the office properly."

Fletcher rumbled as he mused. "Very well, providing you abide by the vote of the Town Meeting."

"Naturally." Russell's smile was quick and puckish. "I would not have asked for their vote if I did not intend to abide by it."

"As you wish," said Fletcher, and returned to his question. "What do you intend to do about Mister Skye?"

"Well, I believe a short interview with him would be the most reasonable way to go about things. Don't you agree?" Russell bordered on feeling light-headed. He had won through.

Fletcher's face creased like an angry baby. "The man is an unrepentant scoundrel."

"Yes, but he will not be stealing from smugglers here. In fact, I suspect that the reason he has come here is that he wishes to be as far from them as possible." He rested his hand on the head of his baton.

"But the man profited from theft!" Fletcher protested as he slapped the report Russell had received from Judge McConnell. "He sold all that smuggled rum!"

"Yes. The rum was illegal and he took it from the men who had smuggled it," Russell said. "But he will not have the opportunity to do that here, and he has brought a great deal of money with him. The theft and the sale of his stolen smuggled rum was not in the Texas Territories, and I do not know if I am required to send him back to Georgia for trial. From what Judge McConnell has said, it isn't likely."

"But how can we trust a man like that?" Fletcher blurted out. "He has stolen; he may well steal again."

"I doubt it," said Russell. "Here he could not conceal the crime, and here it would be discovered at once. We are a little town, and even with all the newcomers, no one could hide an act of that magnitude. If you wish my opinion, I could say it would be wisest to watch him, and unless he does something deserving of suspicion, to give him the benefit of the doubt."

"What is this world coming to, that a man like that can establish himself respectably?" Fletcher demanded of the air. "All right; for the time being there will no action taken against Mister Skye."

"I will have a private chat with him, but nothing more," said Russell.

"I still don't like it," muttered Fletcher.

"Remember the size of his deposit and his underwriting of loans for those rebuilding from the fire before you condemn him." He started toward the door, then paused and looked back. "He might be a thief and a scoundrel, but he is also magnanimous, and the money he has deposited here is almost as much as I have in my account." He gave a little bow. "If you'll excuse me, Mister Fletcher?"

The mayor waved him away without another word.

It was cool that night; a fire burned in the stove at the back of the hall, and the men who came in kept their coats wrapped tightly around them. Most had come from supper, but a few had yet to eat and were anxious to have the Town Meeting over and done with.

Jesse Johnson had driven in that day with two big wagons, and had stopped to see how his brother's building was coming. He had a letter of authorization from Smilin' Jack so that he could vote in his stead. He offered it to Hosea Olfrant, who read it, snorted, and made a notation. "You sit down and wait for the mayor, like the rest of us."

"I got to say something to you," said Jesse, turning scarlet at having to address an official. "That road, Charity Street, on the south side of down, where it dips down? It's going to slide this winter if it isn't recut. I had trouble with the wagons, and once it starts to rain the mud'll make it worse. You can fix it now or fix it in the spring, but if you wait 'til spring, it'll be a lot harder to do." He removed his hat and bowed a little, unsure what else he should do.

Olfrant made another note. "We'll talk about it tonight. But whatever gets voted is the way it'll be."

Jesse nodded several times and withdrew to a seat on the far side, by one of the posts that held up the ceiling. He closed his eyes and wished himself warm.

Hiram Mattington came in a few minutes later, and he carried a packet of messages. "From Ma," he said as he gave it to Olfrant. "She knows she can't vote, but she has a few things she wants mentioned before any voting gets done."

"We'll see about that," said Olfrant warily. He had long since been intimidated by Hepsibah Mattington, even when she was not present. "I'll ask the mayor."

"I told her you'd do it," said Hiram. "And I ain't staying the whole time, so you do it while I'm here."

"Going home?" Olfrant asked, thinking it risky to be abroad after dark.

"No, just as far as Lorinda Dooley's house." He grinned at Olfrant's obvious discomfort. "So you get to it early. Read it over, so's you know what's on her mind."

Olfrant resisted the urge to say he had a good idea of what was on Missus Mattington's mind. Instead he gave a curt "At once," and opened the packet.

Mayor Fletcher came in with his son Frederick and another young man, thicker-bodied than Frederick but with the same look about him. He led the two to the front of the room and sat them in the first row before he took his place at the table.

"I wonder if that's Newton or Horatio?" Russell asked of Liam Cauliffe. "One of them was supposed to be home in the summer. Perhaps he arrived a little late."

"I can't see his face well enough to tell you," said Cauliffe. "I'll have to do something about spectacles, and that's God's truth." He sighed. "And me teaching school."

"Well, you have over eighty pupils, don't you?" Russell asked.

"Eighty-three, all told. Without Miss Rossiter, I couldn't manage the school and still preach on Sunday." He indicated chairs where they could sit. "They'd best find their schoolmaster soon."

"Remind them of it tonight," said Russell. He sat down and removed his hat.

"I hear you bought the cousins' place," Cauliffe said with just enough curiosity that Russell had to answer.

"Yes. Their western border marches with my eastern, and it made sense to me to add it, since I'll have more horses. It gives William a place of his own, as well." He looked a bit uncomfortable.

"Very sensible, all of it," said Cauliffe, nodding sagaciously, "and be damned for a deceiver," he added at his most genial. He might have said more, but George Fletcher was calling the meeting to order.

The first order of business concerned finding a new physician for the town. The men wrangled about the need and the cost and the reliability of physicians; finally Mayor Fletcher's blocky son— Horatio or Newton—rose and said, "Gentlemen, I have business in Baltimore this winter, and there are many excellent physicians there. Also there are medical universities in the area where their graduates are known. If you will grant me the right to speak on behalf of this town, I will endeavor to find you a worthy man."

"Pompous as his father," whispered Cauliffe.

"Still, it's not a bad idea," countered Russell.

A vote was called and of the ninety-one men in attendance, fifty-four voted in favor.

"Say, does anyone know if it's true they've found gold in California?" one of the Smithers boys asked as the votes were counted, and was surprised at the buzz of speculation that filled the hall of the church.

"They say lots of things about California," observed Jesse Johnson laconically.

When the hiring of a schoolmaster was brought up, the same issues were argued, and the mayor's son made a similar offer, which was accepted by fifty of the men at the Town Meeting.

"Now there's the matter of the sheriff," said George Fletcher as he looked in Russell's direction. He paused as the men craned their necks to see that Russell was truly there. Fletcher then recounted the agreement he and the Town Council had struck with Jason Russell almost a year ago. He explained the terms of the probationary period, and then said, "I think we can all agree that Sheriff Russell has done a good job. He observed when he arrived that he is very good at keeping the peace, and I believe he has proven his point. If he is to continue in office, the town will have to pay the full salary of his deputy and provide someone to serve as jailer. That is more than twice the drain on the treasury as the current arrangement. If we renewed our previous terms for another year—"

Russell was on his feet. "Mayor Fletcher," he said cordially, "such a renewal is unacceptable to me. Either you make me sheriff for four years, the same terms as the Town Council serves, or you find someone else to do the job." He nodded to the men around him and sat down again.

"Mayor Fletcher," said Nathaniel Howe as he stood, "we all know that Sheriff Russell is a rich man. They say he's worth more than the whole Town Council put together. Why should he get paid at all? Why can't he do it for the town?"

"Because he's risking his life, you dizzard," said Hiram Mattington. "You read what my Ma sent before you say that again."

Unexpectedly Charles Skye rose. "I know I am a new face at these functions, but I want to say that in all the dealings I have had with Sheriff Russell"—he placed a subtle emphasis on *all*— "I have found him to be a man of excellent judgment and good sense. You are fortunate to have such a lawman in Charity." He started to sit down, and then added, "I am well-off myself, but if I had to do what Mister Russell does, I would expect to be paid for my efforts."

"I have something to add," said Cauliffe.

"Liam, sit down," Russell whispered.

Cauliffe paid him no heed. "I was the one who suggested we bring Jason Russell to Charity. I knew him in Australia and I thought he was a superior lawman. Those who heard what Mister Spaulding said were listening to lies, as well you ought to know. When Russell came, I knew I had not been wrong in my recommendation. I tell you now that if we do not elect him sheriff, we will never find his equal. Think what he has done this last year. He brought the Mayhew gang to justice. He saved many of you from the fire. He apprehended a killer no one else had identified. I say we elect him and pay him whatever sum he asks, and count ourselves fortunate to have him." With that he sat down again, ignoring the cuff on his arm Russell gave him.

Frederick Fletcher stood up. "God knows that if anyone in this room knows how well Sheriff Russell keeps the peace, it's I," he began, and laughed enough to let the others know they could share his amusement. "I have seen him when I was behaving disgracefully; he never abused his position, though I surely gave him cause. His care of my wife in her time of need is well enough known that I do not need to recount it here. His pursuit of justice in my wife's cause was beyond reproach."

Russell stood. "Gentlemen, please. I am deeply appreciative of what you have said; I am pleased you are satisfied with the work I have done in the past. Let me assure you that it is my intention to continue to provide the same service if you elect me. But do not, I implore you, make it impossible for me to perform to your expectations, which will surely happen if you go on in this vein."

"Yes," said George Fletcher. "Commendable reserve. I think we're all aware of the services Sheriff Russell has provided. I don't think there is any reason to delay the vote." He rapped on the table with his new gavel. "All those in favor of electing Jason Russell to a four-year term as sheriff of Charity, raise your hands."

Russell watched with deep satisfaction as eighty-seven hands were counted.

C11516 1408